WHEN THE SAINTS

WHEN THE SAINTS

~A Novel~

SARAH MIAN

HARPER**AVENUE**

Published by Harper Avenue, an imprint of HarperCollins Publishers Ltd

First edition

HarperCollins books may be purchased for educational, business,
or sales promotional use through our Special Markets Department.

HarperCollins Publishers Ltd
2 Bloor Street East, 20th Floor
Toronto, Ontario, Canada
M4W 1A8

www.harpercollins.ca

Library and Archives Canada Cataloguing in Publication
information is available upon request

ISBN 978-1-44343-107-1

Printed and bound in the United States of America
RRD 9 8 7 6 5 4 3 2

The author wishes to acknowledge the support of Arts Nova Scotia
in the creation of the work.

NOVA SCOTIA
NOUVELLE-ÉCOSSE

For my mother.

I

THE RHUBARB LEAVES HAVE GROWN UP TO THE FIRST-floor windows. From the bottom of the driveway, I spy a juice pitcher and some plastic cups sitting on a table on the porch. I strain my ears for voices, but all I'm picking up is the buzz of insects and power lines.

When I get closer, I see cobwebs binding the table to the railing and a grey feather sticking out of the jug. A wool sweater hanging over the back of a chair doesn't stir with the breeze. I squint up at the windows and fight the urge to bolt, pushing my fists into the back pockets of my jeans to anchor myself. A crow starts a staring contest from the roof and I look away first, glancing around at all the beer cans scattered in the grass, wondering what debris was left behind and what's been brought since by kids using the house as a party place.

It's hard to focus with those beady eyes boring into my forehead, so I give up and walk around the side yard to the garage. Thorn bushes catch the hem of my jacket on the slight incline and it takes a few good kicks on the door before I can squeeze inside. Grandpa's shotguns are rusted out and there's a lonesome smell of oil over everything. The dirt floor next to the deep-freeze Daddy used to throw chunks of deer meat into is stained black from years of spilled blood. The wall hook is empty. All the keys are gone, even the one for the disassembled tractor.

Something slides past my foot and vanishes behind a metal jerry can. I push the can aside with my boot, squat down and spy a garter snake coiled back beneath the shelves full of dusty tools. It darts past me and slips outside, and as I'm tracing its path through the weeds I notice the long grass is flattened near the kitchen entrance of the house. As soon as I start wading down there, the crow alights on the awning to keep me in its sights.

I get a familiar jolt as I approach the small round window in the kitchen door. Back in the day, this was the porthole to whatever shitstorm was in swing if Daddy was home. If it was getting dark and my stomach was growling, I used to drag over a sawhorse to stand on and press my face to the glass. Sometimes I could make out a figure slumped over in a chair or catch the shadow of a bottle tipping back. Once, Daddy surprised the hell out of me with his eyeballs right up to mine. I fell backward onto the grass, crawled through the bushes and from a safe distance watched him lurch out the door and trip over the sawhorse, hollering that I was dead meat. While he lay there passed out in the moonlight, I shivered in the trees for an hour until my older brother came home. I watched Bird poke Daddy with a long stick and when Daddy didn't twitch, I sprinted out from my hiding spot. Bird pushed me into the house and locked the door behind us. We stood at the window watching Daddy's belly rising and falling. "Stupid shithead," Bird said. "He won't even remember how he got there." He turned around, snatched Daddy's glass off the table, and I watched the few amber rivulets that missed his mouth go trickling down his neck.

Now I only have to stand on tiptoes to peer inside, but all I can make out are blurry shapes. I try the knob and it's unlocked, so I slowly walk in.

The walls and countertops are scarred with cigarette burns. There are butts on the floor, glasses of mouldy liquid and a shrivelled mouse on a plate. It's like someone hosted the tea party from hell.

I hold my nose and search the room for something familiar. After a few seconds, I spy the rooster clock, the one we got free from an offer on the back of a cereal box. It used to "Cock-a-doodle-doo!" until it startled Daddy one day and he bashed it with his fist. After that, it would only whisper "Cock" every hour followed by a garbled noise like it was being choked. I take it down off the wall, wipe off the grime and wind the little pin in the back, but that bird's finally out of its misery. I carefully hang it back in its place and wander to the next room.

My boots on the floorboards set off a chain reaction of groans and rattles throughout the whole house. In the murky green light, everything looks as if it's under water. The hallway is a jungle of coat hangers and unravelled cassette tapes, piles of fallen plaster and broken Christmas-tree ornaments. Someone booby-trapped the main staircase by nailing a flannel sheet over a missing tread.

Upstairs, the floor's given way in spots. I find where a beam shows through and walk the length of it into the master bed-room. Two white cats are lying on a bare matress. They stare at me, wide-eyed. In the closet, Ma's yellow dress was a banquet for moths. The buttons she kept in the Mason jar on her bureau are stuck together. There are water stains on the walls, wings flap-ping in the attic. Even the clouds are creaking outside.

I pick a sturdy spot and slowly rotate, taking it all in. Before I can even begin to wrap my mind around this mess, I hear a car door slam. I make my way back down the stairs and peer out a window. The RCMP officer I spoke to earlier is parked down on the road and coming up on foot. I open the front door and quickly undo the top few buttons of my blouse. I'll need a place to sleep, and it sure as hell won't be in this house.

"Had to see for myself," I say once he's in earshot.

He takes his hat off. "Sorry, I don't have any more informa-tion for you."

He's lying. I can tell by how fast he drops his eyes. I walk down off the porch and ask, "You know if anyone in town needs a waitress?"

He stares hard at my red boots, tries not to let his eyes slide up my legs. I see he's wearing a wedding ring. A voice cuts through the static on his belt radio and he flicks the volume down with his thumb. "Just head to the tavern. West knows everything any-body knows. You'll get all your answers in one place."

"Who's West?"

"He's been running the Four Horses since Clutch passed."

"He got a girlfriend?"

"Listen, Tabatha." The cop fidgets and puts his hat back on. "Things have been quiet around here."

"You going to give me a ride or not?"

I hear a rustle of feathers and look up to see a whole flock of crows now perched on the rusty telephone wire. They seem to be waiting for a signal. I raise my arm and give them the middle finger, but that wasn't it.

THE MAIN DRAG WAS NEVER A WELCOME PLACE FOR Saints. My stomach tightens as we pass the convenience store I used to steal from right out of the register, and next to it the barbershop with the dirty candy-striped pole Bird once licked on a dare.

Up ahead, I see the big town history mural painted on the stone wall. There's a trick to it where, if you stand in a certain spot, you become another face in the crowd of people cheering for the men come home from war. As we pass it, I see that all the townswomen have been defiled by spray paint. They've all got big tits and tongues hanging out, ready to jump any soldier who still has his legs.

The cop lets me out at the stop sign and drives off without a word. I need to clear my head, so I duck down an alley into the Doyle Street Country Club. That's the name the cops gave to the back lot where kids started congregating to pass around cheap bottles of Great White. By the look of all the empties, the club's still swinging, though the new house beverage is something called Dory 72. The label has a cross-eyed cartoon fisherman with the slogan *Get It in Your Gills*.

I trail my finger along the wavy green line that the big flood stained along the back walls of the buildings, remembering how bits of algae and garbage were stuck to everyone's houses and cars. The day after the storm, my father paddled our family down Main Street in a canoe, pointing out floating baby doll heads and whisky jugs, hooking in the stuff Ma wanted with a ski pole. The cemetery was submerged except for the tallest crosses, and later we heard that some of the bodies went for a ride. One of them floated face up beneath Grandma Jean's kitchen window. She was sure it was Jim Weir, whose funeral she'd been at two weeks before. When she got sick of looking at him, she paid some kids to tether him to their rubber dinghy and tow him down to the station.

I light a cigarette and smoke it down to my fingers while I search for my old graffiti. Someone carved *I fucked your mother last night* into the dumpster, and beneath it someone else scrawled *You wish, Dad.* I wish a few of these kids were hanging around so I could tell them about some of our old hijinks. Like the time some church nuts marched down here preaching the light of the Lord, handing out pamphlets and T-shirts that said, JESUS LISTENS. We ripped the sleeves off the shirts, stole some permanent markers from the pharmacy and added TO METALLICA in thunderbolt letters. Then we sat on the church steps Sunday morning and gave them back to all the people walking in.

I crush out my smoke, crack my neck a few times. Then I pop a piece of gum in my mouth and head back through the alley. I start up the main drag, but I only get as far as the beauty parlour before my stomach seizes up again. One time, my mother and I were walking hand in hand and she stopped short right in front of this door. She had a green and yellow bruise on that day and it was almost pretty, like a fireworks display across one cheek. She said, "I'm going to get me a job and get us out of here." She grabbed my hand, burst through the door and said, "You need workers? I'll do anything that needs doing. I can work sixteen hours a day for the price of eight." And without even looking up from putting perm rods in some old lady's hair, the woman who ran the place, Beula Dean, said to no one in particular, "I'd sooner hire that stray dog that hangs around the library with one eye hanging out of its head."

It was moments like those that forced me to be who I am. If ever I drifted just an inch from being a Saint, something always snapped me right back in my place. The thought of it makes me want to duck into the beauty parlour right now, slice Beula Dean's throat with a razor blade and have a skating party in her blood. But the only person inside is a bored-looking black lady sitting behind the counter reading *Wedding Bells* magazine. She looks up and beckons for me to come in, but I keep moving.

The funeral parlour is boarded up and moved around the corner into what used to be the bowling alley. I don't see any reason why I can't just walk in and ask if anyone in my family cashed in their chips. There's a loud bell that jangles when the door opens and organ music playing on a little boom box behind the desk. I nose around, touching all the display coffins and urns, until a young man with big glasses and hair all combed over to one side emerges from the backroom.

"Hi there. I'm Tabby Saint. I'm curious if you might have buried anybody from my family in the last eleven or so years. I'm just back in town and haven't exactly kept in touch."

"Saint?" The way he looks at me, so spooked, I figure he's going to tell me they all burned up in a fire or something. "We haven't provided any services for Saints."

"Is that because no one died or because they'd sooner dig a hole in the woods than pay your fees?"

He can't seem to pry open his jaw.

"No offence," I add. "I can see them doing that."

"One moment." He opens a door and goes down some stairs. When he comes back, he clears his throat and says, "My father says no Saints have passed on since Jack Saint in 1971."

"People always said we were hard targets. Speaking of which, what'd you do with all those pins and balls when you moved in?"

"We boxed them up and put them out in the parking lot. Some kids carted them off."

I imagine my brothers and sister laying down planks of ply-wood and setting up their own little bowling alley in the front yard, charging other kids lane fees.

He straightens his glasses. "Anything else?"

I take a last look at all the half-open coffins with pink linings and little pillows so shiny they give me a headache. "Just like luxury cars," I say, running my hand down the side of a black casket. "I'll bet the typical dipshit who goes down in one of these showboats spent his years driving a Pinto with bald tires and a driver's-side door that had to be duct-taped shut."

He looks at me blankly.

I wink. "I think I liked the place better when it served beer."

I push the door open and step out onto the sidewalk, and there's this little ringlet-headed thing coming toward me. She's about six years old with a flat nose and juice stains on her neck. She stops and says, "Are you lice? My mother seen you this morning, and she said you're lice."

"That was nice of her." I spit my gum out on the pavement. "Who's your mother?"

"Nancy Roth-MacDonald."

I know that name. Nancy Roth was in my grade. She told her friends my parents were brother and sister and it spread around school like a bad fart. There were a lot of nasty things said about my family that were true; that girl had no good reason to be throwing extra stink into the pot. I bend down to this kid's face and say, "When I was fourteen, my hair hung straight down to my ass and poor Nancy Roth had these little curls stuck to her head like pubic hairs." I wrap a strand of her hair around my finger and wind it up to her scalp. "The meaner she was, the tighter and frizzier those curls got. You think about that."

She hesitates, then pulls away like I scalded her with a hot curling iron.

"Tell your mother I said hi."

THE TAVERN HAS A BRIGHT NEW PAINT JOB, BUT THE men inside are worse than ever. Or maybe they're the same drunks a decade older and uglier, but I can't distinguish one fat ass hanging off the back of a stool from another. I march up to the bar and the bartender finally pries himself from the television set they're all staring at.

"You're West?"

"I am."

"I'm Tabby Saint."

His face twitches like there's a bug crawling across it. "So?"

"So nothing." I take a stool. "Give me a beer."

He doesn't move. The chalkboard on the wall behind him says, *Today's Special: Two Drinks for the Price of Two Drinks.*

"I lived here till I was fourteen years old," I tell him. "I don't remember you."

"I'm from Cable."

"Did you know my father?"

He spits sideways into the sink. "Yeah. I knew your father."

"Where'd he go?"

One of the men snorts and shakes his head. The room falls silent except for the dart game on the television. I eye a basket of stale-looking pretzels sitting on the bar. It's been a while since I've eaten.

"Where's the rest of them gone to?" I ask, taking a handful.

West uncrosses his arms, grabs a bottle of Ten-Penny from the fridge behind him, twists the cap off and smacks it down hard in front of me. "They were smoked out ages ago. Got run across the bridge."

"What for?"

He shrugs, turns back to the television. I can tell I'm not going to get anything more out of him. Not in here, anyway. He's got a broken tooth on the bottom row, but other than that he's decent-looking. Strong arms under his black shirt, full head of hair, copper-coloured eyes.

I wash down a mouthful of pretzel with a swig of beer. "I need a job."

"Oh yeah?" West motions down the line of pasty faces. "Why don't you join the club?"

I hang around for hours watching darts, then pool, then bowling, then darts again, until the last wino picks himself up, takes his ball cap off the coat rack and stumbles out the door. West goes out to empty the trash, comes back in and locks up the fridge, gathers some dirty glasses and sets them in the sink. "You're still here," he says over his shoulder, buttoning his coat.

"You hadn't noticed?"

He leans over and crosses his forearms on the bar. "That guy who left just before Carl came in here wearing a leather jacket that belongs to a friend of mine whose truck was busted into. He must have ripped the tabs off and scuffed it up a little, but it's the same one." He glances down at my cleavage. "Asshole paid me with a hundred-dollar bill, which means he just sold something, and he said his name is Dave. Course, when I pretended the phone was for Dave, he didn't react until I said it twice, and after that he knew I was on to him. Know how I know?"

I shrug.

"Because buddy left right then with a third of beer in his bottle whereas the previous two he drained to the last drop just like you and every other loser in this dump." He takes a mint from the glass dish next to the register and pops it in his mouth. "I notice everything."

"I saw the hundred he paid you with," I say. "I also saw the two fifties in his wallet and the driver's licence that says his last name is Graves. And for the record, I'm no loser, and I don't appreciate you making assumptions based on *my* last name."

He bites down loudly into the mint. Then a smile creeps into his lips as he reaches out and tucks a piece of my hair behind my ear. "Okay then."

THAT NIGHT I WRAP MY LEGS AROUND WEST AND ONCE he's done and snoring I lie awake and walk through each room of our house again in my mind. I can't imagine what would make Daddy leave the place to rot. He used to brag that his father built it with his own hands, which wasn't even true, but he seemed to believe it.

After Grandpa Jack fell drunk in the river and drowned the year I was born, Daddy talked him up like he was the Messiah when really he was a demented alcoholic tyrant who used to beat Daddy with this black horse statue that sat on the mantle. Once, we were riding in our old station wagon and passed a black horse grazing in a field. Daddy started rubbing the left side of his head with the palm of his hand and pressed his boot down on the gas pedal so hard that all the trees slurred together outside the windows. My baby brother Jackie started screaming and Daddy slammed on the brakes, wrenched the car to the side of the road and told Ma she had ten seconds to shut the little bastard up. He pushed in the cigarette lighter as she jumped out and hauled Jackie from his car seat. The lighter popped and Daddy held it up where she could see it as she stood on the side of the highway cooing in Jackie's ear. Then Daddy turned around and stared at Bird and me as he pressed the burning end to the passenger seat, melting a hole where Ma's head had been. I grabbed onto Bird so tight my fingernails made little red half moons in his arm.

WEST MUMBLES A STRING OF WORDS IN HIS SLEEP. I TRY to make out what he's saying. Something about drywall and getting a good deal. Last night when we got back to his place, he told me he'd been waiting a long time for a woman like me to walk into his bar. I asked what he meant by that and he said someone with half a brain. I don't recall saying anything brilliant. Except maybe when I suggested he'd get more women in there if he made a rule that customers have to wear pants that fit. "Just try it for one week," I said. "Put up a big sign: NOW WITH FEWER SWEATY CRACKS."

My eyes are still open and sore when the sun comes up, so I slip out the door and walk down to the river. I manage to find my old spot between the blueberry bushes and the Space Invaders arcade console. I can't believe that thing's still here, lying on its stomach like a beached whale. The neon colours have leached and all the wiring's been gutted, leaving just the box frame. I always wondered how it wound up here. Maybe some kids heisted it, dragged it down here to bash it up for the quarters. Quarters were a hot ticket back in the day because Doreen who worked the corner store used to sell single cigarettes to kids for twenty-five cents. She loved children. She'd knit little leg warmers while she was waiting for customers, had a big stockpile ready in case anyone in town gave birth. "Need a light for that, Baby Bear?" she'd ask, stretching over the counter with her Zippo. She had a script for everything. If someone asked how she was doing, she'd say, "Just another day in paradise." If a man purchased a lottery ticket, she'd say, "If you win, I'm single." Every time. And then she'd laugh so hard it loosened the phlegm in her throat.

The grass is soggy after endless cold spring rains, so I lay my jacket down to sit on. I used to come down here all the time for no reason other than to watch the eddies twirl. Once in a while some flotsam would flash by, like a Dr. Pepper can or a piece of car body. I'd stay until the tide went out and there was just a big bowl of mud. Insects would crawl up and down my arms and I'd pretend I was just another blade of grass.

I tried to disappear on a city bench once, but my face must have a sign on it. Some woman tapped me on the knee and wanted to know if I'd seen her ghost. I told her I didn't have the faintest idea what she was talking about, and she lowered her voice and asked if a woman who looked identical to her went by about twenty minutes ago, perhaps on a bicycle with lightning streaks down the side and a white basket. She took a pen out of her purse and drew me a picture of herself.

At least in small towns, everyone knows who the crazies are and what their deal is. Someone new walks into a corner store and they get the lowdown right away: "Don't say hello to Angus out there or he'll make you listen to him play the spoons for hours." In the city, crazies float around like balloons. You don't know one till she's hovering over you on a park bench.

There's something different in the air here now. When we were kids, the breeze always smelled like the car factory. Maybe it's shut down, because all that's wafting my way is the scent of the pines on the other side of the river. Daddy used to hide out in those woods when the law was on him. I asked Ma once what he did to pass the time and she said something like, "Oh, he's making sure all the birds know he's the king, getting drunk and shitting in the river, probably dreaming up a whole new way to make me wish I was dead."

When I was three years old, I tagged along with Bird as he went trudging in to look for Daddy. He had to tell him that our furnace broke down and Ma needed money to get it fixed. My legs were bare and we didn't get far before some wild animal sunk its teeth into my shin. Bird told everyone it was a king cobra, but it was probably a muskrat.

I squint in the other direction across the old bridge, but I can barely make out the few cars and trucks rumbling through the morning haze.

Grandma Jean, who is my mother's mother, always said that the town of Solace River was a waste of nails from the start, that its sole purpose was to collect assholes. She used to tell us stories about Irish rumbles, grown men pummelling each other over who owned what, everybody taking sides. Her father, Cleary Foster, was a brawler who challenged boxing champs from as far away as Boston to street fights. He'd go around begging shop-keepers to put up the train fare, and when the boxer left Solace River with his face punched through his head, they'd get their money back and more. There were legendary parties every time he won a fight. Cleary himself would preside, buying rounds and throwing bills around, placing small children on his biceps and hoisting them in the air.

After his bare-knuckle days, Cleary bought an automobile, the first Nova Scotian to own one outside of Halifax. He'd drive it around to different towns looking for barroom fights, but no one would take him on. Eventually, he got depressed and crashed the car on purpose, fizzled out his days drinking mouthwash and yelling at the radio announcer. Grandma Jean's mother took all the kids away, and by the time she came back, the house had been looted and there were flies everywhere. Someone had even stepped right over Cleary's corpse to snatch his Crosley radio. The church took up a collection, but she blew it on a flashy car of her own.

"She said it was her due for having put up with all them brawls," Grandma Jean said. "But everyone knew there weren't nothing that woman loved more than the smack of a fist into a jaw. She used to pick up the bloody teeth off the floor and keep them for souvenirs, show them to us kids at the breakfast table while she re-enacted the fight. You'd be sitting there eating oat-meal and the next thing you knew, she'd have you in a headlock." She clicked her tongue. "Point is, the mayor, the farmers, even my own crazy ma weren't nothing but thieves, every last one of them. People say all the trouble started with your father's people, but that's just sweet-smelling bullshit. Garnet Saint didn't invent crime in Solace River."

We used to have a self-portrait of Garnet hanging in our house. I can still see that big nose and the boxy black hat slipping to one side of his head. From what I heard, he was a teenage run-away who wormed his way into a small crew making rum runs from St. Pierre Island to New York during Prohibition until he got kicked out for having a big mouth. Then he tried to break in with the moonshiners on McNabs Island but wound up running a crooked Wheel of Chance on the pleasure grounds.

Grandma Jean said Garnet Saint probably wasn't even Grandpa Jack's real father, but that Jack's mother abandoned him in a Halifax rooming house and Garnet offered to take him off the landlady's hands. He skipped town with little Jack and headed for the Annapolis Valley, never staying in one town long enough for people to catch on to his monkeyshines.

"The baby was his meal ticket," Grandma said. "Garnet fed him nothing but rotten fish and sips of hooch so he'd always be passed out or spitting up. He'd moan that his poor Jack was dying so ladies' charities would give them money for medicine."

They arrived in Solace River around the time Garnet's knees began to wear out. Jack was about seven years old by then. They'd come looking for an old carny buddy of Garnet's, but the man was long dead. They squatted in the old schoolhouse, started stealing chickens and piglets until they had enough of a farm to feed themselves, and for the next ten years scraped by on just the odd con. Garnet had a shed full of painted rocks that he sold to passersby as *Genuine Meteorites!* He also touted his services as a sort of hillbilly clairvoyant, a walking talking farmer's almanac who could tell with a sniff of the air and a coin slapped to his palm which crops would do well that season. Of course, that ruse lasted only one season. Next, he concocted a tincture of pig's blood and tree sap and tried selling it door to door as a cure-all, but by then no one was buying his crap. Garnet swore the joke was on them, claimed Saint's Elixir restored not only the cartilage in his knees but also the muscle in his pants. He and his new-found vitality went around molesting people's wives and daughters until someone did the whole town a favour and beat him to death with a tire iron behind the gas station. Jack was only a young teenager at the time. He went off to war to earn a wage and came back with a sickly little waif who died with my father still inside her. They had to cut Daddy right out of her stomach.

Grandma Jean stitched this all together from jagged scraps of memory and town gossip. My father was like a period at the end of the story, but of course it didn't end there. Why the hell Ma married Daddy, I'll never understand.

After about an hour, I'm sick of thinking about it. I stand up, spit in the river and head back up the road.

WEST IS STANDING BARE-CHESTED IN THE KITCHEN when I let myself in. He gets a hard-on as soon as he sees me. We screw for a while on his reclining chair before he goes to work. A couple of things I learned about him overnight are that he doesn't have a last name and he doesn't drink coffee. I don't think I can trust anyone who doesn't drink coffee.

The door slams and for fun I yell, "Have a good day at work, honey!"

His house is all right even though it hasn't got an upstairs. It's damp and the ceilings are low, but he has some houseplants and you can tell he pushes a mop around now and then. I pour myself a glass of water and read all the magnets on his fridge. *Tim's Autobody. 2-4-1 Pizza.* There's one shaped like a fish that says, *Do Unto Others.* I survey the kitchen and try to imagine it with a nice tablecloth and curtains on the windows. The walls are bare except for a calendar and a small wooden shelf holding a cookbook and a framed picture of an auburn-haired woman with nice tanned legs and her arms around West. I wonder how he messed that up.

I open the cookbook and read the inscription: *Merry Christmas, West! Now learn how to cook and stop mooching scraps at our house.*

In the bathroom, I wipe down the mirror. It's been a while since I've had a good hard look at myself. After I got off the bus in Halifax, I hitchhiked up the 101 and met a nice family from Paradise who offered to let me crash in their teepee while I decided where to go next. The "teepee" was a homemade contraption draped in My Little Pony comforters and tarps. Instead of a firepit, they stuck an electric space heater in there and ran extension cords up to the house. The whole thing was a fire trap and smelled like nail polish remover, but the droopy mattresses piled on top of each other made for the best sleep of my life.

I had high hopes for Paradise based on the name and hung around a couple of weeks to see if anything was going on. Nothing was. Unless you count glow-in-the-dark karaoke in a church basement. The microphone shone electric pink and a heavy-set woman sang "The Rose" into it with such passion that sweat soaked through the underarms of her caftan. She seemed to think I was a secret talent scout from New York City, kept looking over during the solo break to gauge my reaction. Eventually I just admitted to myself that I was inching my way back home, walked to the side of the highway and stuck my thumb out.

I look more like my mother now that I'm finally here. We've got the same stringy hair and that caged-animal look in our eyes. She creeps into my mind more than usual these days. Quick snapshots of her. She used to paint tiny hearts and things on my fingernails before that was popular. She hardly ever laughed, but when she did, it sounded like a rusty motorbike starting up. We'd start imitating it and she'd clam up again.

I poke around in his cabinets. I figure if there's a chance of that redhead coming back and catching me here, finding makeup in a drawer would be a good sign. Women leave behind pots and pans, sometimes clothes, but never makeup. Once you find that shade of lipstick that subtly distracts attention away from the rest of your face, you'd crawl down an outhouse to retrieve it. There's no trace of her.

I fish my purse out from under the bed for my own crusty makeup tubes and use them to freshen up a little, but then I figure I could do with a shower, so I wipe it all off again. The stall is tiny and the walls are wood panelled instead of waterproof so the wood's gone all grey and soft and there's mould in between the slats. The shower head just gives a trickle and the water smells rank. It takes me half the time I'm in there to figure out how to make it run hot, and when I get out, the phone is ringing and ringing.

"Hello?"

"You find the towels?"

"You watching me on a surveillance camera?"

"What?"

"I just got out of your shower. I'm standing here dripping."

"There's a clean towel in the hall closet."

"It's the only thing clean, then," I lie.

"I had to rip off all the tiles to get at the pipes."

"And you still didn't manage to fix the pipes."

"You're welcome to leave any time. Thought you'd left this morning when I woke up."

"You didn't seem disappointed that I hadn't."

"Well, anyway. Wipe the floor up when you're done."

"What? A fancy place like this doesn't have housekeeping service?"

"The door's through the kitchen."

"You home for supper?"

"And lock up when you leave. I like my television."

I hang up and look out the window at a few scraggly trees I don't know the name of. The leaves brushing up against the window are polka-dotted with brown holes and it reminds me of seeing Ma's dress all chewed up in the closet.

Ran out of town.

I sit on the bed staring at my bare thighs and wonder what's happening in Blood Rain. That's the reserve I was living on for a while before I wore out my welcome. I was staying with this guy, Jared, but it didn't work out between us. It wasn't my fault, but they weren't very nice to me when they had that big meeting. A medicine woman there told me I have a soul like a feather and if I don't attach myself to something I'll be floating forever. She said I needed to hang off a cliff or nearly drown to get some weight and when I told her no thanks, she said fine, float forever then. See if I care.

She was probably hoping I'd kill myself by accident. It wouldn't be the first time a stranger tried to put one over on me. I was in a taxicab once headed to a casino and the driver said, "Oh, you're headed to the casino? You might not believe this, but I'm a psychic. If you promise to give me half of what you win, I'll tell you where to put your money down." I know, I know, it sounded like horseshit, but I can't ignore anyone who claims to see the future. Like, if, instead of her floating feather crap, that medicine woman had told me I would someday be impaled by a flying candy cane, I swear I'd have been looking over my shoulder every Christmas. It all goes back to the big flood. A girl even younger than me ran all over school telling everyone to tie a boat to a tree and smoke 'em if you got 'em. It wasn't even supposed to rain that night, and the next day half the town was standing on their rooftops.

So I said to the cabbie, "All right, fine," and he said, "Twenty-six." I went in and put down every cent I had on the number twenty-six, and I couldn't believe it, I won six hundred dollars. I ran whooping back out to the parking lot, handed over his share, and he laughed his ass off at me, said he had nothing to lose either way so he just pulled a number out of his ass. He said, "If you'd lost, I'd have known it as soon as I saw your face. I'd have just taken off and left you standing here." Then he snorted. "Dumb bitch. If I had the power to see winning numbers, why the hell would I be driving this cab?" I stuck my face right up to his and said, "Buddy, if you hadn't played your little trick, I wouldn't have three hundred dollars in my pocket, so how about you take your half and go buy a whore to listen to this crap?"

I take another quick glance at the trees before I stand up. As I'm pulling my clothes back on, I think about how Ma had her yellow dress on all the time because she liked the way it smelled like lemons and so did I. But maybe it just seemed like it smelled like lemons because it was so yellow.

WEST COMES HOME AT A QUARTER AFTER MIDNIGHT. I had planned to greet him lounging naked on the sofa like Cleopatra, but he catches me while I'm rummaging around in his fridge with the cat under my arm, a piece of toast in the other hand and a smoke dangling from my lips.

"I brought you a bouquet of beers," he says.

I kick the fridge door shut and drop the cat. "It must be our anniversary."

"People are talking."

"That's nothing new."

"Everybody wants to know how you turned out."

I prop my cigarette on a pickle jar lid. "Were they all craning their necks to see if I had my chauffeur drop me at the tavern?" I pluck a Schooner from his outstretched hand and wipe the condensation on my blouse.

"I guess because you grew up somewhere else, they wonder if you might've turned yourself around. Who said you could smoke in here?"

"Trust me, I was already grown up when I left here. I got sent to go live with another family, but it wasn't long before they passed me on to Raspberry."

"That home for girls up in New Brunswick?"

"Home for damaged goods is more like it. Everyone in there was either a violent whore, a suicide freak or crazier than the wind."

"I don't think people know about you being in there."

"Guess not. You'd know if they did, right?" I sit down on the sofa and the cat leaps up into my lap.

"So, which were you?"

"What?"

"Violent whore, suicide freak or crazy as the wind?"

"Probably all three." I pick up my smoke, look him over as I inhale. He's gotten handsomer since he left this morning, taller or something. "I had you pegged wrong."

"How so?" he asks.

I chew a fingernail. "Thought you didn't like talking."

"I'm just getting warmed up."

"Aren't bartenders just supposed to listen to people?"

"I wouldn't exactly call reaching into a broken beer fridge fifty times a night bartending." He stretches out on the recliner and finally notices I rearranged his living room set. "Christ almighty, you're making yourself at home, ain't you?"

I HANG OUT AT HIS HOUSE AGAIN THE NEXT DAY. THE paperboy tosses the *Solace River Review* into his neighbour's driveway and I run out and grab it. There's an article on the front page about a local woman who made a fortune selling old junk she found in her basement. I root through West's closets to see if he has any hidden treasure, but he hasn't got much more than a bag of rolled up nickels and a gold chain with an eagle pendant hanging off it. As I'm fixing myself a cup of tea, I notice that the photograph is missing from the shelf, the one of him with the hot redhead.

He comes home early while it's still light out and I make spaghetti from a can with some garlic-buttered toast. We actually sit down at his little table. His chairs don't match; one's wooden country-style and the other's the metal fold-up kind you find in church halls. I wonder if he ever had two matching chairs and, if so, where'd the other one go? I try to picture him getting pissed off in a poker game and cracking it over someone's head, but he doesn't seem the type. This morning he tripped over my purse and apologized even though I was the one who left it lying in the middle of the floor. He bent down and starting picking everything up, and when I tried to explain why I have a rear-view mirror in there, he said it was none of his business and just tossed it in with my toothbrush.

"This is tasty," he says between bites. He picks up his bowl so his fork can reach his mouth faster.

"This? A monkey could make this. You should get some real groceries so I can cook you a roast."

He takes a few bills out of his pocket and tosses them across the table, which is just what I'd hoped he'd do.

"Listen," I say, shoving the money down my sock. "I need to know things."

"Then ask."

"I'm not spreading my legs again until you give me some information."

"Jesus!" He chokes on a noodle and coughs, slams his bowl down. "What the hell is the matter with you? I said ASK."

"Who made my family leave?"

He wipes his mouth on a paper towel and scowls. "Some guys were hired to go out to the house."

"Why?"

"Your father was running some kind of scam."

"So? He was always running a scam."

"I don't know the particulars. He got himself tangled up in a dope rope. Told some rich guys he was going to triple their money. I guess he'd done it before."

"And?"

He shovels another mouthful of food. "And he lost it. Or spent it, or whatever."

Something hits the window and West runs to the door, opens

it and hollers out, "Did one of you little turds just throw something at my house? Well, what's that in your hand, then? Yeah, you better run." He comes back to the table, looks at me blankly.

"Then what?" I prod. "After he stole the money."

He sits. "These men were out for blood, sent a posse out to the house to shake him down."

"Where did my mother go?"

"I don't know, and even if I did, I think I ought to be the one asking the questions."

"Fill your boots."

He leans back in his chair. "You say you haven't seen anyone in your family in, what, ten years?"

"Eleven."

"So, why now?"

"Why not?" I shrug, but it turns into a shiver. "Maybe I want to see them."

He raises an eyebrow then leans forward again, scrapes his fork up the side of his bowl for the last bit of sauce.

I look down into my glass. "Daddy ever rob you?"

"Not really. I cut him off after he stopped paying his tab and he started sneaking beers from the backroom when I wasn't looking. I kicked him out a few times, but he came in one day and settled up, so I told him I'd let him back in as long as he paid cash beer-for-beer. Then I shortchanged him a few times when he was drunk to even things up."

"Well, you've got a bit of thief in you too, then."

I reach over to brush the hair out of his eyes, but he pulls away, balls up his paper towel and tosses it onto his empty side plate.

"I was just getting back what's mine. I ain't no thief."

The house fills with the sound of kids squealing outside and screen doors snapping up and down the street like Christmas crackers. Something hits the window again.

Jared Smoke never sat across a table from me like this. He had a mind like I don't know what, like it was all broken up in sharp pieces flying around in his head. He didn't like it when I looked at him too long or too hard. He had a million secrets. I get the feeling West doesn't have a ton of those. He's staring back at me with those copper-penny eyes and I feel a blush spread across my cheeks and start creeping down my neck. I practically crawl across the table into his lap. Within seconds his belt's undone and we're tangled up on the floor.

My sister Poppy was the baby of the family, born two years after Ma thought Jackie wrecked her womb for good. I can still see the big brown ponytail bobbing on top of her head. We never spent much time together, partly because she was so much younger than me, and partly because she was a crazy little bitch. I remember one afternoon before she was old enough to go to school, she met me coming up the driveway and asked if I'd trade the rocks in her hand for my school bag. I said no, so she whipped the rocks at my face and grabbed it from me. That was Poppy.

She had this squeaky voice and she hated taking baths more than anything. She was always covered in burdocks from running through bushes chasing boys and biting their chins. She had a vast collection of dead things: squirrels, raccoons, beetles. There was always a bird drying out on a windowsill or a caterpillar in the freezer.

Once, when she was about four, she slammed her fist on the dinner table and told Daddy to shut his dirty trap. He looked at her as if he might smash her through the wall, but then he reached across the table, hoisted her out of her seat and planted a big raspberry on her belly. When he plunked her back down, she crossed her arms and said, "And I mean it, Buck."

Another thing she loved, I mean besides dead things and biting people on the face, was marshmallows. Daddy came home once with a stale bag and Poppy inhaled them like they were crack cocaine. Marchellos, she called them. She only had them that one time, but for two years she brought up marchellos to anyone who came to the house, asking if they knew how she might get her hands on some.

I'm trying to remember more stuff about her when West rolls over, sits up and rubs his head. He's done the same thing in the same order every morning since I got here: rolls over, sits up, rubs his head.

"Time is it?" he grunts, guiding my hand to his erection.

"Around nine. Hey, did you know my sister, Poppy?"

"Seen her a few times, but no."

"She pretty?"

"Yeah." He lies back down. "Nice long legs."

"Good for her. I guess Kool-Aid and Cheezies don't stunt your growth after all. Was she still living at home with Ma and Daddy when the shit hit the fan?"

"How come you don't know any of this? You never even phoned them?"

"They never owned a phone."

"So you just left to go live with some other family and that was it?"

My eyes travel to the ceiling. "I'd been arrested a few times. Not for anything serious, just for stupid stuff like stealing under-arm deodorant and busting windows. The cops threatened Ma, said she had to pay a fine for something I did, which was bullshit because I had the right to work it off in community service. But she was a jumble of nerves about it. And she was convinced I'd have a better life if I got far from here. She got this infection in her ears, and while she was in the hospital she met some woman who was bringing her elderly parents back home to live with her in New Brunswick. She confessed to Ma that she didn't know how she was going to get by without some help, so Ma talked me up as some Mother Teresa bed-sitter. Next thing I know, I'm in the back seat of a car headed who knows where."

"What was the woman like?"

"She was adorable. She matched her dress to her earrings, God love her, but I wasn't Mother Teresa. She took one look at me and knew she couldn't leave me alone with her goldfish let alone her parents, so I ended up just being bored and in the way. I stole from her, lied to her, lied about lying. I gave a hand job to her plumber for a ride into the city, came back about a week later high as a shelf, tried to sell her parents some pills. I scared the shit out of all her neighbours. I don't know why she didn't kick me out sooner. I think she felt sorry for my mother. She took me on like some kind of pet project, even tricked me into her church one Sunday."

West fights a smile. "What did she tell you was in there?"

"Her name was Barbara Best. She used to correct the way I talked. If I said I seen her mailman coming, she'd say, You *saw* him. I'd say, What difference does it matter? And she'd say, You mean, *what is* the difference, and *why does* it matter?"

"Worked, though," West says. "You got good grammar."

"One time, we were in town buying milk and she caught me checking out a guitar in a store window. She asked me if I was interested in learning how to play. I told her what my mother always said, that Saints aren't musical people, but Barbara Best said that isn't true, that all people are born musical from the moment they break out of the womb and open up their lungs. She told me, 'Music is everywhere, Tabatha.'" I pause, remembering her face. "I still say that in my head sometimes: Music is everywhere."

"Music is everywhere," West murmurs.

"So we struck a deal that I could have that big red guitar for my birthday if I'd behave until then. My birthday's in June and that was January. I lasted two months until I stole this stupid paperweight shaped like the Eiffel Tower off a teacher's desk and sold it to a student in another class. I didn't think that would count, but it did." I reach my foot up to push back the curtains and sunlight spills into the room. We lie there squinting. "I wish I'd held out. Nobody's ever given me a birthday present my whole life."

"Really? Not even your own mother?"

"She'd bake a cake."

"That's not the same as a big shiny box with your name on it. What about Christmas?"

"Sometimes we had Christmas, if Daddy was around. But our presents weren't wrapped and they didn't come from any store."

"Where'd they come from, then?"

"Other people's houses." I bring my foot back beneath the covers. "Why are you asking me all this?" I ask, and at the same moment he says, "You really gave a hand job to a grown man when you were only fourteen?"

We look at each other.

"Never mind," West sighs. "Don't answer that."

WEST DRIVES AN ORANGE PICKUP TRUCK WITH BLUE doors that probably came off another truck. When we get out and shut the doors, something metal falls off somewhere. Some men would stand around until nightfall searching for the thing, slamming stuff and getting you to "look here" and "hold that" until you have grease all over you, your picnic's ruined and he finally says to just goddamn forget it. But West just circles the truck a few times, pokes his head underneath and shrugs it off.

He follows me through the trees to a wide band of sand where the sun is actually shining for once and, as soon as he glimpses water, strips down and starts running. I sit on a rock and watch his bare ass vanish into the lake. He surfaces with a howl, flicks his hair back and comes shivering back out with one hand over his crotch, shaking icy water on me as he plunks down on the sand.

"Cold enough to freeze the balls off a pool table, but beats swimming in the river with the townies," he says. "How come you know this spot and I don't?"

"Ma and Daddy used to take us here in summertime. They'd get frisky right in front of us. We'd cook beer-can chicken over a bonfire and Daddy would throw us in the lake over our heads and make us swim back to shore. One time, my little brother Jackie had a leech stuck to him and wouldn't let anyone pull it off. We chased him up and down the sand until Daddy yelled, 'Look at the fucking mermaid!,' ripped the leech off Jackie's leg and took it over to the fire on a stick. We all cheered while it fried."

"Sounds like good family fun."

"Everyone was less of an asshole here. Even Daddy. At home, his moods could change on a dime. If he came through the door, one of us would put this plastic shark toy on top of the mailbox so the rest of us would know to stay gone. He used to sit us down and make us tell him all the bad things we did while he was away. If we said we hadn't done anything, he hit twice as hard. One time, we saw a cop car coming and ran up to the house, but instead of warning Daddy, we told him Poppy fell down the cellar so he'd go check it out and have no escape when the cops busted in. Things were always better when he was gone. But we paid for that stunt when he got out. He whipped Poppy and me with her skipping rope, tied Bird and Jackie up in a blanket and dropped them out the second-floor window."

West takes my hand in his and squeezes it. I sit there with my hand trapped under his until I can't take it anymore. I slide it out and pretend to slap a mosquito on my neck.

"Come on." I jump to my feet.

We splash around knee-deep until the sun starts to sink and paint the lake in all my favourite colours. Our eyes follow all the gold threads sewing up the clouds and it's only when West says, "I think I'll drive home like this," that I remember he's still buck-naked.

He takes the long way back, past hidden driveways and an abandoned church with a tree growing out of its roof. A hitch-hiker appears out of nowhere and West slows to pull over.

"You're not wearing any clothes," I remind him.

"Shit!" He accelerates, sticks his head out the window and hollers, "Sorry, buddy!"

BACK IN THE FIRST GRADE, WE PLAYED A GAME CALLED musical chairs. It was stressful as hell. I was convinced if I was the one left without a seat at the end of the song, it'd mark me an outsider for life. My heart would pound out of my chest, and when the music stopped I'd lunge for those orange plastic seats like a mountain lion on bennies. There wasn't even a prize except to sit there looking smug, but I've got to hand it to those teachers: it was good practice for getting your hands on what's up for grabs.

I wake up after West's gone to work and it takes me a while to realize the thumping noise I'm hearing is the wind beating itself against the back wall. Through the window, I spy a huge pair of panties float past and get twisted up in a hedge. I sit up for a better look and see all kinds of clothes drifting into West's yard. There are blouses and skirts in near flight like flat, deranged birds.

I run out in just an old T-shirt of West's to chase after them, and when my arms are nearly full, I run back inside and drop my little pile on the floor. I try on a few things, but nothing fits right, so I find some rusty kitchen scissors and a sewing kit in a drawer and spend hours cutting and ironing and sewing. By the time West comes home, we've got a new set of yellow curtains and an apron.

"What's this?" he asks.

I put the apron on to show it off.

"Where'd you get all the fabric?"

"It blew into the yard. The wind must have stripped somebody's clothesline."

"Tabby!" He glances down at the leftover sleeves and zippers on the table and bites his thumb. "You can't go around swiping things from the neighbours. What do you suppose some woman's going to think when she walks by and sees her favourite dress hanging in my window?"

"Don't the curtains look nice?"

"Yes, they're real nice," he says, softening. "That ain't the point." He throws his coat over the chair. "Sit down. I got something to tell you." He plunks himself across from me then leaps back up and starts unloading beers into the fridge.

"You're making me nervous," I say.

"I got a lead on your sister. She's turning tricks in Jubilant. It might not be true, but that's what people are saying."

I went to Jubilant once. My mother had a friend named Bev who got married and moved there with her husband, and we drove four hours to go visit her. She had one of those macramé owls hanging on the wall and used a scallop shell as an ashtray for her roaches. The way she pronounced her husband Daryl's name drove me nuts. "No, honey, that's Deerull's chair." Nobody was allowed to sit in Deerull's velour chair, even though he was out in the middle of the Bay of Fundy on a lobster boat. She even vacuumed where I sat and made sure all the grooves went in the same direction. Her little house was right on the shore where it smelled like sulphur. We spent the night and I kept sneaking out of my sleeping bag to look out the window. I saw mermaids in the shadows pulling themselves up the sand by their forearms and woke Ma to tell her. She told me I was dreaming, but I was certain that in the morning we'd see their silvery paths and find them all lying bloated and sick on the concrete basement floor.

I imagine Poppy lying under some fat, hairy trucker as I watch West admire the new curtains out of the corner of his eye.

"West, you're a good person."

"Why can't I get a roast, then?"

"I needed an apron first. You can't cook a roast without an apron."

"You're running out of excuses."

"You'll get your roast."

On Sunday, I get up before dawn and pack us a lunch of bologna sandwiches and apples then climb back into bed. West had a bad night at the tavern. A couple of guys got into a fight over a woman and he had to break it up. He came home late in a rotten mood all covered in blood.

"It's this town," I say. "I've been wanting to stab someone since I got off the bus." I roll over. "So, was she gorgeous?"

"Oh, Christ. She had an ass down to her ankles and a big old camel toe in front."

"Sounds like you had a good look."

"You can see her in all her glory with your own eyes if you ever come down to visit."

"Yeah, right. And have to listen to what everybody has to say?" I lift his hand to inspect the bandages. "You want to help me find my sister or what?"

"Not really."

"How about I go on my own?"

"In my truck?"

"What—you scared I'll take off with it?"

"Something like that."

"You think I want your piece-of-shit Frankentruck? I used to drive a *Mustang*, asshole." I find my panties in the sheets, shove them into my purse and pull on my jeans, yanking the fly up so it makes a good loud *ziiiiip*. West walks out of the room and I figure that's it, but then he comes back in and tosses the keys on the nightstand.

"Fine."

"Forget it. I don't want it."

"Take the damn truck before I change my mind." I move to grab the keys and he adds, "Just leave something behind so I know you're coming back."

I dump out my purse on the bed and rummage through the pile. I find the little red plastic envelope and gingerly remove my autographed Randy "Macho Man" Savage card.

"Sentimental value," I say, handing it over.

"Jesus Christ," West says. "That's not going to cut it."

"Why not?"

He turns it over a few times. "This means that much to you?"

"Did you know that Macho Man's real name is Randy Mario Poffo?"

"No."

"Do you know who Leaping Lanny Poffo is?"

"Ain't he the WWF wrestler who used to write poems on Frisbees and chuck them out to the crowd?"

"Did you know that the Poffo brothers got their start right here in Atlantic Grand Prix Wrestling?"

West massages his eyebrows. "No."

"Before WWF, they fought each other in an International Title Match in Truro, and guess who got to see it? It was the only time my family ever left Solace River. I was only six years old, but I still remember every move. You know what a moonsault is?"

"No."

I stand up on the bed. "Want me to show you?"

2

THE BRIDGE HAS A NEW SIGN ON IT: ERNIE ELLS BRIDGE.
I guess that means Ernie's cashed in his chips. He didn't live too
far from our house. He used to ride his Supercycle down here
every morning and wave at the cars that crossed the river. It was
part of his routine. From nine in the morning till noon, he stood
on the bridge waving at cars. Then he'd go home and let all his
cats run around the yard while he counted them, 1-2-3-4-5-6,
over and over again. After that he'd hide and wait for Mrs. Glen
on her afternoon walk. He'd get behind a bush or a tree, jump out
at her and yell, "I get a kick out of you!" She hated it, but there
was only one road. Ernie wasn't that great a hider anyway.

Mrs. Glen was always talking to whoever would listen
about how her husband died in a factory accident. She must
have told Ernie the date of their wedding anniversary because
he boasted to everyone in town that he had a surprise planned.
He put on a ski mask and a pair of yellow dish gloves, climbed
the tree at the edge of his property and waited over an hour.

When Mrs. Glen was right underneath him, he jumped down, hollering, "I get a kick out of yoooooooooooou!" He almost kicked her in the head. She had an anxiety attack and Ernie wasn't sure what to do, so he came up and banged on our door. Ma went down and helped Mrs. Glen up to the house. I was in the kitchen when they came in. I watched Mrs. Glen's heavy makeup lift off her skin in beads of sweat until it hovered over her face like a mask. She wouldn't sit on our chair until I laid her sweater on it, and she didn't trust our water, so Ma had to boil it for her. At one point she turned to me and said, "Which one are you?" I told her I was Tabby, and right in front of Ma she asked me, "Do all your brothers and sisters have the same father?" As she was leaving, Jackie loudly asked Ma why she didn't tell the bitch to go fuck herself. Ma waited till the door was closed after Mrs. Glen before she turned to him and hissed, "Because it's her anniversary with her dead husband."

I guess they named the bridge after Ernie simply because he liked to stand on it and wave at cars. If Mrs. Glen's still around, I wonder what she thinks of that. Her poor husband got pressed into paper by two forklifts, and Ernie gets all the glory. That alone might have killed her.

Just off the exit ramp, I see a giant square rock on the side of the highway that some bored hick painted to look like a Rubik's cube. Most of the squares are almost faded off, but I can still make out the colours. Two sides of the cube are partially solved, which, if you've ever tried to crack one of those bastards, doesn't mean shit. Even if you get five sides lined up, you end up having to break them up again to line up the sixth. The only way to solve it is to peel off the stickers and re-stick them when no one's looking.

Three oncoming cars in a row flick their lights to tip me off there's a cop hiding around the bend. West's headlight knob is jerry-rigged with a wine cork and I don't want to mess with it too much, so after I pass the cop car I pass on the warning by pointing my index finger in the air and rotating it like a siren.

This has to be the most unscenic stretch of highway. The only thing distinguishing one long run of trees from another is the occasional Christmas tree farm, and the only difference between those trees and the rest of the forest is signs that say CHRISTMAS TREES. Around the halfway point, my stomach starts to growl and I turn off the highway looking for a nice place to park while I eat my lunch. I pass an old Mi'kmaq burial ground, a one-truck volunteer fire station, a sign telling me to Choose Life. There's grass growing up through the pavement in some spots. Finally, I spy a small farm. I pull over and walk up to the fence, hold out my apple and wait for one of the ponies to trot over. I'm stroking her nose with those big horsey eyelashes brushing my fingers and the rain holding off and West's big truck parked behind me, and I realize part of me is waiting for the farmer to come out here and yell for me to get the hell off his property. I have to remind myself I'm not fourteen anymore and nobody way out here's going to know I'm a Saint unless I tell them myself.

I get back in the truck and eat the bologna sandwiches while I listen to the country stillness. I keep trying to remember the tune of this old church hymn Ma used to hum low and quiet at the foot of our beds. She didn't think she had a voice for singing, so she'd speak the lyrics. It was maybe what church was like if your mother delivered the sermon in her nightgown and all you could see was the tip of her Export "A" glowing in the dark. Even when the verses were punctuated by Jackie's farts, she would just keep droning on in that creepy voice. Ma was never one for brightening the mood. If you skinned your knee, she'd say, "Course you did." If you asked if it might rain, she'd say, "Only if you don't want it to."

I wonder if there really is such a thing as blood ties. Even though I always thought of my family as just a pack of wolves forced to live together in that big drafty shack, I do feel something pull on me every now and then. I imagine there's a long string holding us together, stretching and fraying as the years drag on. Maybe that's why I'm driving through the armpit of nowhere trying to find a sister I haven't seen since she was ten years old and who may well spread her legs for a living. I guess I'm afraid the string's about to finally snap.

DOWNTOWN JUBILANT MAKES SOLACE RIVER LOOK LIKE Shangri-La. Some of the shops even have bars on their windows. West says stories of trouble in Jubilant have swamped the news ever since the lobster population started to dwindle. A few weeks ago, some fishermen surrounded a truck delivering cheap US lobsters to the processing plant and busted a few of the driver's ribs, and last summer there was a murder over trapping turf.

West said the dead guy's boat washed up so full of gunshot holes it looked like a hunk of Swiss cheese.

It's early afternoon when I pull into town, but dusk is settling in by the time I find out where Poppy lives. The owners of the feed store give me directions. I walked in as they were closing and the old man said he never heard of Poppy Saint. "She's leggy," I said. "Probably swears a lot, doesn't dress for the weather." His wife came out, wiped off her hands and drew me a map on a piece of cardboard.

I crawl along in the truck with the windows rolled down so I can see the numbers on the houses. There are homemade protest signs in people's windows with slogans like FEELING THE PINCH? or TRY ON OUR RUBBER BOOTS FOR A DAY AND SEA HOW IT FEELS. Some homes have dulse laid out to dry on the rooftops and fishing buoys piled on the lawns. I'm hoping one of these hard-working places is Poppy's, but of course she's in the rusty trailer up at the edge of the woods.

I park at the end of the long driveway and take my time getting out, hoping she'll see me before I have to walk up and knock on the door. The air is much cooler and damper here. I can't see the ocean, but I can smell it.

There's a swing set on Poppy's lawn made from the back seat of a car and a broken plastic swan planter full of Popsicle wrappers and beer caps. The wrought iron steps aren't attached to the trailer, just propped up against it. The paint is chipped on the mailbox nailed to the exterior wall, and the name says *Saint*. It feels like a punch to look at it, that ugly peeling name.

After a long minute, a woman comes to the door. She looks

like an ashtray that's been left out in the rain. Her eyeglasses are hanging around her neck on one of those granny strings. She puts them on roughly and stares at me from behind the screen, takes a drag of her smoke.

"Poppy?" I say stupidly.

"She ain't here."

"I'm Poppy's sister."

"She don't got no sister."

"She used to."

The woman retreats inside and stubs out her cigarette. Then she comes back and looks at me again, moves her tongue around in her mouth as if to make sure her teeth are in there.

"Tabby?"

"Hi, Ma."

I stand there with the fog falling between us like a curtain until she finally opens the door. The interior light floods the steps, and I follow her inside. There's a permeating smell of microwave cooking mixing with the general bouquet of cigarette smoke. The chesterfield looks like a werewolf got hold of it, stuffing coming out at all the seams.

"What a dump."

"Nice of you to say." Ma lights a fresh cigarette from her blouse pocket and lowers herself into a faded armchair. I remembered her being so pretty, but now she's all slumped and puffy-faced. Her hair looks like she cut it with a pocket knife.

"Sorry."

She avoids my eyes. "My God, Tabby. Where have you been all these years?"

She puts down the cigarette. "Come here. Let me hold you." Neither of us makes a move and finally she picks her smoke back up. "Poppy disappeared. Went to work one night five weeks ago and never came back."

I ask Ma what line of work Poppy's in, but she won't answer. So I ask if she gets paid by the hour and Ma picks up a cloth and starts wiping the table as if somebody just spilled something. Not that there's anything to spill. She didn't offer me coffee.

Poppy takes off like this every once in a while, Ma says, but never for more than a week because of her kids. Janis and Swimmer. Janis is five and wears sunglasses in the house. Swimmer is three. He's got a big round head and eyes so huge they remind me of peanut butter cups. They pretend to be shy at first, peeking around the corner, but then they march in and curl up on either side of me like little bookends.

"So, where've you been living?" Ma asks.

"All over New Brunswick, but I came back and met a guy in Solace River."

"Solace River?" Ma freezes. "Why the hell would you go back there?"

"I was looking for you."

She picks up the cloth again. "This man of yours. He got a job?"

"Of course," I say, like I'm so used to having a man, let alone one with a job. "He runs his own business."

"Good." She nods. "Good for you."

"Where's Daddy?"

"He's in hospital waiting to die." She wrings the cloth in her hands. "They say he's got colon cancer. He might be dead already for all I know."

"How can you not know?"

"We cut ties a long time ago."

"Oh." I can't seem to find an emotion. "What about Bird and Jackie?"

Janis tugs on my arm. "I got a picture of you."

"Of me? I haven't even got one of those."

She pulls on my arm. "Come on. I'll show it to you."

I follow her down the short hallway into a tiny bedroom crammed with toys. The purple walls are covered in personalized stamps, gold stars with her name inside them. I can tell she tried to stamp up the whole room with JANIS! but the ink faded and wore out. There are a few stray stars on the dresser and ceiling like the faded embers of a dream.

She hauls out a pink plastic cash register from under the bunk bed, removes some old, sticky photographs from the drawer and slaps them into my palm.

The photo on top is one of all of us in front of our house: Daddy, Ma, Bird, Jackie, Poppy and me. We look like we're in a police lineup. I wonder who took the picture, and why on that particular day. I flip through the stack and find the one of just me. I'm wearing a dress with a hole in it and my hair is so blond it's almost invisible.

"I hated those shoes," I say.

There's a used Q-tip stuck to the photograph and when I pull it off, a piece of my little leg comes with it.

46

"Gross." Janis screws up her face. "You can keep that one."

"Thanks," I say, tucking it into my purse.

I walk out of the room when Ma comes in to get the kids ready for bed, and Janis yells after me, "Will you still be here when it's morning? If you are, I can learn you how to do two somersaults in a row."

"You can do two somersaults in a row?"

"Probably four."

"Then how come you're only going to show me how to do two?"

She doesn't get back to me on that, so I head for the living room. Ten minutes later, Ma comes with an armful of wool blankets and some flannel sheets. "You can have the bedroom," she says.

"I'm not going to take your bed."

"It ain't mine. It's Poppy's."

"I'll be fine on the sofa."

She watches me make it up before shuffling off. I can't sleep, and I can tell she can't either. She coughs constantly and the bedsprings squeak every time she rolls over. When I glance at the clock, it's barely nine. When we were kids, Ma never went to bed before 2 a.m. She'd sit at the kitchen table drinking coffee, doing word search puzzles and thinking up worst-case scenarios. I trudged past her once on the way to the bathroom and she reminded me I couldn't flush the toilet because the well was almost dry. Then she said, "Tabby, if the house catches fire and none of you can get out, give the kids all the pink pills in my bottom drawer." I nodded, squinting against the kitchen light, and by the time I realized I'd just agreed to poison Poppy and Jackie to death, she'd licked her finger and flipped to the next puzzle.

There are so many things I want to ask her now. I consider knocking on her door, but every time I sit up, I chicken out and lie back down.

In the morning, Janis drops a piece of toast on my chest from over the back of the sofa and it scares the living shit out of me.

"Shhh," Janis whispers. "Grandma's sleeping." She climbs under the blanket with me and chews loudly, raining crumbs all over both of us.

"This is delicious," I whisper. "You're a good cook." I lift up her sunglasses and see my baby sister Poppy looking back at me.

"What's the matter?"

"You look just like your mother."

"Why are you making a sad face?"

"I miss her, I guess."

Janis sighs, her mouth circled in strawberry jam. "I miss her too."

A cat jumps on top of us. When I put my hand out to pet it, Janis says, "I wouldn't do that if I were you."

I sit up so fast, I knock Janis to the floor.

"That's Gord the Ferret," she says as it slithers away. "We got him for our pet so he would kill the rat, but Swimmer's more scared of Gord than the rat, so Grandma put Gord out to the woods, but he keeps on coming back in here whenever he feels like it." She throws a hunk of toast at its face. "He always has poop and bugs on him."

I look around at the room in daylight. Aside from the ratty

furniture, there's a stereo, a lamp, a stand-up ashtray, a peeling plastic rocking horse on springs, and that's about it. The grey carpet is just about worn through to the plywood floor underneath, and the whole place needs a bucket of bleach.

Janis gets up and straddles the plastic horse, bounces on it a few times for my benefit. Then she stands up on its back and starts to lift one shaky leg in the air behind her like a figure skater. I realize I should probably stop the show, but I'm not sure what the safety rules are around here. Before I can speak up, she loses her balance and crashes down on the saddle. If it hurt, she doesn't let on. I look away and she follows my gaze to matching velvet paintings of palm trees hanging on the wall.

"Those are some pictures of Toronto. Mama says when we get there, we'll be rich. Everyone there has white cars and gold teeth. We might go soon if the bad people come."

"Bad people?"

"They think she stoled their money, but it wasn't her. It was Petunia."

"Who?"

"PET-OO-NEE-YA. She's always getting in trouble. Mama had to sleep in jail one time because of her."

"Have you ever met Petunia?"

"Nope. Don't want to neither."

Petunia my ass. "Hey, Janis." I glance at the clock. "Do you think Ma would mind if you came with me to run some errands?"

"Mind?" Janis leaps off the horse like she's going to Disney World. "She'll be glad to get rid of me!"

She changes into elastic-waist blue jeans but leaves her pyjama top on. I offer to comb some of the tangles out of her long brown pigtails, but she won't let me. I leave a note for Ma and just as we're going out the door, Swimmer stumbles into the hallway. His head is so much larger than the rest of him that he walks like a drunk, all leaned over toward one wall.

"You stay here with your cartoon shows, Swimmer," Janis says, pushing him back into the bedroom and shutting the door. "Quick, before he gets out!" she yells.

"Can't Swimmer come too?"

Janis looks as if she might cry if I insist, so I don't. She runs out ahead of me and hauls the truck door open all by herself. When I get in, she's touching the knobs on the dash, careful not to turn any, though I can tell she's dying to. She takes a good long survey of the bench seat and pats the vinyl.

"Nice ride."

"Thanks. It's not mine, though."

"I know. What's your man's name?"

"West." I feel a little guilty for letting on like he's my boyfriend. She nods. "That's a good name."

"Speaking of names," I say, changing the subject. "Are you a Saint?"

"Yup. But I ain't no saint. That's what Ma says. She says *saint* means someone who's good all the time."

"Have you ever had a different last name?"

"Nope."

"You know who your father is?"

"His name is Bruce or Barty. Something stupid like that."

"You ever met him?"

"Nope."

"Do you wish you had a daddy?"

She shrugs. "It don't make no difference."

She's a Saint all right, I think, revving up the truck.

JUBILANT ISN'T MUCH OF A TOWN. JANIS GIVES ME THE lowdown. It's got a movie theatre that only shows movies on Saturday nights, and the duct-taped popcorn machine catches on fire when it gets too hot. The trains are all gone. Janis said they ripped up all the tracks and made footpaths that nobody can walk on because of all the ATV riders hot-rodding up and down.

"Ran buddy's foot right over. There was blood squirting out of him like this!" She flings her fingers in every direction.

"You saw it?"

"And we got one of them nail salons, but I never been in there."

"Do you think they paint little pictures on people's finger-nails? Your grandma used to do that. She could even make shooting stars."

I wonder if Ma remembers when she used to do my nails. She would get out her blow-dryer and dry them one at a time. Maybe she'd be rich now if she'd started her own business.

Janis points out Frosty's Convenience Store in case I need any Cracker Jack. There's a giant neon orange sign in the window: *We Cash EI Cheques!* We come to a stoplight and I turn left onto the main street of town, drive along a row of faded businesses with the ocean whitecapping between them until I find the salon. I easily nab a place to park and we go inside. The sign on the wall lists prices for hair, nails, waxing, body piercing and pet portraits. There's a camera set up on a tripod in the corner next to a shelf of props, including chef hats and bow ties. Janis shakes her head no when I ask her if she knows the woman cleaning the sink.

"Hi there!" I call out. "This one needs her nails done."

The woman lays down her towel, comes over, picks up Janis's hand and examines it like a surgeon. "All right, honey. Come over here with me and have a seat."

"I'm getting my nails done?" Janis can hardly sit still. She chooses turquoise with glow-in-the-dark ladybugs. Every time the woman finishes a nail, Janis whispers, "Oh. My. God."

"You hiring?" I ask, trying to imagine how I'd get a cat to hold still while I drape it in a feather boa.

"No one is."

"Well, there goes that idea. I'd planned on popping into a few gift shops after this, figuring they might need someone to hand-paint *Bay of Fundy* on all those conch shells they import from the Bahamas."

The back window looks out onto a rain-slickened wharf where some fishermen are stacking traps. I watch them finish the job and start goofing off, scooping up mussel shells and tossing them at each other. It quickly leads to a shoving match.

"You ever have Poppy Saint in here getting her nails done?"

The woman pauses with her nail brush mid-air and stares at me.

"Poppy's this little girl's mother before you say anything," I say. "She's gone AWOL and we can't find her."

"She's been in here once or twice. I haven't seen her lately. You want to ask Lyle Kenzie."

"Who's he, now?"

"He hangs out down at Jody's."

"Jody's? Is that around here?"

She points with her free hand down the street. When she finishes up, I pay her with the money West gave me for truck emergencies. She hands Janis a coupon for 10 percent off a pet portrait, but Janis hands it back and says, "My dog got run over by the garbage truck." The woman turns white, apologizes to us twice. When we get back on the road, Janis tells me she never had a dog.

"Why'd you say you did?"

She tilts her sunglasses down to look me in the eye. "Because if I said I don't got no dog, she'd say, 'Well then, honey, give it to your friend.' I only know one kid that got a dog and I wouldn't give that girl a used fart."

"What's a used fart?"

"A fart that's already used. My mama called the mailman a used fart because he keeps giving us flyers with toys on them, and Swimmer sees them and wants her to go buy them all."

"But how do you use a fart?"

"You fart, then you smell it, then when someone else smells it, it's already used."

"She called him that to his face?"

"Yup. She hates his guts ever since he told on her."

"Told on her for what?"

"For leaving me and Swimmer alone when he was just a baby. I hotted up the milk in the microwave and when he pooped in his diaper, I chucked it out the window so it didn't stink him up."

I lean to put my arm around her, but she straightens up and slaps my hand. I put it back on the wheel and she relaxes again.

JODY'S GARAGE IS A BUSINESS ATTACHED TO SOMEONE'S house. It's empty except for some old cars in various stages of dismantle and a sea of fast-food wrappers. I whisper to Janis that the place smells like a used fart. She nods sagely. When we walk out, some woman sticks her head out the front door of the house and yells, "They're all down at the diner!" so we get back in the car.

Dot's Daughter's Diner is long and narrow, half full of customers who stare outright at whoever walks in. Janis holds up her nails and tells the woman at the cash register, "They glow in the dark. If the power goes out, you'll know where I'm at, so I can't steal nothing."

We grab a booth.

"Have you been in here before?" I ask Janis.

She nods. "Grandma brings us here when my mother forgets to cook dinner."

I look around. One whole wall is plastered in photographs of customers posing with their meals. At the centre is a framed eight-by-ten of a bemused-looking Rita MacNeil holding up a bowl and spoon. The inscription says *Cape Breton's First Lady of Song Getting Her Mac 'N' Cheese On.*

"Is your mother in any of these pictures?"

Janis shakes her head. "They tried to get us in their camera, but Mama wouldn't let them. She said she'd bring them in one of her mug shots."

I laugh.

"What?"

"Do you know what a mug shot is?"

"Yup. It's a picture of a lady sitting in a lawn chair drinking coffee."

The laminated menu posted above the table informs us that customers come to Jubilant from far and wide to taste Dot's legendary recipes handed down to her daughter. I glance around, but no one in here looks like they're from farther down the road than the old fish meal factory I saw yesterday. The rest of the menu is barely legible from all the revisions made with a ball-point pen. Most of the fixes are to prices, but I notice someone crossed out the words "home-cooked" in *Home-cooked lasagna – just like Dot used to make!* It's a thinker. I keep running my finger down the list. A scary set of quotation marks were added to *Try Our World Famous Fresh-From-The-Boat Lobster Roll.* Not to "world famous," or even "fresh-from-the-boat," but to "lobster."

The waitress comes over with her pencil.

"You must be Dot's daughter," I say.

She rolls her eyes.

"I don't suppose you're hiring?"

"I don't suppose I am."

"We'll have a double order of Tater Dots and a smile."

"And a milkshake." Janis swings her legs.

"Strawberry okay?" The waitress lowers her pad. "We're all out of chocolate."

Janis mumbles something that sounds suspiciously like "Bullshit."

"Has Janis's mother been in here today, by any chance?" I ask quickly.

"No."

"How about yesterday?"

"Haven't seen her in ages."

"Is one of those men over there Lyle Kenzie?"

She follows my gaze. "Black baseball cap." She walks off, comes back a few minutes later with the milkshake and a look that tells me I better not ask any more questions that aren't about the food.

"I hope Dot has more than one daughter," I whisper to Janis. "This one's kind of crusty."

Janis ignores the straw and takes a big sip from the rim of her shake, coating half her face in it. "She forgot the smile. You should order another one. Ask for one that looks like this." She sets down her heavy glass and stretches her mouth into an exaggerated grimace.

"How's the milkshake?" I ask, feeling my stomach gnaw on itself. "Better than the service?"

She shimmies her shoulders, which I take it means yes. She seems to have a whole set of moves. Pumping her fist up and down means, Drive! Putting her hands together in prayer means, Please stop asking me questions.

"I was going to order strawberry anyway," she says when she comes up for air. "My mother says I should try every kind."

"Well," I say, glancing over my shoulder at Lyle Kenzie, "she certainly practises what she preaches." I lower my voice. "Do you know the man in the black baseball hat?"

"He's been over at our trailer."

"Farewell to Nova Scotia" is playing on the jukebox and it's stuck on the line "But still there was no rest for me ... But still there was no rest for me ... But still there was no rest for me ..." Janis hops down, picks up a hammer lying next to the machine and gives the side of the jukebox a good whack. It skips to the next song.

"That's what the hammer's there for," she tells me.

I keep my eye on Lyle Kenzie as he puts on his jacket. He's staring right back at me.

"Sit tight a minute, okay?" I tell Janis. I get up and walk outside.

Lyle pauses in the doorway a moment before letting the screen creak closed. "You looking for me?" He adjusts the pasty beer gut flopping over the waistband of his jeans and reaches into a grease-stained shirt pocket for cigarettes.

"I'm looking for Poppy Saint."

"You and me both." He lights a smoke, jams his lighter back in his pocket.

"My name is Opal Kent. I work for the police department." I try not to blink. Opal Kent was one of my favourite characters when I lived in a group home and got addicted to soaps. She had steel-blue eyes and a matching blazer.

"You're a cop?"

"I'm a private investigator working with the Jubilant Police Department."

He sneers and starts walking away toward a new Ford truck.

I follow him and say, "Miss Saint should be easy to find, but if you want to make it easier by giving me an address or a phone number, I'll put you down as a false lead. I've been watching that garage for two days now, and I think you know what I mean when I say that I wouldn't want to have to disclose what goes on in there. The cops are only interested in Poppy at this point."

It's a stab in the dark, but Jody's must be the base for something shady, because Lyle blinks like crazy for a few seconds then goes into his truck and scrawls something on a piece of paper. He comes back and shoves it at me. "I don't know anything about what she's been up to and if she says I do, she's a fucking liar."

He glances in the rear-view at least four times as he pulls away. I stand watching until the roar of his souped-up engine fades down the road. Then I go back inside and slide in across from Janis.

"That was easy," I say.

She slurps her straw on the bottom of her empty glass. "Mama said that Lyle's about as bright as the hooks on Grandma's bra."

I glance down at the table. The Tater Dots arrived while I was outside and now they're just a plate of crumbs. I sigh and scoop some up with my fingers. "Grandma's still alive?"

"You just talked to her last night. Wasn't no ghost."

"Oh, right. I thought you meant my grandma."

"Great-Grandma Jean? She choked on a Mars bar and died at the table."

"You were there?"

"Nope, it wasn't our table. She never lived with us. She does now, though. She's in a box in our trailer."

"What?"

"They took her to the fire place and burned her up so she looked like dirt. Once Swimmer was driving his Dinky trucks through her on the kitchen floor. We had to scoop her back into the box, and now there's a few Cheerios in there with her."

"Janis, you are a source of information."

MA IS WAITING FOR US OUTSIDE THE TRAILER. SEEING her shocks me all over again. She looks like she's wearing an old-lady costume. When Janis runs inside to show off to Swimmer about her fingernails, I fill Ma in on what happened.

"Lyle Kenzie is small-time," she says. "Don't let him scare you."

"He doesn't scare me. I scared him. Who is he?"

"I used to think he was her boyfriend. She was checking in with him all the time. But I think he's a contact."

"Pills, pipe or needle?"

She averts her eyes. "I don't know exactly. It don't make her see things or nothing like that, and she won't do it in front of the kids. But she needs to have it. That's what she always says. She needs to have it, just like food. She says she wishes she never got it in her blood because now she can't get through the day without taking something." She shakes her head. "I'll never understand it."

We stand there with our arms crossed, staring down at the dirt.

"There's something I got to show you just down the road." Ma says. She looks at me kind of funny and lights a cigarette, takes three or four hauls on it before crushing it out with her heel. She goes to the door and tells Janis we'll be right back, locks it with her key. We start walking, Ma and me, and it's sort of like the reunion I'd once imagined: me all grown up and Ma with grey in her hair, strolling down a sunset road.

"I'm taking you to your brother."

"Which one?"

"Bird."

"Bird! Really? What I remember most about Bird are the whoppers he'd come up with. Like that time you asked him where he got that brand new gold watch with the price tag still on it and he said he found it in the empty ice cooler out back of the Kwikway. Or when he said he failed math because the teacher added up his marks wrong. Remember how he used to kiss people's mothers on the hand when he met them?" I laugh. "Does he still have all that long blond hair?"

I keep rambling until Ma stops short in front of a little blue house and puts her hands on my shoulders. "Now, Tabby. Don't you say nothing about it."

"About what?"

She goes up the stairs and in through the screen door, and I follow. We enter a dank room with wallpaper that's been ripped to shreds in two-inch-wide strips at waist height along every wall. The ceiling fan is missing two paddles and the cord that makes it spin is so long it drags on the brown shag carpet. Three men are sitting around a table drinking rye. The one with his back to us is slumped in a wheelchair. The man on his right has an eye patch and a good eye that won't hold still, and the squat, fat man on the left doesn't seem to be wearing any pants.

"Hey, Birdie!" Ma trots over, scoots in behind the wheelchair, leans down and kisses him on the cheek.

I come at the table from the other side so I can see his face. He has a scar that runs from his left temple all the way across to his right jawline. It looks like an eel, all grey and rubbery. There's a bald spot on the back of his head with a flaky rash on it and his fingernails are bruised black, as if he slammed every one of them in a drawer. He's drooling all over his shirt front.

Ma pats his head. "What are you boys doing? Getting in trouble?"

"Nothing," the fat one says. Now I see he's not even wearing underpants. Just a T-shirt, like Winnie-the-Pooh.

"This is Tabby," Ma tells him. "She's Bird's sister."

"Hi, Bird," I say, trying to hold a smile. "Do you remember me?"

His tongue dangles out of the corner of his mouth as he shakes his head side to side.

"That's okay," I say finally.

He keeps his eyes on me as he slowly reaches his arm out, grabs hold of an edge of wallpaper and tears it off in a long line. Ma leaves the room to check the cupboards, and the rest of us go mute until she comes back and sets a bowl of soup down in front of each of the men. She ties a dishrag around Bird's neck and starts to feed him with a plastic ladle. After he slurps a few mouthfuls, she taps the elbow of the man with the eye patch and says, "Go ahead and eat your soup, Stanley. Tabby won't bite you."

When they finish eating, Ma washes the dishes while I dry. She tells me Bird's not fit to live on his own, but he won't go to a facility. She tried to take him once and he spit on the nurses and broke a television set. "I asked around and heard about these two living here with an older brother. Bird gets a disability cheque every month, so I told the man we could pay a little rent and I'd help out with the cleaning and meals. Bird moved in the next week and the brother said he was going on a fishing trip. That's the last we seen of him." Ma dabs the cloth on some soup spills. "I stayed here for a little while, but then I had to move to the trailer after Poppy took off. Now I go back and forth all the damn day trying to keep everyone fed."

I hear a loud noise and poke my head in the other room. Winnie-the-Pooh has a hold of Bird's wheelchair handles, trying to dump him out onto the floor. I tell Ma and she takes her time finishing the dishes before going to break it up. She comes back in with a Game Boy device in her hand.

"I'm taking this away from them for good. It's a fight in a can." She shows me the video screen. "See these bars falling down? You got to move them around real fast to make them fit together before the next ones come." She keeps demonstrating until I ask if it's time to leave.

When we're finally outside, I take a big breath of air and walk away as fast as I can.

"Why didn't you warn me, Ma?" I yell. "What the hell happened to him?"

"He got jumped. Lost the use of his legs and half his brain. Some days I think he's better off. The way he was going, someone would've killed him by now."

"Who jumped him?"

"It started right after we moved here, some pissing contest. There was probably a woman involved, 'cause you know there always is. Bird was getting even with somebody every other month. Now he's fine most of the time, except for when the cards come out. He gets a temper when he can't keep the rules straight. I just feel bad about his little girls. Their mother took them away out west after he got out of the hospital. Every once in a while he'll ask where they are, but mostly he forgets about them, which is best for everybody."

"How is that best for *anybody*?"

She doesn't have an answer. "It's a hard life, Tabby. I always blamed your father for everything, but it's been just as bad with him gone."

"Should I even ask about Jackie?"

"Jackie's around. He's hell-bent on finding out who did this to Bird. But he's doing all right, works construction, don't even smoke no more. His girlfriend says he watches fishing shows and goes to bed early most nights."

"Can I call him?"

"Of course."

"He doesn't speak through a voice box or have a glass eye or anything?"

"Well."

"What?"

"He's about to become a father."

"Jesus. You scared me."

"You don't think that's scary?"

BEFORE I SETTLE IN ON THE SOFA FOR THE NIGHT, I GIVE West a call from the telephone in the kitchen.

"I'm going to go see my other brother, Jackie, tomorrow night," I whisper. "If you don't need your truck right away."

"I guess not."

I fiddle with the mustard-coloured phone cord. "I lied. I never drove a Mustang."

"Mustangs aren't that great."

"I have a five-year-old niece, Janis. She likes your name."

"Oh yeah?"

I try to think of what to say next. "Your voice sounds good on the phone. Just like angel food cake."

"Angel food cake does sound good. Maybe that's for dessert after my roast."

3

It's ten miles to Jackie's. He's throwing a party to welcome me. When I pull up, all his friends turn and wave. I get out of the truck and Jackie leaps down from the deck. He takes his cap off like we're in church or something. The black hair plastered to his forehead is still thick and shiny as ever. Ma used to say Jackie stole all the good genes, but I'm not sure there were any. He just looks like he came from some other family. He's got suede grey eyes framed with thick lashes. When he was born, Daddy took one look at him and accused Ma of fucking around.

"Scabby Tabby." Jackie punches my arm.

"Black Jack."

He does up a couple of buttons on his flannel shirt before he picks me up off the ground in a bear hug. "It's some good to see you, girl. I thought you were history." He turns and yells up to the deck, "Everybody, this here's my big sister, Tabby. I don't want to see her without a beer in her hand for the rest of the night."

A petite brunette greets me at the top of the stairs with a cold one, but Jackie grabs her arm. "Not that piss," he says. He fishes in the cooler and tosses me an Oland's instead.

"I'm Jackie's girlfriend, Jewell," she says. "It's so nice to meet you." She's tiny everywhere except for the baby bulge under her tight ivory dress.

"You are not my girlfriend," he says, pinching her ass.

She glares at him. "You want a wife, keep it up. I'll make you put a ring on this finger so fast it'll make your dick spin."

In the same breath she starts chirping away to me about the weather and Jackie excuses himself to get barbecue sauce. I notice the woman who did Janis's nails is standing on the other side of the deck. She sees me at the same time and waves.

"You met Tabby the other day, right, Kim?" Jewell says to her.

"That's right." The woman finishes chewing a mouthful of potato chips. "How's your little niece doing?" she asks me. "I didn't clue in that the two of you are Jackie's people until you mentioned Poppy."

"Thanks for that tip on Lyle." I pull the paper out of my purse. "He gave me this."

She walks over and takes a look. "Don't know it. But you should bring Jackie with you if you go. I wouldn't trust Lyle."

"Why not?"

"Because he's Lyle." She picks up a lock of my hair and rubs the ends between her fingers. "Is the humidity fucking with your hair? When I first moved to Jubilant, I swear, I almost shaved my head."

Before I can ask anything else about Lyle, she walks down off the deck. I watch her rummage in the trunk of a car and pull out a whole salon. She tucks her Calypso Berry Breezer in her cleavage to free up both hands and comes hauling everything up the stairs.

"I take it all home with me at night because the shop gets broken into at least once a month," she says breathlessly. She plucks the cooler from her boobs. "Nobody comes to me for hair anymore. They all go to this skank Gina for extensions. I don't do them because everyone wants them out as soon as they're in, and you end up working twice and getting paid once. But Gina wears sweatpants with her own name written on the ass, so she's not about to do the math."

She pushes me inside to Jackie's kitchen table, sweeps Jewell's dog-eared novels and knitting needles to the side, and the next thing I know I'm sitting on a stool with a garbage bag pinned around my neck. While she's snipping away, Jackie hoists himself up on the counter and starts asking me every question he can think of.

"You got a house?"

"Sort of."

"Kids?"

"No, but I see you're about to have one."

Kim cuts in and says, "Jackie's fathered just about the whole elementary school."

He grins. "I got to work seventy hours a week to pay for all their fancy sneakers."

"You must love being a daddy."

"I love making love. But not every woman tells you she's setting a trap. Most of them kids I didn't know I was making till their mothers' bellies swelled up and they showed up on my doorstep with their palms out." He clams up as Jewell comes in and slides coasters under our drinks.

"Jackie," I say when she goes back outside. "Do you have shit for brains? It's called a condom."

"Oh my God!" He falls off the counter, laughing. "I swear to Christ, that's the last thing you said to me before you left home a million years ago."

"It's probably true," I tell Kim. "And he was only eleven."

I look around at his walls. He's got a Jack Daniel's calendar with Jewell's prenatal appointments scrawled on it and a pay phone mounted next to the fridge, which he tells me is the kids' college fund. Someone actually drops a quarter in it and makes a call while we're sitting there. I don't know how he rigged that up, but it's proof enough he's Daddy's son.

I glance at a photograph of him and Bird taped to the refrigerator. Their arms are slung around each other's shoulders, hunting rifles down at their sides. Bird looks big and solid, at least a foot taller than Jackie.

"We used to go up to the hunting cabin," Jackie says, pointing to the photo with his bottle. "Bird shot four pheasants that day and rubbed it in my face for months. Now I tell him that was me. He don't remember." His smile fades and he takes a long swallow of beer. "You seen him?"

"Yesterday," I say.

He doesn't say any more. Kim brushes some highlights in my hair, talks to me about her Labrador retrievers while they're developing. Then she leads me to the sink, rinses it all out and fluffs my hair with her fingers as she blow-dries.

"Tabby!" Jackie whistles. "You look like a supermodel."

I go look in the bathroom mirror, come back smiling. "Holy shit, Kim, how can I thank you?"

She unclips the plastic bag from my shoulders and gathers up her supplies. "See that sawed-off turd over there in the workboots?" She points to a snaggle-toothed kid drinking out of a mug that says SEX IS BETTER THAN GRASS IF YOU HAVE THE RIGHT PUSHER. "Don't let him near me."

She heads for the deck and, sure enough, he's hot on her heels. I tap his shoulder, introduce myself, and for the next two hours get the long version of his whole life story. His last name's Miller and since everybody calls his older brother Miller, he got stuck with Miller Lite. He's the only game hawker in the Maritimes, training his falcon eight hours a day and getting paid zero dollars and zero cents for all his hard work. I feign interest as he shows me all his claw marks and peck scars. Secretly, I'm staring at the reflection of my new hairstyle in every available surface, including the metal toaster.

"So, anyways," Miller Lite says, reapplying the Band-Aid he pulled back to show me his infected neck gouge. "You should come over sometime and see my bird." He plucks a badly rolled joint from behind his ear and lights the wrong end.

Jackie overhears on his way to take a leak. He thumps Miller Lite on the back and says, "Sorry, man, my sister's only interested in seeing guys' dicks if they're over three inches."

"Aw, fuck's sakes, Jackie," Miller Lite says, coughing out billows of smoke. "Why you got to tell everybody everything for?"

JACKIE NAVIGATES THE WAY TO BLUEBELLES. HE RECOG-
nized the address. He says his friends call it Blue Balls because
married men go there after work to watch the dancers before
driving home to their homely wives.

"Course, you can buy some relief in the backroom," he says,
twisting his cap in his hands.

"So, who's Lyle Kenzie?"

Jackie sticks his hat back on his head. "Just some fat fucking
loser who can't even be an alcoholic right."

"There's a right way?"

"You don't get drunk on every kind of booze there is. You
pick one staple. I seen that guy one time with a rum and egg-
nog sprinkled with fucking nutmeg, sipping it out of a cinnamon
stick."

"Who is he to Poppy?"

"I don't know. She got herself mixed up in that skid soup
down at the autobody shop. Probably buys drugs off him."

"When's the last time you saw her?"

He traces his finger in the dust on the dashboard. "Been about
three months. She says she's fine, but she ain't. I've given up on
her, tell you the truth. Ma watches them kids and they seem like
they're doing all right. I help out some, and Poppy sends money
when she's been gone a while."

"Not this time."

"Well." Jackie sits up straighter. "Jewell won at bingo last week.
I'll borrow some if I have to."

"How'd you nab a good girl like Jewell?"

"She's from Fiddle Bay, came up to Jubilant to see her cousin.

I was driving by and seen this tight denim ass walking into the bar, ran in after it."

"Well, there's a heartwarming bedtime story for the baby."

"By the time she found out I was bad news, we'd already soaked the sheets a few times. It was too late then, she was hooked. But I ain't telling my baby boy none of that."

"How do you know it's a boy?"

"Every one of them has a pecker so far. Bad little fuckers, but some good-looking. There's only three of them, by the way. Kim was just putting you on."

"Three different mothers, I suppose."

"Carla, Chrissie, Cora Lee—the three Cs. All batshit crazy."

A house appears between the trees. The family who lives there is sitting out in lawn chairs facing the road instead of the sunset on the lake behind them. I wish I was one of them, all settled in with a lapdog and a Corona. One of them points at the truck and I imagine they're playing a game, trying to guess where people are going. I wonder if it would occur to anyone we're a long-lost brother-sister duo trying to track down a missing hooker.

"It's time I got a real job," I say out loud.

"You never had a job?"

"I spent four years in Raspberry. No one hires juvenile delinquents who don't even have a social insurance number."

"What?" Jackie turns. "I thought you moved to easy street."

I shake my head no and he keeps staring. When we were kids, the older sister of one of Jackie's friends got sent to Raspberry. Cher was a typical small-town bad girl, too cool for school but not so tough you wouldn't bum a light off her and slip it in your pocket. When she came back months later, she'd shaved the words FUCK OFF into one side of her head and choked out her boyfriend with his belt when she found out he'd cheated.

"I've worked before," I say. "Just not for a paycheque. I cleaned motel rooms, harvested pot, was a tattoo guinea pig, things like that. One summer, the Tilt-A-Whirl operator at the Bill Lynch Show used to let me take over for him when he went to jerk off. He only paid me in ride tickets, but he'd give me a whole whack. I'd go out to the parking lot and sell them half price."

"Tabby, what in God's name is a tattoo guinea pig?"

"Some guy was starting up a tattoo business and he used me to test out different inks and designs. I got a few on my ass that I'm trying to hide from West."

"West? That the bartender?"

"Yeah."

Jackie looks at me, shakes his head and snorts. "Jesus Christ. You know you can't put any of that on a resumé, right?"

"Oh, come on. I don't have to get specific. I'll say I've been a canine handler, a gardener, a carnival relief worker and an artist's assistant. They want my resumé, I'll bend over."

"Carnival relief worker." He grins. "I think I missed you a whole lot."

The sun dives behind the trees and the clouds start to roll themselves into in a giant ball. In the half-light, the two-lane highway shimmers.

"Look at that," I say, pointing. "So pretty."

Jackie squints ahead. "That's busted glass. From drunk-driving idiots."

"Oh."

He taps his knuckles on the windowpane then sighs and takes a bag of chewing tobacco out of his pocket. "Don't tell Jewell. This shit was supposed to help me quit smoking. Now I can't stop." He paws in the bag and scoops a bit under his lip.

We drive on in silence while I debate how to bring up Daddy.

"So, what was it like at home after I left?"

"Same as when you were around. Except Daddy got even meaner and Ma got harder with him. They were fighting all the time and we just scattered. We'd come home to eat sometimes, but we were each of us hatching escape plans. Bird and I started working construction when I was fifteen. Poppy had older boyfriends she'd crash with. Eventually Daddy pissed off the wrong side of the dock. He had a line on some grade A dope, convinced a few businessmen to give him a fuckload of money, bought as much as he could, then sold it to a skipper headed to the States. He skimmed so much money off the top there was no way he was getting away with it. He gave them back even less money than they'd put up, the moron. Next day, a gang showed up at the house with knives, axes, you name it. Daddy took off and they went after him, told Ma they'd be back for the rest of us. She was afraid if she called the police, they might find something of Daddy's in the house to pin on her and she'd wind up in jail with no way to keep after us. So she phoned that old friend of hers, Bev, and got her to come pack us in her car and bring us to Jubilant. Bev dropped us at the Salvation Army and told Ma to lose her number. After a few months, we got enough money together to buy that trailer. Bird and I used to hitchhike back and forth to sneak Ma's things out of the house and bring them to her. We did that for years."

"What happened to all the money?"

"Fucked if I know. You know Daddy can't hang on to a dollar to save his life. He probably blew it all in a week."

I ponder it. "You should have saved Ma's good dress."

"What?"

"Her yellow dress. It's still hanging in the closet."

"You went in there? It ain't safe, Tabby. The floor's ready to cave."

"It was like you all evaporated."

"Spooked you, did it?"

"It takes a hell of a lot more than that."

The marquee appears ahead: KLASSY LADYS, $6. Behind it, on the facade of the blue warehouse, is a painted silhouette of a busty woman bending at the waist with her hands on her hips. She's naked except for a bonnet tied around her neck.

"Why the bonnet?"

Jackie looks up at it and shrugs. He finds an empty coffee cup on the floor and spits into it. "Why not, I guess."

A soft rain is now falling on the thirty or so cars in the lot. We park, and when we walk in, a few men whip around to make sure I'm not married to any of them. The stools and walls are painted neon blue and there's a permeating stench of vomit. The woman dancing around the pole isn't even trying not to look pissed off about it. We seat ourselves in the corner and wait for a server. After five minutes, a woman in fringed leather underpants struts over with a tray. She sprays our vinyl tablecloth and wipes off the red wine ring left by the last customer.

"Evening, madam." Jackie tilts his hat back. "We'll take two glasses of your finest vintage."

She snaps two beers open and parks them in front of us. "Anything else?"

"Poppy Saint working tonight?"

"No."

"She around lately?"

"No."

"You know where she's at?" He's doing a bad job of looking casual, tapping his foot like crazy.

"He's her brother," I interrupt, "not some jealous boyfriend. She's got a sick kid she needs to know about."

She hesitates. "We ain't allowed to tell customers nothing about the dancers."

"We just want to know what nights she dances."

"She ain't danced here in a while."

"Then she's not a dancer."

Jackie looks up at her from under his long lashes. "You got kids?"

She drops her shoulders. "Poppy's here on weekends. But you ask anyone about it, they'll say she don't work here no more."

She walks off and Jackie examines his bottle to see if anything's floating in it. "Now what?"

"I guess we come this weekend and you go into the back-room."

"Fuck that." He almost drops his beer. "All I need is one person to see me go back there and half of Jubilant will know it. Jewell will go mental."

I chew a fingernail, thinking. "We'll bring Ma with us, get her to vouch for you."

"Fine." He pushes his bottle away. "Let's get out of this shithole."

I drain half my beer and we walk back into the drizzle, inhaling the fresh sea air. I wait till we're back on the road before I say, "Ma says you're staying out of trouble for a reason."

"What does that mean?"

"You tell me."

The rain starts whipping in sheets and the windshield wipers don't work right. I have to pull over twice because I can't see two feet in front of us. Jackie doesn't say a word to me, just sits there staring straight ahead. When I finally drop him off, he leaps out of the truck then turns around and holds the door open, letting in the rain.

"Tabby, I'm staying out of trouble because I got kids that are starting to copy everything I do." He drums his palms on the roof. "Okay?"

"Okay."

He shuts the door without making eye contact, and I watch him walk across the wet grass with his hands in his pockets. Even the back of his neck looks guilty.

JANIS CAN'T GET OVER MY NEW HAIR. SHE STRETCHES out on the carpet with her arms folded under her head and says, "You look just like a beauty pageant runner-up."

"Gee, thanks. I always wanted to be second-best."

"Now hold on." She tilts her sunglasses down on her nose. "Runner-up means the best."

"Runner-up means second-best."

"No, it's the winner, because you run-her-up to get her crown. This girl at my church group is always talking about how her dog was the runner-up at the dog show. Her mother must have gave that judge a hundred bucks, because that dumb dog is always barking his head off and his fur is all mashed up like this." She whisks her hands through Swimmer's hair until it stands up in all different directions.

Swimmer points at me. "Lello."

"*Yellow*, Swimmer." Janis grabs his ears and yanks his face up close to hers. Her head looks tiny in comparison. "Y-E-L-O!" She lets go and he falls over backward. "He likes blondies," she says to me. "He got a big dirty crush on Dolly Pardon and we have to listen to Kenny and Dolly's Christmas record even when it's summer out."

"Dolly Parton," I correct.

"Yup. Dolly Pardon."

Swimmer starts singing a version of "With Bells On," adding in jazz hands and fancy kicks. Janis covers her ears and rolls under the sofa.

AFTER SUPPER, MA AND I PUT THE KIDS IN THE CAR AND drive to Jackie's place. When we walk in, Jewell's got a bucket of crayons and large pieces of paper laid out on the table. She's frying up grilled cheese sandwiches and pressing them into heart shapes with a cookie cutter.

"Where's everybody going?" Janis asks, keeping her coat on.

"Bingo," Ma tells her. "Auntie Jewell's going to look after you."

"Hey, Janis the Menace," Jewell says, opening the freezer. "Jackie bought you some of that bubble gum ice cream that rots your teeth. Come have a look."

Janis is on to us. "You tell that Poppy Saint to get her butt back here," she says, crossing her arms. "Tell her Janis said Swimmer's only a dawdler and he needs his mama."

He stumbles over sucking his fingers and leans against his sister, staring up at us with his big, solemn eyes. Jewell unzips their coats and steers them to the table while we duck out.

"I might strangle Poppy if we find her," Ma threatens.

"Has she always been such a train wreck?" I toss Jackie West's keys as Ma and I get in the other side of the truck.

"Not always," Jackie says. "She had Janis when she was only sixteen and was headed nowhere, but then she had to go to court-ordered night school. Halfway through, she actually started reading her books and finished with straight Bs. We couldn't believe it. Then she took a course to be one of those people who do makeovers on dead people—"

"Somebody who gets dead bodies spiffed up for the funeral," Ma cuts in.

"Right," Jackie says, backing the truck out of the driveway. "She got the certificate, but nobody would hire her."

"Why not?"

"Because Daddy blackmailed the funeral home in Solace and word gets around."

"I was just in there the other day. How'd he manage that?"

"He found out they were burying bodies in expensive coffins then bringing them back up and wrapping them in burlap. They'd stick the bodies back in the ground, clean up the caskets and resell them. That's why all them corpses went bobbing around after the flood."

"How'd Daddy find that out?"

"Who knows? Crooks can probably smell each other like dogs."

"What's any of that got to do with Poppy? She's not Daddy."

Jackie sighs. "Shit, Tabby, if life was fair, I'd have grown up playing Little League and going to Grandma's house for Sunday ham."

Ma glares at him. "But instead you beat kids up with a baseball bat and called your grandma a fat whore."

I don't know why that strikes me funny. I start to giggle, then I'm shaking with laughter. Jackie snorts then Ma joins in and the three of us are howling all the way down the highway.

"She *was* a fat whore," Jackie squeaks between breaths, wiping his eyes.

"I know it!" Ma bellows, and off we go again.

BLUEBELLES IS BUSY. IT'S LIKE THE GROCERY STORE ON sample day, greasy men hovering and salivating over the goods. We grab a table and a server finally comes over, doesn't bother with hello, just informs us beer costs a dollar more on weekends. Ma asks for a cup of tea, but they don't serve that, so Jackie orders her a virgin pina colada. The waitress brings it in a plastic wineglass with a fake orange wheel glued to the rim. Ma looks at it like it might bite her.

"Ma," Jackie says. "How did you get through all them years with Daddy without a stiff drink?"

"I don't know." She glances around at all the customers tipping bottles to their lips. "I figured somebody had to stay dry or we'd all just wash away."

Jackie looks uncomfortable sitting beside his mother in a place like this. He waves over another waitress. "Excuse me, can I get me some action in the backroom tonight?"

She doesn't even stop. "You got to talk to Charlie."

"Okay." He stands up and taps her arm. "Where's Charlie at?"

She gestures to the ammunition belt full of shooters slung around her waist. "I'm busy, hon. Give me ten minutes."

"He's on a weekend pass," I interrupt. "He hasn't got many minutes left."

She snaps her fingers. "Come on, then."

Jackie shoots me a dirty look and follows her across the floor.

Ma nervously turns a beer coaster around on the tabletop. "Look at this place," she says. "Good lord. There's a woman over there with the ass cut out of her pants. What's the point of that?"

A new dancer appears onstage slathered in oil. Ma stares, transfixed, then says, "I don't want Janis and Swimmer to grow up the way you did." Her words hang between us as the woman starts to writhe around in chains. "I know that must have been hard. I never stopped praying for you, Tabby. I told myself you were okay, that you had been brought up right by that woman. I thought she put you in a nice house with a pretty pink bedroom. I figured you had a new life and you were better than us now and didn't want to come back. I had no clue how to find you."

"Not that you tried."

"Maybe you didn't go to a fancy school and you're not wearing a fur coat or nothing like that, but you seem like you got a lot going for you."

"You think they have pretty pink bedrooms at the Raspberry Home for Damaged Goods? That's where I grew up."

Ma makes a sound in her throat like a cat trying to heave up a furball then reaches in her purse and finds a crumpled tissue, wipes the mascara under her eyes before it runs. All her hair is grey under these blue lights. "You ever get into the drugs?" she asks me.

"I tried. They were hard to get in Raspberry."

"How long were you in there?"

"Four years." I raise my voice over the music so she'll hear every word. "Then I was in a group home for a while, but I ran away and crashed in an abandoned building in Saint John with a bunch of crackheads. They used to go around collecting broken electronics in shopping carts. They'd take the wires out and fry the plastic casings off on a little hibachi, sell the copper for a few bucks at a metal salvage place. That was their whole goal in life: find some old tape decks, fry the wires, sell them, buy drugs, fry their brains. You really want to see what drugs can do to people, take a walk through one of those places."

Ma taps two cigarettes out of her pack, offers me one. "You think Poppy could wind up like that?"

"Sure," I say, digging in my pocket for my lighter. "One of the junkies I met in there grew up in a mansion in Ontario. If it can happen to her, it can happen to anyone. When I met her, she'd scratched almost all of the skin off her face and neck and thought she was on fire all the time. She'd scream at people to put out the flames."

"How could you live with those junkies?"

"I didn't have a choice. But after a few days I hitched a ride with a girl who took me out to a pot farm outside Oromocto. She introduced me to her brother, a tattoo artist, and I wound up moving in with him. He was all right. He had a few problems."

Ma leans in for a light. "What kind of problems?"

"Nothing serious. He had a thing for women's shoes. He'd buy new pairs and get me to wear them around for a few weeks. Then I'd have to give them back."

"Why?"

"He liked the smell."

"That's disgusting, Tabby."

"What did I care? He gave me a place to stay, food to eat, let me drive his car around. And every two weeks or so I got a tattoo and a flashy new pair of heels. I was spoiled rotten if you think about it."

"I don't want to think about it."

I eye her mocktail. "You going to drink that?"

She pushes it over and I take a few sips between drags on the cigarette, all the while glancing toward the back door.

"What about you?" I ask.

"What about me?"

"When did you and Daddy split?"

"After we came to Jubilant, I couldn't even smell his farts on the wind. About a year later, he showed up on the doorstep. I told him I was done with him, called the cops on him so he'd leave. He came back maybe two or three times after that, but I wouldn't let him past the steps. Then, a few months ago, he called me up to tell me he caught the cancer. He was expecting me to rush over and be his bed nurse, gave me some big fish tale about how he never loved any other woman. I told him to go die on the cross. The Mounties had a warrant on him and heard he'd been lurking around Jubilant, came over to the trailer to ask me if I'd seen him. I didn't tell them nothing, but a few weeks later they called to tell me he was in hospital, said they took one look at him and knew it wasn't worth the taxpayers' money dragging him through the courts." Ma grips the edge of the table. "Here comes Jackie."

I stamp out my cigarette and watch Jackie weave through the crowd toward us.

"She don't believe me that you're with us, Tabby," he says when he reaches our table. "I told her to meet us at the back door in two minutes and I'd prove it."

"Is she going to come out?" I grab my purse.

"I don't know." He glances over his shoulder. "Let's talk out-side. The bouncer's all over my ass."

"What happened?" Ma asks as we hurry out to the truck.

"I asked for Poppy, and they took me to a room. She came in and when she saw it was me, she tried to bolt. I had to put her in a chokehold. I told her what Janis said about Swimmer needing his mother around. She kind of fell apart then, started crying and talking crazy. She's all messed up."

"What kind of crazy?"

"Junkie crazy. Who's out to get her and shit."

"Who *is* out to get her?"

Jackie ushers us into the truck and drives it around to the back of the building. We sit staring at the grey door lit by a No Entry sign. The breeze rustling through the trees behind us sounds like a deck of cards being shuffled. Jackie twists the brim of his hat and Ma starts humming one of her old church songs.

"Come on, Jackie," Ma whispers. "Pray with us."

"How do you know I'm not?"

"Because you're my son."

The door opens and there she is. My heart shoots up to the roof then crashes down to my knees. Her eyes are like two dark tunnels. She's got long spindly legs and tall clacky heels on. She keeps trying to pull down her skin-tight dress to cover her thighs.

"Jackie?" She squints into the headlights. Her voice is high like a little girl's.

He keeps the engine running as he opens his door and steps out. Ma gets out the other door.

"Poppy," Ma says, "it's time to come home and get yourself better. I can't take care of those kids by myself."

Poppy clutches one arm, shivering. "I will. Just not right now."

"Right now!" Jackie yells at her. "I'll throw you in the god-damn back if I have to."

She cranes her neck to try to see beyond him. She's ready to run back inside, so I get out of the truck and take a few steps. She clicks up on those heels and puts her face right up to mine. Even in the dim light, I can see the holes in her arms.

"This ain't Tabby," she says. "How much did you pay this bitch?"

"Forget it," Jackie says to Ma. "She don't want her kids. You'll have to give them to social services. Let's go."

Poppy tries to slap him, but he ducks.

"Get in the fucking truck!" he hollers.

A scream erupts from Poppy that echoes across the parking lot and gives me gooseflesh all down my back. I heard the same sound once before when a cat got caught in one of the rabbit snares behind our house. We watch her kick off her shiny shoes one at a time and hurl them at the back wall of Bluebelles. Then she limps over and gets in the fucking truck.

"Stop being so dramatic," Ma scolds.

We all squeeze in around her and Ma hauls a seat belt out from between the vinyl cushions, reaching over my lap to try to clip it over Poppy's waist. Jackie peels us out of there before he even has his door shut. With the four of us packed in like sardines, he can barely manoeuvre his arms to steer.

"I remember you." Poppy's eyes are so glazed it's hard to tell if she's looking at me. She drops her head on my shoulder, smearing makeup on my shirt. "You were sitting on our old roof with a towel tied around you like a cape. I watched you fly away, sailing over the hills." She lifts her bony arm and tries to make a wave motion.

Ma and Jackie sit like statues.

85

When we get back to the trailer, Poppy teeters down the hall to the kids' room and doesn't come back out. Jackie decides to stay the night in case she tries to take off. We watch *Wheel of Fortune* reruns in the living room and around 1 a.m., Ma stands up and says she's going to bed.

"One of you better stay awake," she advises.

After her door shuts, Jackie says, "So, tell me about this West guy. He don't mind that you used to be a Saint?"

"I'm still a Saint. I didn't walk into some presto-chango chamber." I hand him one of my blankets.

"Buddy must be pretty serious lending you his truck like that. Before I met Jewell, I wouldn't let a woman leave a box of tampons at my place, never mind take something with her."

I chew on my thumbnail. "How did you know Jewell was the one?"

He twists around trying to get comfortable on the floor. "She was leaving town, so I told her I was dying. Then I couldn't think of what I was dying from, so I told her she couldn't leave because I needed help moving a fridge. She said, 'Fine, let's move it,' so I told her it wasn't getting delivered till Wednesday. Then she asks me why the delivery person can't help me move it, so I said *he* was dying. Finally, she just yelled, 'Jackie, are you asking me to stay?' and I was like, Holy shit, I think I am."

I bust out laughing and Ma shushes us from the bedroom.

"This time is different." He stretches his arms over his head and stares up at the ceiling. "I'm going to be the best dad in Jubilant."

"In all of Jubilant?" I mock.

He catches the cushion I toss at him and puts it under his

head. Neither of us trusts the other not to fall asleep, so we both lie awake all night. When it's almost daylight, I drag myself to the kitchen to make coffee. Jackie joins me and we drink the whole pot in silence. I'm brewing another as Jewell arrives with the kids.

"Is she here?" Janis hollers, practically kicking the door down. She takes off down the hall, sliding on her socks and smacking into the wall at the other end.

Jewell comes in behind her, balancing Swimmer on one hip. She sets him down and holds his hands up in the air to show us his purple-stained fingers. "I left my craft supplies out and when I got off the phone, Janis was playing nail parlour, putting fabric dye on his fingernails with a paintbrush." She eases down on a chair and gives Jackie a once over. "How did it go?"

We all pause, listening to Poppy murmuring something to Janis. Swimmer toddles down the hall toward her voice.

"She's here at least," Jackie says.

Janis comes out after a few minutes and tells us, "She looks like a chew toy. Lord knows what she's been up to."

Jewell has to leave for a doctor's appointment and Jackie tells her to go on ahead, he wants to stick around a bit. Ma wakes up and makes toast and eggs for everybody, but it's past noon when Poppy finally emerges. Her clothes are wearing her, she's so skeletal. I connect all the pointy bones with my eyes, but I can't seem to find the sister I remember.

"I thought I dreamed you," she says to me. She sits down on the sofa with Swimmer glued at her side. She grabs his hand and asks us, "What the hell is this all over him?"

Janis inspects her work. "I think he looks rich."

"Did you sleep?" I ask Poppy.

"I don't sleep." She sticks her bony fingers in her hair and works at the tangles. "I just worry."

"You let us do the worrying," Ma says. "You just try to eat something."

"I have to go out for a while."

Jackie pulls the truck keys out of his pocket. "I'll take you."

"I'm coming too!" Janis yells.

Poppy changes the subject. "Your tooth's fixed," she says to me. She touches one of her own front teeth as her eyes drift along my face. "I used to be better-looking than this."

Jackie cuts in. "Pops, you get off them drugs and get healthy and you'll be that gorgeous bombshell everybody used to talk about."

I get up to get her some coffee and Ma whispers to me in the kitchen, "She's probably going to get itchy soon."

Every time we ask Poppy when she wants to leave on that errand, she stalls us. Jackie is already hours late for work. He calls to say he's not coming in, but the boss says two guys phoned in sick already. Jackie hangs up and curses.

"They're coming to get me."

"Don't worry," I say. "I'll tackle Poppy if she tries anything."

Ten minutes later, we hear a honk and when I walk him out, Jackie puts one arm around me and then the other. He hasn't given me a real hug since he was the same size as Swimmer and it makes us both blush. He jogs down to meet a yellow truck and the second it pulls away, Poppy comes out and stands beside me. She squints in the weak light, rubbing her hands up and down her ribs.

"I'll just be gone for an hour or two, Tabby. I got to get something in me."

"How about you get your shit together instead? If you choose a needle over your own kids, then you're not the Poppy Saint I remember. That girl had guts."

She picks up a handful of rocks and squeezes them in her fist. "You got no idea what I'm going through."

"Yeah, I do."

She searches my face. "Drugs?"

"The other thing. What you have to do to get them. Not the shakes, not vomiting—nothing can be worse than selling yourself. If you can live through that night after night, you can make it through detox easy."

The screen door bangs open and Janis comes charging at us, slamming into Poppy's thighs. Poppy opens her hand and the rocks fall to her feet.

"I thought you left," Janis yells at her. "Please, don't go again. I promise I'll stop putting hot dogs in the toilet. I'll get a job so you can stay home with Swimmer."

"A job?" Poppy says. "Doing what?"

"Walking pets."

"You hate pets."

"I don't have to be their friend. I just have to put a rope on their neck and pull them up and down the driveway till they're wore out." Janis tugs Poppy's T-shirt. "Let's go back inside!"

As Janis pulls her back up to the trailer, Poppy turns and claws at me with her eyes.

"I FOUND MY SISTER," I WHISPER INTO THE PHONE.
"She'd taken off on a drug bender. But we got her back home and
she's going to a methadone clinic."

"No shit."

"Jackie knew about one downtown and talked her into giving
it a try. It took us forever to get her through the door, but once she
got a dose in her, it calmed her down a lot. The nurse wanted her
to check into the hospital because of her weight and everything,
but Poppy told her she'd sneak out to score if she isn't with her
kids, so they agreed to let her come in for a regular appointment
each day. Do you mind if I stay in Jubilant a few more nights just
to be sure she keeps at it?"

West sighs. I picture him standing in the hallway with one
knee bent, foot against the wall. He's probably got a beer in one
hand, receiver tucked under his chin.

"Why the sigh? Still think I'm going to steal your truck?"

"Nah. I'm just horny."

Now I see him fiddling with the phone cord, massaging his
neck.

"It's all right," he says. "I was already bored and horny out of
my mind before you ever walked into the Four Horses."

"You're good to me, West. It's too bad you don't drink coffee."

"Sure I do. I just have to be in the mood for it." He pauses.
"Speaking of in the mood for it, you alone over there?"

Janis comes around the corner and yells, "Who are you talking to? Is that your man?"

I cover the receiver as fast as I can.

"Can I talk to him?" Janis asks.

I uncover the receiver. "Janis wants to say hello."

"Put her on."

Janis drags over a chair and gets comfortable. I stand there listening to her gab to him for over ten minutes about his views on everything from snowstorms to men who have ponytails. She probably learned more about him than I have. I let her keep talking until she brings the conversation around to the fact that I spilled a Pepsi in his truck.

THAT NIGHT, WHILE MA'S PLAYING GAME BOY AND THE rest of us are zoned out in front of the television, Lyle Kenzie's Ford comes roaring up the driveway. He's banging on the door before we have time to react. Poppy grabs the kids and runs to the bedroom. I try to lock the door, but it's too late. He pushes his way in, knocking me aside. I look through the open door and see another man out in the truck.

"Where's she at?" Lyle hollers.

"There's kids in here, Lyle," Ma tells him.

"She needs to pay up."

Ma tries to block the hallway, but he pushes past her. I'm right on his heels as he goes down and swings the kids' bedroom door open. Janis and Swimmer are sitting on top of the toy chest.

"Where's your mother at?"

"I ain't talking," Janis says.

"Don't sauce me," Lyle says.

"The cops are on their way!" Ma yells from the front room.

Lyle turns and walks right past me back to the living room, peers out the window into the darkness. He slides back the front of his coat to reveal a revolver tucked into the front of his pants.

"Seven eighty-two," I say loudly, pretending to speak into a wire. "We got a 782. Lyle Kenzie and accomplice."

Lyle snaps his head in my direction and finally recognizes me. He lunges, eyes flaring, then changes his mind and runs out the door, threatening something I can't make out. Ma and I go to the window and watch the truck swerve out of the driveway.

"What's a 782?" Ma asks. She doesn't seem fazed, which tells me this has happened before. She goes back to check on the kids, and I phone the police for real. About twenty minutes later, a car arrives. The cop who gets out looks about ten years old.

"Your stairs aren't safe," he scolds, as if we haven't got bigger fish to fry. He takes his hat off and Ma brings him a glass of Kool-Aid. He sits on the sofa and sticks it between his knees, taps his cigarette ashes into it while he fills out the paperwork.

Janis tells him, "My mama's skinny as a piece of paper, so I said to my brother Swimmer, let's get her into the toy box. Then that Lyle Kenzie comes in to bust some heads. You want to write down what he said to me? He said, 'You keep sassing me, I'll show you my gun,' and I said, 'Whoop-dee-doo, where'd you get your gun, Walmart?'"

"Janis Jean," Poppy interrupts. "You're telling a tale."

Janis blushes and sticks her hands on her hips. "Well, I might not remember everything exactly as what happened."

The cop stops writing, tells us they don't have enough men on duty for him to stick around. He's gone before Jackie shows up.

"How many times have I told you to keep this door locked?" Jackie yells at Ma. "I'm going to nail the goddamn windows shut, too."

She presses Pause on the Game Boy. "How are we supposed to get fresh air in here?"

"You're letting people in here with guns and you're worried about fresh air?"

"I didn't let him in." Ma yanks off her glasses and they drop around her neck. "He barged in."

Jackie gets some tools from his car. Janis tags along behind him, giving him her version of events. This time Lyle told her he was going to blow the place to smithereens.

"You see headlights, you call me," Jackie tells us. "Don't wait." He glances at the kids. "And no more smoking in here. Go outside."

"I don't smoke!" Janis says. "It's bad for your lunges."

"Lungs," Jackie corrects her.

"Lunges."

"Whatever," Jackie says. "It's bad for them too."

I DRIVE DOWN TO THE STATION FIRST THING THE NEXT morning. When I give my name, the clerk smirks.

"This must be the first time a Saint ever walked in here of their own accord."

I smile sweetly. "But probably not the first time one of them spits in your coffee as soon as you turn your back."

He makes me sit in the waiting room for almost an hour before he calls out, "You can talk to Detective Surette now if you want."

"You mean this man right here who's been sitting around watching the sports highlights all morning?"

Surette has some grey in his black moustache, but a boyish, round face. He gestures me into his office. There's an Acadian flag mounted on his desk next to a brass trophy shaped like a man with his service pistol drawn.

"How can I help you?"

I sit down and set my purse on my lap. "I know you read the report. You want one less prostitute turning tricks for drugs, you got it. But now you've got to keep her safe."

"I don't *have* to do anything." He switches off the television and eases into his chair. "She did right. Now you should get her out of Jubilant so she won't have to look over her shoulder every five minutes." He catches my expression and says, "Yes, I've got my own interests in mind too. You take your brothers with you and we can work something out." He picks up and peels a spotted banana, takes two bites of it then tosses it in a wastebasket.

"What does that mean?"

"It means if you need help with a moving truck or a new place to live, something like that, you let me know."

"Why would I do that?"

"Sometimes your brothers are the shit, sometimes they're the fan. Either way, I'm the one cleaning up the mess. Right now I got no bigger problems to solve than this." He taps a half-finished crossword puzzle. "And that's the way I like it."

He catches me eyeing his trophy and pushes it closer to my

side of the desk. "I got this one for Working My Ass Off." He shows me how the buttocks slide off the man, grabs a tissue and polishes the brass butt cheeks before clicking them back into place. Then he opens a drawer, pulls out another trophy and sets it in front of me. "The Baby's Bottom Award. For smoothness in a crisis."

"What was the crisis?" I ask. "Tim Hortons run out of Boston creams?"

"I'll wager it had something to do with brother number one or brother number two." He offers me a piece of gum, but I refuse. He unwraps a piece and I sit there watching him blow an enormous bubble, fighting the urge to reach over and pop it with my finger.

"You got any awards not about your ass?" I ask finally.

He reaches down near his feet and hoists a homemade ceramic penis onto the desk.

I stomp back out to the truck and sit there fuming. He's right. The only thing we can do is leave. But where are we supposed to go? No one wants us. It's the story of the Saints, and it goes all the way back to Garnet Saint and his travelling shit show. Grandpa Jack may have been a thieving drunk from birth, but Daddy had a good woman who actually believed he deserved a chance. He could have got a proper job, paid his taxes, put food on our table. What did he do instead? Tried to be the biggest asshole in the world. It's probably the only thing he ever succeeded at.

I start the engine and start heading back to the trailer, but before I get to the intersection I pull a U-turn and speed back through town. Some awful venom is welling up in my throat. I roll down the window and spit a few times, but I can't get rid of it.

Jubilant has only one hospital. It's in an old building that used to be a nuthouse and it still reeks of crazy. The hallways are painted that yellow-green colour that makes anyone feel sick who didn't come in that way. When I ask for Wendell Saint, every nurse in earshot stops what they're doing and turns to look. He's on the top floor in the far left corner, as far away from the nurses' station as possible, and I'm sure there's a good reason for that. I go up and stand in the doorway of his room, summoning all my nerve.

"Hi, Daddy."

THE MORNING BARBARA BEST CAME TO WHISK ME AWAY, Ma insisted she and I wait out in the driveway. Daddy was getting out of jail any day and Ma was afraid if he showed up before Barbara's Volvo pulled in, he'd raise holy hell and refuse to let me leave. Probably because he had so few of them, Daddy had always counted us amongst his personal possessions. Ma was his. Bird, Jackie, Poppy and I were his. His to ignore, or order around or use as scapegoats. His to demand an audience of when he had a joke to tell, and to smash a fist into if we didn't laugh hard enough.

"She showed me pictures of where you're going," Ma said, glancing up the road every three seconds. "Some nice. It's like a house you see people living in on a TV show."

I stood there holding a ratty backpack of Bird's that had only one strap, half listening as she ran through a list of things I should and shouldn't do: Keep my head down in the car until the car is over the bridge. When I'm wiping the old people's asses, sing a song in my head and picture a field of daisies. Eat everything they put in front of me, even if I've never seen it before. Don't ever, ever, tell anyone who my father is.

Part of me was secretly thrilled that I might become a different person for real, not just in my pretend games. Maybe I'd be a girl who wore brand name jeans and had a horse in a barn whose tail I could brush whenever I felt like it. My new friends would have names like Victoria and Cindy and they'd invite me to sleepovers where the worst crime a dare could lead to would be swiping macaroons from the pantry. I'd start over, just like Ma said.

I hadn't argued with her when she told me I was shipping out. Nobody in our house was eating enough, and wherever I was headed couldn't be any more miserable. I'd always wondered what it was like to be in a normal family, one that watched movies together and could make it through a whole board game without someone hurling another player into the wall. I'd see kids at school take out Velcro lunch bags with their names on them, talking about how their grandparents brought them to PEI to see Anne of Green Gables' house. The only place Grandma Jean ever took us was the Legion parking lot. She was watching us for the day and said she was just going to pop in and say hello to Gladys. She came running out three hours later, big braless tits swinging under her light blue World's Greatest Grandmother

T-shirt, yelling, "SHIT, YOU FELLERS, I FORGOT ALL ABOUT YAS!" By then Bird and Jackie were jumping from roof to roof on parked cars and Poppy had eaten a thyroid pill she dug out from between the seats.

So, I was intrigued. But I hadn't even met this Barbara woman, and the way Ma was talking, it was as if we were never going to see each other again.

"Your father's heart is going to break when he finds out you ran away."

"Ran away?"

I glared at her, slung the backpack over my shoulder and stormed down to the foot of the driveway. I didn't look back and she didn't follow, but I could hear her up there sobbing like a professional mourner.

Barbara Best arrived right on time. I jumped into the spotless back seat and told her to drive away fast.

"Shouldn't I speak with your mother?" she asked.

"She's too emotional. She said we should just go."

Barbara Best waved up at Ma. As she started to drive off, I looked back and saw Ma running down the driveway flailing her arms. Barbara was already firing a hundred questions at me and didn't hear my mother yelling for her to stop. For the next eleven years of my life, I'd wonder if my mother was trying to call the whole thing off.

"So, Tabatha, what do you like to eat?"

I opened my mouth then closed it again. I was about to say anything my mother didn't kill herself.

"Pizza."

"Well, I've got ham and potatoes ready for the oven back home. Hopefully that'll do for tonight."

My stomach growled, and Barbara laughed. "Goodness gracious!"

I realized right then we weren't going to get along. Goodness gracious? What an asshole. Plus, she had a whole rack of Billy Joel cassettes.

On the way out of town, we got stuck behind the Acadian Lines coach that stopped once a day outside the library. Passengers spilled out of its grey belly and started crossing the road right in front of Barbara's car, so we just had to sit there and wait. I snuck a few glances at the bus shelter I'd smashed up a few weeks before. They still hadn't replaced the glass, just duct-taped some cardboard in its place.

"What are your hobbies? Do you enjoy gardening?"

Obviously she'd failed to notice our pop bottle tree.

"Sure."

Somehow I knew before he stepped off the bus that my father was on board. He was wearing a wrinkled old suit, carrying a garbage bag slung over one shoulder. He had a day-old shiner and his knuckles were bandaged up, which might make another man seem tough but only made him look more pathetic. I suddenly realized that he must cause as much trouble in jail as out of it, that Daddy was Daddy no matter where he went. He just couldn't shut off the tap.

I watched him bum a smoke off the bus driver and lean against a tree trunk to light it with a pack of soggy matches. Barbara Best followed my gaze and said, "Lock your door, Tabatha. You never know with these characters." She tapped her fingers impatiently on the wheel and a half second before her open-toed sandal met the gas pedal, Daddy finally looked over. His face broke into a gap-toothed smile when he saw me. His eyes flicked to Barbara in the driver's seat and then his mouth hardened. He gave me a questioning look and I gave him the finger.

While Barbara Best rambled about how a seed needs to be nurtured in the right soil, I twisted around and watched through the back window as my father walked out into the road and grew smaller and smaller and smaller.

"WRONG ROOM."

"I'm your daughter—Tabby."

He turns his head to look, blinks a few times and tries to sit up. "Holy whoredust. Where the fuck did you come from? Am I dead? Where's your mother at?"

I walk in and stand at the side of his bed, behold the patron Saint of Shitville.

"How are you, Daddy?"

"I thought I was fine, but now I think I'm cracking up." His voice is ragged from years of smoking outside in a T-shirt. It sounds like sandpaper running over his vocal chords. He closes his eyes and presses his palms against his lids. Then his eyes fly open again and he reaches over and tries to touch my face.

I flinch.

"You look like me, around the eyes. In the jaw, too." He stares. "Are you really here? I'm dying, you know."

"I heard."

"The doctors say there's nothing they can do. They're crooks, every one of them." He struggles again to sit up. "Fucking flapjacks! My girl Tabby is here to visit me. I must be almost dead. Where have you been?"

"A lot of places."

"Bad places, I bet. Me too, girl. This place is the worst of them. Your mother left me here at the mercy of these goons."

"I can't say I blame her, Daddy. You never took care of *her*. You beat her and left her whenever you felt like it."

"As soon as I got too weak to hold my own dick, she made a break for it. After all them good years."

"What good years? Am I supposed to feel sorry for you? After you put us all through hell and made us all ashamed to be who we are?"

"Nobody can make you ashamed of who you are except yourself. You're not too stupid to know that, girl." He gives up trying to sit up and falls back on the pillow.

"Don't tell me what I know."

I grip his bed rail, remembering the time he slammed my face into the sink because I didn't want to brush my teeth and my front tooth broke in half. I didn't smile again until I was fifteen years old and some welfare-sponsored dentist came to Raspberry. I'm blinded with rage for a few seconds, and then I can almost see it seeping out of me, black and pooling on

Daddy's white sheets. I watch my right hand fly out and grab his throat. It pushes down hard on his Adam's apple and he starts laughing. His face goes from blue to crimson and he's laughing. He's not struggling, and I have to ease up or kill him. I release my grip and he coughs and coughs. A nurse sticks her head in, but Daddy waves her off.

"Tabby Cat, listen to me," he manages. "I'm not right. In my head and my heart, I've never been right. My father beat the human out of me. If I knew what sorry was, I'd be sorry for the things I done." He sighs. "I just fuck and fight and eat. That's it. I don't feel nothing. Can't even fuck anymore. You can kill me right now. I'd rather it was you than Doctor Donkey Dick."

"I'm not going to kill you, you asshole. I'm going to let you lie there thinking about how you shovelled so much shit on top of us we'll never climb out from under it."

"You hate me, do you?" He blinks. "Do you love me a little bit, too?"

Before I open my mouth to answer that, something Ma once told me jumps into my head. She said when Daddy found out she was pregnant with Bird, he wouldn't leave her side. He sang songs to her belly and built a crib out of an old chicken coop. That's how Bird got his name.

Daddy's small eyes case my face, studying his own blue eyes, his own mouth. Then he reaches down and shoves his hand between the mattress and the bed frame. "I got something for your mother. Come help me."

I push his arm out of the way and slide my hand in until

my fingertips touch something. I nudge it into my grasp, work it forward and pull out a soft wad of bills.

"Stick that in your purse and don't talk to any of those crooks on the way out." He pats my hand and closes his lids. "You look just like me. Not like your sister. She looks like a beggar. Nothing worse than one of those."

When I get to the door, he opens his eyes again. "Hey, girl."

I pause.

"There's a lot more where that came from."

I GET IN THE TRUCK AND COUNT IT QUICKLY. THERE'S over two thousand dollars. My hands shake as I roll up the bills and stick them down my boot. I press the gas and peel out of there, speeding toward the highway turnoff. My heart's pounding in my ears as I try to form a plan. If I drive to Yarmouth, I can catch the ferry to Bar Harbor. I heard it's easy to find work in the States, and no one will know me.

I'm almost to the end of the ramp when I glimpse Janis's little purple jacket scrunched up on the passenger-side floor. I hesitate then slam on the brakes. The tires lift up a cloud of dust that slowly settles on the windshield.

I think of a story Daddy once told me about Grandpa Jack. He was walking home from school one day and saw a four-year-old girl crying on her porch. She ran up to him and pleaded for help, said she'd gone out in the yard to feed the chickens and her grandmother forgot she was outside and locked the door by mistake. She'd yelled through the window, but the old woman couldn't remember how to undo the latch. Jack went and got a slim jim. He came back and pried the latch, told the little girl to take her granny to lie down in one of the bedrooms while he strolled around the house taking whatever valuables he could find. When the little girl emerged from the room, he told her never to tell anyone he'd been inside their house. "If you even tell a kitty cat that you saw me," he said, "I'll come back and kill your granny in the night."

Grandpa Jack told Daddy it was as if Garnet had taken over his body. Garnet wouldn't think twice about doing something like that to people so helpless. He'd call it Lady Luck. Daddy told me it was the only time he saw his father regret anything he'd done. But did that story make Daddy pause for thought any time he caught himself pulling a Grandpa Jack? Fuck no. He was probably worse than Jack and Garnet put together. And he didn't even have the decency to call it opportunity. He'd come home with someone else's engine in his truck and act like he'd had no choice.

I was about to pull a Daddy, and I hate us both for it. I whip the truck around in a U-turn and head back down the ramp. It's one-way, but I'm not worried about oncoming cars. Anyone smart enough to leave this town left long ago. I check the rear-view mirror all the way to the trailer, and when I pull in the driveway, I wait a few minutes to be sure no one's on my tail. It's so quiet a deer pokes its head out of the trees at the end of the lot.

I open the truck door and it sprints off. I stare at the empty space where it was standing. Then I walk up to the trailer and mount the rickety stairs.

"Which one of you has been praying for a miracle?" I ask, bursting inside.

Swimmer is perched on the sofa, sucking on his fingers. He pops them out of his mouth and raises his pale little hand in the air.

4

Before I head back to Solace River, I drive Poppy to get a month's worth of groceries then hand the rest of the cash to Ma.

"That bastard!" She drops to her knees. "He had all that money all this time? What was he going to do with it? And us here with kids nearly starving to death and Bird needing a decent chair." She slaps the floor a few times with her palm. "Why does he punish me like this? Why? After all the years I lied for him and cooked for him and acted as his goddamned whipping post."

"Daddy is not right, Ma. He said so himself. He's like that doll Poppy had that came out of the factory without ears or a nose."

"I remember that ugly thing," Poppy says. "What was her name?"

"Bernadette."

"Bernadette!" she shrieks. She follows me to the bedroom, sits on the bed as I whisk a brush through my wet hair. "You're going back to that man in those ratty jeans?" She goes to the closet and rummages around, grabs a dress from the back. It's cornflower blue with tiny white flowers. "Here. This don't fit me no more."

It slides down over my curves like a glove. Poppy catches my eye in the full-length mirror hanging on her closet door and gives me a sad smile. She pulls a blow-dryer out of a drawer and offers to dry my hair, but her hands are shaking so bad she can barely hold on to it. She rips the plug from the wall, swearing under her breath.

"I bet you wish you never came back," she says. "If I was you, I'd have been gone by now."

"I'll be back. Jackie's going to sleep here every night until I am and Detective Surette has a cruiser driving by every few hours to check on things. I saw one go past this afternoon."

She sits down again, knees and elbows vibrating slightly out of sync. "I feel like I don't know a thing about my own sister."

Sitting this close, I notice grey spots on her front teeth. The whites of her eyes are a dull yellow.

"We'll have lots of time, you and I. And Jackie. I guess I'll never know Bird."

"I can tell you about him." She perks up. "He loved playing cards like he does now, only nobody could beat him. Sometimes he'd let me win and pretend to be all pissed off, but I knew he lost on purpose. His friends were all half scared of him. He had a temper like Daddy. But I wasn't scared of him. He was a good brother. Good father, too. At Christmas he would spoil those girls rotten. If one asked for ham and the other wanted turkey, he'd go out and get both."

My smile sinks as I remember what Christmas was like at

our house. I grab Poppy's hand, but it's so slight I'm afraid I'll break a bone. I let go and it falls back in her lap with a soft thud.

"Poppy, you gave Janis and Swimmer the name Saint for a reason. You must have believed things would get better, that someday they'd be wearing it like a purple heart instead of a badge of shame."

"It ain't that." She shrugs one sharp shoulder. "I just wanted them to be all mine, same name and everything in case anyone tried to take them." Her eyes glaze as she wanders into some torture chamber in her head. "They shouldn't even have let me bring Swimmer home from the hospital. I was so high, I don't even remember him coming out of me."

I look down at the bedspread.

"I'm so sick and tired of being who I am," she says.

"Then start being who you're going to be."

She nods and grabs my hand this time, squeezes it hard.

WHEN WEST WALKS INTO HIS KITCHEN, I'M STANDING there in Poppy's pretty dress, hauling a steaming pan out of the oven. His roast has all the trimmings: turnip, carrots and rosemary potatoes. He tosses his jumble of keys onto the table and circles me like I'm a new model car on the showroom floor.

"You're making me nervous," I say. "Do you like it or not?"

"I love it … all of it. The dress, the food. I feel like I just got out of prison or something."

I set the pan on the stove and feel his breath on the back of my neck. He starts kissing my neck and I detach myself from the erection growing in his jeans.

"Come on now." I push him into a chair. "You've been asking for this roast since I met you."

I grab some plates out of the cupboard and serve him a heaping helping. When I sit down across from him, he's got this lovesick look on his face.

"What?"

"I feel like we should say grace or something." I think he's joking, but he closes his eyes and says, "Dear Lord, thank you for this roast, *finally*. It looks goddamn delicious. And thank you for keeping hothead hicks out of my tavern and helping Tabby find her sister in Jubilant. Oh, and for her walking into my life and the good sex and all that. Amen."

I hold my breath as he takes a bite. He must approve because he cleans his plate before I finish my roll.

"Where'd you learn to cook?" he asks after his second helping.

"Barbara Best. It was the only thing she did that interested me. I didn't even know the names of most of the vegetables she had in her garden because I'd only ever eaten them out of cans. One day Barbara picked a pea pod, slit open the casing with her fingernail to show me where peas come from. It just about blew my mind."

West goes quiet the way he often does when I talk about my past, and I wish I knew what he was thinking. After dessert, I come back from the bathroom and he's got my homemade apron on, standing over a sink of soapy water scrubbing dishes. I grab a beer and hoist myself up on the counter.

"How's the truck running?" he asks.

"Pretty good, considering it's old enough to have an eight-track player." I dangle his key chain in the air and he pulls my wrestling card out of his back pocket. We switch. "I've been wondering about our old house," I say, examining Macho Man for creases. "Do you think the land still belongs to Ma? She says she never paid any taxes, but she's still got the deed. Think that counts for anything?"

"I'll ask around, see what I can find out."

"Holy shit," I say, pointing at the wall with my beer. "You flipped your calendar to the right month."

"All by myself."

I notice he's been keeping the place a little neater. The afghan is neatly folded on the back of the sofa and it looks like he watered and trimmed the plants. I take a sip of beer and swallow hard.

"So now that you have your truck back, are you going to ask me to find another place to stay?"

West sticks his hands back in the suds and pulls up a fistful of cutlery. I watch him diligently clean each piece. Then he dries his hands on the apron, hangs it on the stove handle and takes me by the hand. I let him lead me down the hall to the bedroom, where he opens a drawer in the nightstand, removes some scented candles and lights each one with a Zippo. I watch as he starts setting them around the room.

"What's all this?"

"A romantic gesture."

"Oh. I don't think I've ever had one of those. Someone spray-painted my name under an overpass once."

"Tabby." West tosses the lighter on his dresser. "Shut up."

After all the wicks have burned down, I lie naked next to West trying to picture him walking around the general store sniffing different candles, dropping the ones he liked into a store basket.

"Thank you for the romantic gesture," I whisper, and he murmurs, "You're welcome," even though I was sure he was asleep. Then he says, "Can I ask you something?"

"What?"

"Is there a tattoo of two horses doing it on your backside?"

"No." I flip over.

"Are you sure?"

"They're unicorns."

"Oh, okay, then. Good night."

He snorts into his pillow until I hit him with it.

THE NEXT DAY, WHILE HE'S AT WORK, I TAKE A WALK TO the old house. A couple of cars slow down to offer me a ride, but the drivers are both men in sunglasses who look like they have too much time on their hands. I'm in no mood for perverts, so I tell them I'm out walking for exercise. The one with the bumper sticker that reads SOLACE RIVER PRAYER AND COUPON CLUB yells, "Lezzie!" as he pulls away.

It's a long way around the river and I have a lot of time to think. I've been dreaming about Raspberry lately. Two nights ago I dreamt that I got a notice in the mail saying I'd been selected at random to win an all-expenses-paid vacation there.

How I actually ended up there is no less ridiculous. I was on probation when I left Solace River for vandalizing the bus shelter, a small detail Ma forgot to mention to Barbara Best, so I was probably in violation for missing my check-ins with the lame hockey jersey–wearing probation officer they assigned me to. All I know is Barbara made some calls and went to meet with someone at the courthouse. When she came back, she sat me down and told me I had to go to a detention centre where they had some programs I might benefit from. Then she put me in her car and drove me out to the country like some feral animal she had to release back into the wild. She wouldn't even pull over to let me pee. She'd decided Raspberry would be better for me than my own family and I have no idea by what channels of incompetence no one investigated that claim. Barbara knew about Daddy's law troubles from Ma and she was certain I'd end up a career criminal if I went back. I guess no one told her juvenile homes are career criminal factories.

During the ride, she pulled out an envelope full of cash and said that, when I was a little older and out on my own, I should use it to get some therapy.

"Gee, thanks, Babs," I said, stuffing it in my back pocket. "Just let me out in front, so you can get back to bedazzling bingo daubers or fingering yourself to Billy Joel or whatever."

She insisted she had to escort me inside. In the lobby, she tried to give me an honest-to-goodness hug. That's what she called it. I staggered back about six feet. There was no way I was going to let anyone touch me who was wearing peach heels that matched the buttons on her cardigan. She frowned and clicked away, back to the land of dry-cleaned underpants and stackable Tupperware.

They made me sign a contract as part of the admission

process. I had to sit and read three pages of rules out loud until my eyes rolled back in my head. They left me alone to think about it "very seriously" and I took out the little pocket knife they hadn't found in my inside pocket, sliced my finger and signed it in blood. No one there could take a joke. When they came back in, I was sent for a strip search and a psychiatric evaluation.

Barbara Best sent a few letters sealed with fruity scratch 'n' sniff stickers, but I chucked them out without opening them. I thought about writing to Ma with no return address, but all letters had to be sent through Raspberry and I couldn't be sure they wouldn't add their stamp. I didn't want my mother to know I was in there. She'd never sleep again. Plus, if Daddy ever found out where I was, he'd probably spring me just to make me sorry I'd left.

OUR ROAD STILL ISN'T PAVED. EVERYONE ALWAYS CALLED it the Old Solace River Road, but now it has a street sign. I never noticed this last week. Victory Road. I wonder what that's about. The only victory I know of on this road involved a court battle over whether it's sanitary to run a daycare out of a barn.

After ten minutes walking along the riverside, I hear voices. I round the bend and see a group of kids doing bottle tokes on the road near our house. They freeze when they see me coming, but as I start up the driveway, one of them calls out, "Hey! Do you know whose house that is?"

I turn to see a girl who's about the age I was when I left home. She's wearing a miniskirt, sitting on an anthill.

"Why?" I cross my arms.

"Everyone says they're still in there, hiding in the walls."

"Everyone should smoke less pot, then."

I feel all their eyes on my back as I head up and around the side of the house out of their sight. I find a busted plastic chair lying on its side, drag it down the grass and plant it upright. It pinches my ass as I sit.

"Jesus Christ," I say out loud. "We're a goddamn ghost story."

I turn my face toward the breeze, trying to block out the memories playing like little horror films along the outer walls of the house. Even with my eyes closed, I see my brothers throwing chicken bones at each other, setting fire to anything they could get their hands on, baby Poppy toddling out to the road in a dirty homemade diaper, Ma yelling at her to come back, Daddy gunning his truck up the driveway and almost clipping her. I see fights, broken glass, cold meals, all of us pissing into the wind any time we tried to spin our bits of straw into gold.

What a childhood. We had no books, no toys from our own decade. The only thing I owned that was truly mine was a little marble I found in the river reeds. I keep it on me at all times, rubbing it between my fingers trying to wear it down enough to free the colours locked inside.

I had one friend, but that only lasted a month. Kids at school normally kept their distance, but Summer's family moved here from Prince Edward Island and didn't know any better. One day she came over to play, and when her mother arrived to pick her up, Ma was coming out of the woods holding a rabbit she'd just killed, blood dripping all down one arm. At the same time, Bird and Jackie were showing off, playing a game where one of them would spit straight up in the air and the other would catch it in his mouth. Her mother looked as if she was going to have a heart attack. After that, Summer was only allowed to talk to me at school, and when she had a birthday party I didn't get invited.

Ma said that birthday parties were no fun. She said all the little girls feel like shit if they aren't wearing the prettiest dress or if the gift they brought isn't the best one, and that I should be glad I didn't have to go. I felt like shit anyway. I wanted to go to a party. I wasn't even sure if I was crying because I wasn't invited or because, if I had been, I wouldn't have had a dress to wear or a gift to bring.

Soon after, I invented Tough Girl. I'd wear all black and scare kids at the playground by freezing my arms in the snow and putting out cigarettes on my wrists. I told them Summer had a restraining order on me and that was why we didn't hang out anymore. They didn't even know who Summer was. They barely knew who I was, except that I was dirt-road people. That's how we classify people in Solace River: you're either up the hill, across the bridge, before the bridge or dirt road. Whenever I told other kids that I lived up the dirt road, they took a step backward and looked at me like I probably ate my own shit for breakfast. If I added Saint onto that, they'd scatter like pigeons.

Not long after, I became Truck Driver. In the back field behind the garage we had an old pickup that didn't run anymore, and I'd make like it was an eighteen-wheeler, put on one of Daddy's mesh caps and go to Sacramento, Australia, Moose Jaw, any place I liked the name of. I'd make up stories about how

I really had to gun it to save the day. Once, I was carrying a load of hay for a bunch of starving horses in Russia and showed up in the nick of time before they all dropped dead.

In my truck-driving days, Daddy had a friend named Terry Profit who used to come by to borrow tools. If Daddy wasn't around, he sometimes slept on our sofa for a few days. One night I heard him try to go into Ma's bedroom, but the door was locked. He knocked and knocked, but she wouldn't let him in. The next day, he was going into the garage and saw me playing in the truck. He strolled up and tapped on the window, asked if he could catch a lift. At first he said I was a damn good driver and checked the map for me to be sure we'd make it into Paris by nightfall. He said we even had time to stop at the next exit for cheeseburgers, and when I pulled in at the truck stop, he said, "Paris is the city of love, you know. We better start practising." Then he pushed his hand down my shorts. I started to scream, but he put his other hand over my mouth and held it there. It smelled like the compost bucket after it had been left steaming in the sun a few days.

Terry Profit's the reason I didn't get the red guitar Barbara Best promised me if I stayed out of trouble. She got me enrolled in school in New Brunswick and one of my new teachers had a paperweight on her desk shaped like the Eiffel Tower. It had *Paris: City of Love* written on it in pink cursive and I swiped it because I couldn't stand looking at it every day.

Anyway, after what happened to Truck Driver, I went back to being just Tabby. I started drinking with the older kids down at the country club and walking home along the river letting the moonlight on the water mess with my eyes. I'd see all kinds of things swimming in there. Sea witches, lampreys. Once, when I was stoned, I saw Grandpa Jack floating by on his back, singing the executioner's song. I said hi and he stopped, turned his head and looked right at me.

I GET UP FROM THE PLASTIC CHAIR AND WALK IN BEHIND the garage. That old truck's still sitting back there, rusting away. I kick a path up to it through the scratchy brush. A crow sitting on the back fender doesn't hop down until I'm three feet from it.

The weeds that barely tickled the truck tires have almost grown over the hood. I part them and haul open the door, climb in onto the dirty leather seats. As soon as I slam the door shut and place my hands on the wheel, I smell Terry Profit's breath. I push down on the handle, but it sticks and I have to elbow it as hard as I can. The door flies open and dumps me onto the grass. I lay there cursing as the crow stares down at me from a crabapple tree.

"What the fuck are you looking at?"

It doesn't flinch. I pick up a piece of pipe lying in the grass, scramble to my feet and smash out the centre of the windshield before busting the side mirrors and headlights. I spin around to swing at the crow, but the branch is empty.

From up here, the house looks even more wretched. The roof is shifted so far over to one side it'd slide right off if I blew on it. The rotted eaves are hanging off in sections where they haven't already fallen. I wish the whole thing would collapse right now, sink into the ground and disappear forever.

I find a good throwing rock, run a few steps and whip it up at one of the broken upstairs windows. I miss, find another rock, and on the second try shatter the glass completely. Stray cats come flying out from all directions. I start picking up whatever's lying around the yard and chucking it until I've broken every window on two sides.

Then I set my sights on the bottle tree. Various bottles that held various liquids are still shoved onto branches, stunting the growth of leaves. Ma said that soon after she moved in here Grandma Jean came over with a box of empties and a superstition about evil spirits diving down the bottlenecks, getting trapped in the glass and frying up in the hot sun. Too bad the demon was already inside the house with his gnarly, stinky feet up on the sofa. The tree's no bigger than I am and I easily pick off the bottles. I line them up by the door then blast them one by one against it, christening the sinking ship.

I'm sweaty and panting as I stumble into the house, kick over some kitchen chairs, grab the rooster clock off the wall and smash its face into the cupboards. I put all my weight against the refrigerator that's all leaned over in the hallway with its door hanging open, but it won't budge. Finally, I give up and slump down on the floor next to it.

"Tabby? What's going on in there?"

I spring to my feet as West pokes his head in.

"Don't come in!" I trip over all the stuff I knocked over and push him back outdoors.

"I went to the house and you were gone, so I figured you might be here. I was just wondering if you might want to grab some lunch."

I walk back to his truck and get in. He follows and we sit staring through the windshield at the house. After a while, some of the cats re-emerge from the bushes with their tails raised. One of them slips back inside through a hole in the side wall and the rest follow.

"I called the town office," West says. "It's still yours."

I turn to look in his eyes and see the same copper swirls that were inside my marble. I focus on them until my fists unclench. Then I look back at the caved-in facade of the house, the wisps of curtains billowing in and out of the upstairs windows.

WHEN I TURNED EIGHTEEN, THEY KICKED ME OUT OF Raspberry and stuck me in a halfway house. The supervisor who was supposed to live with us only stopped in once a week to make sure we hadn't burned the place down, which would have been easy since it was practically made of cardboard. If someone coughed in the next room, it sounded louder than if they were sitting right next to you. The carpets were stapled to the floor and the windows were covered by clear plastic curtains stained yellow from all the nicotine. There was only enough hot water per day for one person to bathe, and if you tried to be that person, everyone else would bang on the door and scream for you to get the fuck out so they could take a shit.

The women who lived there were harder than the hardest

bitches at Raspberry. Especially Simone. Simone had four kids living with different relatives and she never talked about them, never
visited them. She used to freebase at a flophouse and come back
ranting about how the cops were the worst criminals out there,
how they stole her fur coat and raped her in a paddy wagon. When
she was in really bad shape, she pulled out her hair and carved up
her arms and legs with knives. There were big clumps of dyed red
hair all over the place. She flipped between being sickly sweet to
me, almost motherly, and threatening to murder me in my sleep.

"You looking for a job, Tobey?" she asked me one night.

Sometimes I was Tammy or Abby.

"Yeah," I said. "Why?"

"I know this motel owner. He only pays four bucks an hour,
but he hires under the table."

She took me straight down to meet Enzo. He showed us
how the chambermaids emptied the ashtrays and wiped the
pubic hairs off the toilet seats, where to dump the empty wine
bottles and used condoms. He said he'd try us out for a day and
see how we did. He gave Simone the room next door to clean and
assigned me to another way around back.

I'd never been in a motel room. I poked around a bit, wondering what kind of people stayed there. The vacuum cleaner looked
as if it was made in the 1800s and the towels were bleached stiff
as boards. There was a Bible in the drawer that someone had
taken a ballpoint pen to and made crazy notes in the margins.
There were little doll-sized bottles of shampoo and conditioner
and I hid a few of them in my pockets.

As I was stripping the sheets from the bed, Enzo came in

and shut the door behind him. I heard him unzip his pants, but before I could turn around, he got hold of my wrists. I tried to kick him off, but he leaned on me with all his weight and pinned me to the bed. I screamed and bit at his hand as he tried to cover my mouth with it and used the other to work my jean skirt up, yank my underwear to the side and jam himself inside me. Once he stopped thrusting, I told him I was calling the cops.

"You think they'll believe you? Your friend, she lies to police all the time. Don't be stupid." He buckled his belt. "You clean rooms for me and, for a little while every day, you and I will have our time together. I'll pay you seven dollars an hour, three dollars more than I pay the other girls."

He left, and I wailed into the pillow until I was hollowed out. I stared at the small round bloodstain on the sheet and watched my arm reach out, rip the sheet off the bed and throw it in the trash. When Enzo came back an hour later, I was scrubbing the sink in the bathroom just like he showed me. I looked at both our faces in the mirror and, in a voice I didn't recognize, said, "Ten dollars an hour."

Once I'd made a hundred and sixty dollars, I ran away from the halfway house and Enzo. For a long time, I couldn't look at a man when he took his clothes off. I'd close my eyes or stare at a wall. It even happened sometimes with Jared Smoke, who looked like a god when he was naked. The first touch of his skin on mine and my hands would clench into fists.

I TURN MY HEAD AND STARE AT WEST. HIS MOUTH IS parted just a little and he's snoring as usual. I lift the sheet and see his penis slumped to one side, the skin of his scrotum comically darker than the rest of him. I reach my hand out and let it hover a moment. The trail of hair is soft and warm. He's got a freckle pattern on his chest that looks like a bird sitting on a branch. I connect the dots with my finger. There's a little scar on his jaw and another above his right eyebrow. I kiss it, and he opens one eye.

"You're the best person I ever met, West."

"Christ," he murmurs. "You must have met all the wrong people."

I roll on top of him and we lock eyes for a few seconds. Then we're all mouths and limbs everywhere and my skin feels as if it's melting into his as I let him inside me. I'm building up to a blinding orgasm when there's a knock at the front door.

"The hell?" West cranes his neck, trying to see sideways out the window. He gets up on his knees for a better look. "Shit. It's my cousin. Stay here." He hauls on a pair of jeans, zips the fly and heads down the hall.

I don't know what to do, so I just stay still and listen to his muffled voice say, "Hey, Danny, come on in."

Danny is heavy-footed.

"What's going on, West?"

"Not much. Did you get your bike running?"

"Tommy says you're shacked up with some woman. Says you gave her your truck."

"Tell Tommy to fuck himself."

"Have you been talking to Abriel?"

"No," West answers. "And keep your voice down."

They turn as I appear half dressed in one of West's button-up shirts.

"Tabby, this is my cousin Danny."

Danny is tall with sandy hair, could be mistaken for West but for a wider face and small, bloodshot eyes.

"You look alike," I tell them.

"Yeah." West scratches the stubble on his cheek. "I don't know who got the shit end of that stick." He's trying to look casual, but I can see him gripping the counter behind him. "Want some coffee, Danny? If not, I got stuff to do."

"You kicking me out?" Danny asks.

"Not if I don't have to."

Danny picks up the salt shaker off the table and rolls it around in his fingers. "Abriel wants to talk to you."

"Abriel has a phone."

Danny smacks the shaker down, taps a smoke from his shirt pocket pack and sticks it in his lips. He lights it and blows a smoke ring that hangs in the air. He looks me up and down as he pokes his finger through the hole. "How about you let me have a go with her? See if she's worth it."

West pushes himself off the counter, but before he can grab him by the throat, Danny turns and bangs out through the screen door, slamming it so hard he almost knocks it off the hinges. West runs out in his bare feet. I follow and see him yelling something, saliva flying from his teeth, but the sound is swallowed as Danny starts up his motorcycle. West flips the bird as the Honda Shadow tears off down the street.

"What was that all about?" I ask.

West wipes the spit off his mouth. "I got something to tell you."

He steers me back into the house and starts making coffee, which he never does. He pours us each a cup and motions to the table, sets the mugs down and sits across from me. He smooths his eyebrows with his fingers, takes a sip, places his hands on his knees to try to stop their bouncing.

"Tabby, I'm married."

UNTIL ABOUT A MONTH AGO, I WAS LIVING IN A SORT OF commune making necklaces and key chains to sell at a weekend flea market. People paid a lot for them because the teenage boy who worked our table was irresistible. He was about fifteen years old with dimples and long, shiny black hair. He'd offer to try the necklaces on middle-aged women and their mothers, tying the leather ends around their saggy necks and tilting his hand mirror at different angles, whispering silky compliments in their ears. The women would walk away in their mint green slacks, smiling and stroking their new feather pendants while he counted their money.

I watched this happen over and over from where I was originally selling hubcaps at a table nearby. How I got doing that was, this tattoo artist I was living with had a buddy who offered to take me out to the countryside near the Miramichi. He said, "Come on, we'll start a business together." I imagined a little country store with quilts and pots of honey, but we wound up selling old junk and watching black-and-white Alfred Hitchcock movies all day. I can't even recall the guy's name. Victor, maybe. Vince? Everyone called him Scrounge.

Anyway, I'd been at the market for a few weeks when the necklace kid came strolling over. He brought me a hot black tea in a paper cup and asked me about the different hubcaps. He started telling me about the commune where he lived, and when I had a million questions about it, he offered to bring me out and meet everyone. I went with him after work and we got drunk on dandelion wine with ten or so others. They were living in a big old cabin and several outbuildings. The cabin was strung with patio lights and had a moose skull mounted over the door. They had a well and a few generators. Most of the people living there were potheads with university degrees. I couldn't figure out why they'd choose this over sitting at a desk somewhere with free heat.

Still, it was better than what Scrounge and I had going on. We were staying at the tiny, low-ceilinged house of his grandmother's sister. Every room was filled with her "children," dolls of all kinds arranged into scenes of birthday parties, sock hops, chess matches—and, more disturbingly, hair-pulling cat fights, a funeral for a dead baby and what looked like the intervention of a freckle-faced boy standing with his head bent in shame before a semicircle of former friends.

I asked the old lady which doll was her favourite and she scowled. "I don't play favourites." I winked at her, said, "Sure you do." She turned red from her neck all the way up to her forehead, hobbled quickly out of the room, slamming through the saloon doors into her kitchen, where I heard her pouring Black Seal rum into the measuring cup she used as a drinking glass.

So when the commune said I could stay if I didn't mind making key chains and shitting in an ice cream bucket, I told them, "Making key chains and shitting in random places happen to be two of my God-given talents." They thought I was joking.

The kid's real name was The Kid. I didn't believe him, so he showed me his birth certificate. His full name was Billy The Kid Billyboy, so I could see why he went with The Kid. He could shimmy up onto the roof in seconds. You'd be standing next to him then hear a whistle and he'd be up there grinning down at you. He could also do roundhouse kicks, burp the whole alphabet and get you to agree to just about anything. He was the only person at the commune who didn't start every sentence with the word "when": "When Robbie gets back," "When I get out west," "When I get my money." He was an expert on hot-air balloons because his grandfather used to operate one for a tour company. The old man would take vacationers up and sail them over farmhouses and rivers, stand mute in the corner working the propane valves while couples kissed and snapped photos with expensive cameras. The Kid got to go up sometimes after hours on Sunday evenings. His grandfather would hoist him on his shoulders to get him up even higher, show him all their land being swallowed by pavement.

The Kid and I got along like river stones. When I told him about all the things that happened to me before and after I left home, he put both his arms around me and sobbed. Then, to cheer us both up, he tried to fart "O Canada," but he never got past a sombre trumpeted O.

At the start of trout season, his uncle showed up with a van full of fishing gear and vinyl records. The Kid introduced us and the uncle said we could have the albums to sell at the market because he'd converted to CDs. While I rummaged through the stacks, he kept looking up the back of my shorts and talking to me about fishing, like I cared. He asked me if I wanted to come along on the trip. He was sexy as hell and had decent taste in music, so I said yes. After the weekend, he asked me if I wanted to come live with him at Blood Rain.

When The Kid and I said so long, I gave him my marble and made him promise not to lose it. He held it up to the sun, watching the light play through it. Then he came running after the van, leaping and hamming it up. The uncle and I watched in the rear-view mirror, laughing. His uncle told me The Kid had an identical twin who died at birth. "Imagine two of him!" he yelled over the engine.

I smiled, thinking one twin could burp the alphabet while the other burped it backward. Then the van hit a bump in the road. The water in the fish bucket slopped over and I looked back and saw a big ugly trout sliding down the metal floor toward us. The uncle managed to keep one hand on the wheel while he reached back, scooped it up, took aim and plopped that sucker right back into the bucket. That's when I fell for him.

Jared Smoke was the kind of man who could screw three times in a row if you were up for it. And you would be. He had washboard abs and his hair was as soft as kitten fur. He lived on the reserve in a converted office with linoleum floors and fluorescent ceiling lights. The washroom was down the hall from his apartment and it still said MEN on the door. To bathe, you had to boil water and put it in a basin in the basement laundry room. He had musical instruments everywhere and I'd sing along whenever he picked one up. He said I had a pretty voice.

When I found out he was married, I locked myself in the bathroom and tried to loosen the knot in my stomach by making myself cry. I'd been deluding myself since we met that we were starting a real relationship. I even daydreamed we might fall in love and make little babies to sing to. He said, "I didn't think you'd care," and then, "Don't worry, she's not coming back." So I stayed. About two weeks after I arrived, his grandmother called on the phone and they yelled at each other in their language. Then his sister came over and told us the band council was waiting down the road to talk to us.

Jared and I walked into the room together and when he saw all their faces, he dropped my hand and sat two chairs away from me. When they finally spoke, he didn't translate even though he said he would.

Afterward, I grabbed my jacket and purse from his place. I was too embarrassed to go around collecting my other junk. Jared drove me to the bus station and gave me forty dollars. I sat on a bench inside and looked up at the electronic board to see which buses were arriving and where they were going next. The first one that lit up on the screen was headed to Halifax. Through the windows, I watched Jared Smoke fiddle with the radio station to find a good song. He pulled away singing and probably never thought about me again.

WEST RIPS UP A PAPER NAPKIN AND ROLLS THE SHREDS into a hard little ball. "I don't know why she said yes when I asked her to marry me. Neither does she."

I picture them tying the knot in a barn strung with white twinkle lights. I think back to the photograph I saw of her the first night I slept here. I bet she wore a dress short enough to show off the calves of those tanned legs. I try not to imagine the same legs twisted around West in the bed I've been sleeping in, but I do anyway.

"After the wedding, she wanted me to buy the tavern, so I did, and right after that she wanted me to buy the pawnshop across the street. She was furious that I wouldn't do it. She hated my clothes, hated this house, couldn't stand me breathing next to her. Some rich guy came to town a few years ago to buy horses, and five minutes later she was taking off with him. I haven't seen her since."

I finally get my vocal cords to work. "Have you talked to her?"

"She calls me once every three months or so to make sure I'm still miserable." West reaches his hand across the table, but I draw my chair back. "If she walked in the door right now, I'd tell her to go to hell."

"Why are you still married to her?"

"I guess I didn't have a good reason to bother with the paperwork."

I catch a glimpse of my homemade curtains hanging on his window and feel my stomach tie itself in that familiar slip knot. I look away to the shadows sliding like ghosts across the cupboards and wonder if there's any hard booze behind their doors.

"I need a cigarette."

West leaves the room and I hear him rummaging around in

the hall closet, taking things down off the shelf. He comes back and hands me a frumpy-looking Peter Jackson.

"I quit ages ago, but I hid a pack on myself in case the world's about to end."

"Did your wife make you quit?"

He squats down beside my chair and clears his throat like he's about to give a speech, but then he drops his head and sighs. We stay like that, me sitting, him squatting, neither of us speaking, until the afternoon sun starts to die on the linoleum. Finally, he stands back up, ankles cracking. "I guess I should start supper." I feel him studying the top of my head. "Tabby, I would have told you sooner, but I didn't see the point."

"You didn't think I'd care that you're married?"

"I'm only married by law. It don't mean shit. She left."

"Your cousin said she wants to talk to you."

"Her brother Tommy is a buddy of Danny's. The little piss stain's always trying to get her to come back to Solace to help take care of their mother. It ain't going to happen, and even if it did, she wouldn't be welcome here."

I get up, walk down the hall and lie down on his bed, trying to decide if I should leave right this minute. I squeeze my eyes shut, picture this wife of his prancing around, lounging next to him on the sofa watching TV. For all I know, he's using me to make her jealous. Why else would he let a stranger practically move in overnight and drive around in his truck? Maybe he even invited Danny to drop by, hoping he'd find me here

When I open my eyes, West is standing in the doorway.

"Hit me." He taps his cheek. "Come on, give me a good whack

so we can get past this and eat chicken strips." He paws around in a drawer and pulls out a Halloween devil mask, yanks it down over his head.

"Why do you have that thing?"

The devil tilts his hideous mug closer and closer. "Hit me," his voice insists.

So I do. I knock him right off the bed.

"*Jesus fuckmongering ass witch.* Was that just your hand?" He tries to laugh, but it makes him wince. "I've taken knuckle rings with less bite."

I reach down, pull up his mask and gasp. There's a mass of swelling already forming under his cheekbone.

"What?" He grabs his top lip and hauls it to one side. "Am I missing some teeth? Maybe you better hit me again to make sure."

I tell him I need some time alone to think and he pulls himself up off the floor, closing the bedroom door behind him. After he leaves for work, I go out to the kitchen and eat a few of the chicken fingers he left for me on the stove. They're pretty good.

I take a bath then sit on the sofa flipping through West's cookbook. Finally, I shut it and dig through my purse looking for the phone number I wrote down. I dial the trailer and it only rings once before Ma picks up.

"Oh, Tabby. I thought you were the police."

"The police? Why?"

"Swimmer's gone."

"Gone? What do you mean?"

"As soon as I went over to Bird's, Poppy took off to buy drugs. She left the kids in the car at some dealer's house and Janis fell asleep. Swimmer took off from the back seat and no one's seen him."

"Since when?"

"Since five hours ago."

"Oh my God."

I hang up and step into my boots, run down the road to the tavern. When I tell West about Swimmer, he kicks everyone out and snaps off the lights. We're on the highway within five minutes.

"Floor it."

"I am." The engine rattles. "This is as fast as she goes." West glances in the rear-view mirror. "Shit, did I lock the register?"

We arrive in Jubilant a few minutes after midnight. There's a cop car parked in Poppy's driveway. I hurry inside and find Ma sitting on the sofa with Jewell. A police officer is on the phone in the kitchen.

"No news," Jewell whispers before I ask. "Poppy's in the hospital having a nervous breakdown. Jackie's out searching. We just got Janis to sleep."

Ma looks like she's been punched in both eyes, her lids are so swollen. I ask her if she's all right and Jewell pats her hand, looks at me and shakes her head no. I go to the kitchen cupboard where Ma keeps a carton of Export "A"s, grab two packs, slip one in my jacket and tear the wrapping off the other. I remove the silver paper on the left-hand side the way she prefers, light one and bring it out to the waiting V of her fingers.

"West is with me," I tell her. "We're going to see what we can find out."

"She was right off Wharf Road," Jewell says. "We've already been up and down there fifty times."

I go back out to the truck and tell West, "We need to hear what people in town are saying. Is there a bar around?"

"The Hug 'n' Slug," he says, backing out. "The owner was ready to board it up a while back, but I guess he's still turning the sign on."

I chew a fingernail down to the skin, staring into everyone's yards as we pass. We pull up in front of a square building with bars on the windows and a sign hanging over the door that says *The Lighthouse*. I've driven past it a few times. The paint used to be blue, but the salt air turned it a pale turquoise. It's almost pretty in the moonlight.

An electric buzzer sounds when we walk in and the bartender's hand darts beneath the counter where he probably keeps his weapon. There are six or seven people seated, a few more shooting pool.

"Lazlo around?" West asks.

"Nope."

We sit at the bar and order a couple of drafts. The bartender relaxes a little and pulls down two glasses, keeps a steady eye on us as he pours.

"We heard there's a kid missing," West says. "Seen posters up at the Irving station."

A man sitting at the bar turns to look at us. "It's that little feller belongs to that stripper." He fishes the straw out of his glass and tosses it on the bar, takes two quick sips. "I recognize you."

"I run the tavern in Solace River."

"The Punch 'n' Kick?"

West removes his coat and slings it a little too hard over the stool back. "The Four Horses."

"That's right." The man taps his cheek then points to the shiner I gave West. "Looks like someone got the better of you."

A woman clomps up and whispers something in the man's ear. She leans down so far the ends of her peroxide blond hair dip into his drink. I look away from her saggy cleavage down at her leopard print pumps.

"Nice shoes."

"Got these at Frenchy's for four bucks." She picks up one freckled foot in the air and rotates it. The blurry mermaid tattooed on her ankle gyrates its tail. "Who the fuck are you?"

"Tabby. He's West."

She catches her balance. "I'm Angela, this is Bernie, and over there are a bunch of shitheads not worth knowing."

"We were just saying it's a shame about the missing little boy."

"They ain't going to find that kid. That woman has enemies. They want her brother and all them gone."

"Angela, quit your drunk talk." The bartender snatches her empty glass.

"Smoke?" I show her my pack of cigarettes, hop off my stool. "Let's go outside."

The street is deserted. She sparks the cigarette I give her off the lighter dangling from her key chain. Her key chain charm is a leopard print pump exactly like the ones she's wearing.

"Your man's some good-looking, though, Jesus." She inhales sharply and holds it in as she says, "You two walked in and I almost fell out of my chair."

"Well, he's not really mine. He's married."

"Fuck him, then." She blows out. "It ain't worth it."

"I do fuck him." I sigh. "And trust me, it's worth it."

She snorts and careens on her heels. "I like you. You should stick around. I'll warn you, though." She points at me with the burning tip of the cigarette. "This place is boring as shit. I mean, *look* at it." She gestures up the drizzly street, flinging her smoke in the air. I watch her stumble back and forth trying to fish it from the sidewalk crack. She finally manages to pinch it between her fingers and brings it back to her mouth, coating the filter in hot pink lipstick.

"So, this missing boy," I say. "You know something?"

"Troy and them were all up at his place yelling at each other, and it sounded like they were talking about where to stash some kid. I only go up there to buy grass off Kay, right?" She blows out a long stream of smoke. "They just ignore me."

"You didn't call the cops?"

"Fuck, no. They're probably taking better care of him than his mother does. Anyways, I know better. Those assholes would bury me."

"Why do you think they took him?"

"Probably to get back at somebody for something. Either way, the kid's going to social services. I know, because it happened to me, right?" Her veined blue eyes drift away up the street. When she looks back at me, they're shining. "They won't even fucking let me see my own fucking *kid*."

WEST AND I HEAD BACK TO THE TRAILER AND SLEEP IN the truck. In the morning, we drive to the truck stop for breakfast and I call Ma from the pay phone. Janis answers and says Swimmer's still gone and Grandma can't talk right now because she's crying too much. I tell her to try to cheer Grandma up and we'll check in later.

West parks outside the Lighthouse until the Open light switches on, then goes in hoping to catch the owner. Twenty minutes go by and I fall back to sleep on the sun-warmed seats. The door snaps open and I sit up with a start.

"Laz knows this Troy guy," West says, sliding back behind the wheel. "Says he wouldn't be surprised if that's who's behind this."

"Okay. What do we do?"

He squints toward the dock railing where some boats are heading out to open water. Then he turns the key in the ignition. "We'll have to send the cops up there."

At the police station, we find out they have only one car out searching for Swimmer. The officer in charge gets winded just from standing up from his chair. The two middle buttons of his uniform shirt pop open. West gives him the address for Troy, but he tells us there's nothing he can do without a search warrant.

"You got a woman in a bar saying she heard people at that house arguing about where to stash a kid." West rubs the knees of his jeans. "Don't you think it's worth looking into?"

The officer picks some crud out of the corner of his eye with his pinky finger. "Sir, let me explain this to you one more time. Even if I wanted to check it out, I can't enter private property without a search warrant."

I cut in. "Shouldn't you at least issue some kind of press release with Swimmer's photograph?"

"Truthfully, we're not considering this a missing person case yet."

"What? Why the hell not?"

"Because it's not the first time your sister's lost track of her son. Last year, we got a call from some woman a kilometre away saying he just turned up on her lawn, playing with her dog."

"He's been gone overnight. If he was playing with somebody's dog, they'd have called by now, for Christ sake."

He shrugs. "Maybe, maybe not. It could be someone who knows his mother and hasn't got around to bringing him home yet."

"Are you kidding me?" West looks about ready to put the guy in a headlock. "What if you're wrong? What if this was your kid?"

"Sir," the cop begins, but doesn't continue.

I stand up. "Let's go."

West kicks the door on our way out and yells, "Fucking Keystone Cops!" He tells me about an RCMP officer in Solace River, the only one he trusts enough to call when a fight gets out of hand at the tavern. We find a pay phone and the dispatcher puts him through. He talks for a while and, when he hangs up, tells me the Mountie might have a jurisdiction issue but said he'll see what he can do.

We drive to the playground for a quick look before we head back to the trailer. No one's home when we pull in. I dig the spare key out of the swan planter and we go inside, try to make small talk, but we're too drained. Our voices trail off and we just sit in silence. West's eyes travel around the trailer and I bet he's wondering where I get off making comments about his place.

Just before dusk, a Toyota Tercel rolls up the driveway. Jackie gets out, goes around and helps Ma out of the passenger seat. Janis climbs out the back and it takes her three tries to slam the door shut. Swimmer's still missing. I can see it in their eyes.

"Janis, this is West," I say once she kicks her sneakers off.

She stands there on the carpet, eyeing him from behind her sunglasses. "You're him."

"I'm him."

"You can't meet Swimmer, because he escaped."

West nods. "That's okay. I'll meet him when he gets back."

"He'll be back on Tuesday because that's when we watch the Muppets show." She points at Jackie and Ma. "This is Uncle Jackie and this is my grandmother. Just call her Grandma."

West shakes their hands, but they barely register him.

"We been at the hospital trying to get more information out of Poppy," Jackie says. "She's hopped up on something, trying to claw out the windows. They had to restrain her twice because she's so goddamn skinny, she squirms right out of the straps."

"Who's Troy?" I ask.

Jackie flinches. "Who said Troy?"

"Some woman in the Lighthouse said Troy was out to get Poppy. Who is he?"

Jackie sniffs his armpit, says he needs to take a shower and walks away down the hall.

Ma sets her purse on the table. "Poppy said those low-lifes at the drug house wouldn't let her leave, wanted to know why the cops were looking for her and whose names she's been giving out. They closed the drapes and wouldn't let her check on the kids, started forcing pills down her throat and asking her the same questions over and over. She doesn't know how much time passed before she heard Janis screaming at her through the cat flap."

"Oh shit." I feel the blood drain from my face. "I made Lyle think the cops are after Poppy."

"This ain't Lyle," Ma says. "It's Troy. This ain't the first time he used Poppy to get at Jackie. When she was just a dancer, he fed her drugs like candy one weekend, convinced her she could make a thousand a night doing what she shouldn't. He's the reason she got addicted in the first place."

Janis lies down on the kitchen floor and doesn't say a word while I boil spaghetti noodles and West chops up whatever he can find in the fridge. I have about ten questions for Jackie, but after he jumps out of the shower he heads straight down to the pay phone at Frosty's to call Jewell. I ask him why he doesn't just use the phone here and he says he doesn't want to tie up the line in case the cops call.

"Use your head," he snaps at me, jabbing his index finger to his temple.

I keep thinking about what Ma said. Troy would have to be one demented motherfucker to snatch a kid. I bet West is thinking the same thing. He's been slicing the brown spots off the same onion for five minutes.

When Jackie finally comes back, he rigs up a police scanner in the kitchen and stays glued to it all night. The rest of us eat in the living room, staring blankly at the television while we chew.

"Is Swimmer eating supper?" Janis asks.

"Of course he is," I say. "He's got it all over his face as usual."

"And on his arms," she says.

"And on his shirt."

She rips off a hunk of bread. "He's wearing his Smurfs shirt," she says with her mouth full. "I remembered that to the fuzz."

AFTER SUPPER, WEST TELLS ME HE'S GOT TO HEAD BACK to Solace River and check on the tavern. He keeps his back to me as he puts his boots on and I get the feeling he's had enough. Maybe he's finally realized why people keep ten paces back from anyone named Saint. Part of me wants to jump in the truck with him and forget I ever found Poppy's trailer in the first place. I take my coat off the hook.

"You should stay," he whispers.

I peer around the corner at Ma slumped in a chair, Jackie resting his head on his arms at the kitchen table. West starts to say more, but Janis pops up between us.

"Can you look for my brother at Saw-liss River?" she asks West. "He might go fishing, so you should look for a kid sitting with a stick in the water." She spreads her arms wide. "His head is this big."

West tells her he'll keep his eyes peeled and heads out. Janis follows me to the front window, waving to West as he starts up his engine. At the foot of the driveway he gives a weak honk, and then he's gone. I still have my coat in my hand.

"There goes a good man," Janis says.

"How do you know?"

"Trust me."

The full moon is so low in the sky, it looks like the opening to a tunnel through the trees. Janis stares at it, nose pressed to the glass. "You think there's wolfs out there eating Swimmer's brains?"

"No, honey. They don't eat humans."

"They do too. I seen it on Uncle Jackie's TV. They eat us raw. But I don't think they'd want to eat Swimmer because he smells too bad." She breathes a circle of condensation. "Some wolfs take real babies and make them into wolf babies. So when Swimmer comes back, he might walk like a dog and eat out of garbage cans."

WHEN THE POLICE FINALLY PHONE, THEY TELL US THEY went up to Troy's residence and no one was there. The doors were locked and the cars gone. They finally contacted all the Maritime police agencies and alerted the media, and I bet it's only because West made that phone call to the Solace River detachment.

Ma goes to lie down and doesn't come back out. I knock on the bedroom door to ask if I can borrow her car and she says fine, if I can get it started. She drives a hatchback with two missing side mirrors. I try the key, pumping the gas until the engine finally turns over. The safety inspection expired four years ago and there's a hole in the floor so big you can see the gravel in the driveway. An air freshener shaped like a lobster hangs from the rear-view mirror. I sniff it out of curiosity, but the scent's all worn off.

It's been a while since I drove stick and it takes a minute to catch it in gear. I jerk all the way down the driveway but have it under control by the time I pass Frosty's. Thinking about Poppy going to score after she was half clean gets me so worked up I almost take out a purple mailbox.

It starts raining as I pull into the hospital parking lot. I get out and stand in the drops, staring up at Poppy's lighted window and grinding my teeth. She's sleeping when I get up there, so I sit down in the hallway with my back against the wall and wait until a nurse goes in to check her meds. When the woman comes back out, she tells me Poppy's awake. I walk in, keeping my distance. Poppy's arms and face are scratched up and bruised.

"Someone beat you up before I got the chance?"

She squints at me. "I did. I hit myself in the face until they shot me up with tranquilizers." She wrenches herself into a sitting position. "Where's my baby?"

"No one knows."

Her eyes are red slits. "Please kill me."

She looks dead already or I'd seriously consider it. Her skin is so pale, she practically disappears against the sheets except for the black and yellow holes in her arms. Twenty-one years old and all washed up. I can't stand to look at her.

"That's the second time someone said that to me in this hospital. You both want the easy way out."

I turn and walk out of the room to the stairwell, jog two stairs at a time up four flights to the top floor, push open the heavy door and march to the end of the hall. The door to 404A is closed, but I kick it open and barge in. Daddy's rank breath makes it easy to find him in the darkness. I switch on the lamp, stand over him for a few seconds and listen to his chest whistle. I can only imagine what demented dreams slosh around his head.

It takes me a few minutes to unhook all the tubes. I figure out how to release the foot brake on his bed then guide it out into the hallway. He doesn't wake up until the elevator doors are sliding open.

"The hell?"

A nurse comes around the corner and yells at us to stop just as the doors are closing. Before we get down to the second floor, Daddy starts struggling and demands I take him back to his room. I tell him to shut his trap just like he said to me a thousand times. The doors open and I wheel his bed quickly down the hall. When I'm almost to Poppy's room, I break into a run and heave Daddy right through the open door.

"You deserve each other!" I yell.

A loud bang echoes into the hallway as his bed crashes into hers and slams it into the wall. Nurses come running, Poppy's screaming like she's being doused in acid, Daddy hollers, "WHAT IN THE FLYING FUCK?" and I turn and walk right out of the hospital.

5

THE CLOCK IN THE FRONT ROOM OF THE TRAILER IS ticking too loud. It's like Chinese water torture.

"Ma," I say. "We have to leave."

"And go where?"

"Back to Solace River."

She's been sitting in her ratty maroon bathrobe staring out the window at nothing all day. Ever since Swimmer's face appeared on page two of the *Jubilant Herald*, people have started driving by to get a look at the missing boy's trailer. Some dick-heads in a minivan stop at the foot of the driveway and point at us. I point right back.

Ma sighs. "In the old days, when something like this happened, the neighbours would come over with casseroles and ciga-rettes, offering to pick up prescriptions or do the dishes. It was like that when I was a little girl."

I try to close the curtains, but her fingers reach out and

tighten around my wrist like an eagle talon. I debate whether to tell her the problem is us, not the town.

"Whatever happened to your friend Bev?" I ask instead.

"When I shacked up with Wendell, I lost all my friends, one by one. They couldn't sit still around him, kept turning around to make sure their purses were still hanging off the back of their chairs. But not Bev. She used to come by to check on us when your father was in jail. She didn't want no trouble, though. After those men came out to the house, she brought us to Jubilant, but was scared shitless they were going to show up on her porch next. She always said she had no idea why I hooked up with a man like that, but Tabby, he could dance, and my God, he was so funny. He made me laugh so hard one night I pissed my new jeans."

"But then the fangs came out." I summon the nerve to ask her the question I've been wondering about for years. "So why did you stay with him?"

Janis looks up. She's been drawing pictures of Swimmer to put up on phone poles. In every one of them he's dancing to music notes rising out of a grey rectangle that's supposed to be the stereo. She waits for Ma to answer.

Ma picks up the cold mug of tea sitting on the window ledge. "I didn't. I left."

"No, you lost your home and couldn't go back."

"Well, I didn't let him in *here*, did I?" She sets the mug down with a bang and I can tell she's determined to have that tally point.

"But why'd you stay with him before all that? Back when he beat you, beat your kids, took off or was in jail half the time?"

146

Her eyes drift back out the window where a three-legged cat is hobbling along the ditch. I think she isn't going to answer me, but then she says, "He used to cry sometimes at night. He didn't mean to hurt you. He just couldn't change." She blinks a few times. "In the old house, the bathroom doorknob was wrong. You had to turn the knob left instead of right. Your father could never keep that straight. Even if he'd just been in there, he'd keep turning it to the right, getting all worked up, hollering that it wouldn't open, and I'd have to come show him again. He had some damage, I think, from his father."

"Like Uncle Bird," Janis says, wagging a brown crayon back and forth on the paper to make Swimmer's hair.

"Oh my God!" Ma leaps up. "I forgot to feed Bird! Shit! It's been two days. Janis, fetch my bra!"

"Sit down, Ma. I'll go."

"Really?" She sinks back on the sofa. "Would you mind?"

Janis watches me put on my boots. "Want me to come show you where they keep the tuna fish cans?"

"Nah, you stay here and finish the posters."

I gulp in the fresh air as I step outside. The sky looks like Solace River after a rainfall, clouds curdling into pale green clusters. I cut across the backyards instead of taking the road.

I think about what Poppy said, that if she was me she'd have taken off by now. I don't know myself what's holding me here. All I know is that after I got kicked out of Blood Rain, I'd never felt more like an outsider in my life. I started imagining some happy movie ending in which my family had been watching the horizon for years, that as soon as they saw my face they'd shed tears of joy and dig out the good china. We'd feast on ham and scalloped potatoes as they hung on my every word, taking turns refreshing my drink.

I should have at least questioned myself on the good china. I mean, Christ, where would Ma have kept it—in the chest next to the good white linens?

Through the side window, I make out the shape of Bird's head, and when I walk in, I find all three Musketeers seated at the table.

"Hey, gang," I say. "You had anything to eat today?"

Three sets of eyes stare back at me.

"I'll fix you something, okay?"

The fat one mumbles something about it being goddamn time. He's wearing pants today, thank God. I go into the kitchen and open the cupboards. They've got cans of soup, some old crackers, Shake 'n Bake mixture and mouldy bread. There's a forty of spiced rum in the fridge, half a bag of onions and three jars of homemade pickles. In the freezer, I find a whole chicken, so I defrost it in the microwave, season it with the Shake 'n Bake and stick it in the oven.

"It'll be ready soon," I say, coming back to the table. "What are you playing?"

"Gin rummy," the fat one finally answers.

"You ever play crazy eights?"

"Gin rummy," he repeats.

The one with the eye patch turns to stare at him with his good eye. "Crazy eights."

I sit and show them the simplest rules of the game. We play a few hands and even Bird catches on, solemnly laying down each card. When the chicken is ready, I serve it to them with fried onions and pickles on the side. I have to cut up Bird's into little tiny pieces and feed it to him. Sitting this close, I notice how strong his body odour is. I find the washroom, and the bathtub looks as if no one's been using it. I clean it with dish detergent then fill it halfway.

"Come on, Bird." I wheel him away from his empty plate. "Let's get you in the bath." I park him in the washroom and pull his shirt off over his head. "Can you stand up?"

He sticks his spindly arms straight out. I take them and hoist him up a little out of the chair. I'm not sure that's the best move, so I sit him back down and pull his pants and underpants down and shimmy them over his feet. Then we try again. Eventually, I have him standing naked, holding on to me. His skin is hanging slack on his bones and he seems so shrunken. In the photograph I saw on Jackie's fridge, Bird towered over Jackie. Now he's my height and probably weighs about the same.

He reeks so bad I have to hold my breath while trying to lower him into the tub without dropping him. Once he's seated, I gently grab his ankles and stretch his legs out in front of him. He smiles as all the warm water wraps around his body.

"How's that?" I ask.

He points to the taps, so I run a little more hot water. I find a skinny bar of soap, wipe the crud off it with some toilet paper, then use it to lather his chest and shoulders. I clean his whole head and face and then each arm. Then I slap the soap in his

149

hand and get him to clean the rest. I have to tell him in parts: Clean your legs. Clean your knees. Clean your privates. Clean your belly. I watch him and think about how for all these years I was so pissed off about not having a family to take care of me, it never occurred to me I was getting off scot-free of taking care of them.

When we're done, Bird leans back in the water and closes his eyes. For a moment, he looks like any normal man. I sit on the toilet seat lid and study the war museum of his body. He's got a crooked forearm from the time Daddy chucked him and Jackie out the window like a sack of garbage, and there are tattoos of his daughters' names branded on either side of his sunken chest. Up close, the scarred flesh across his face is so shiny I can practically see my reflection in it. For some reason he's missing half his ring finger. I lean in for a better look and his eyes fly open.

"Tabby got bit by a king cobra."

I'm stunned for a second. "Yes, she did." I lift my pant leg to show him the scar.

He blinks at it for a while. Then his tongue rolls out of the side of his mouth as he smiles at me.

SWIMMER HAS BEEN GONE FOUR NIGHTS NOW. MA HAS the police scanner on all the time. Janis had a nightmare about naked vampires lying in bathtubs and now she won't go pee without a steak knife in her hand. Sitting around doing nothing is making me stir-crazy. I tell Ma I'm going to buy toilet paper and take off in her car.

Troy's house is a beige, two-storey rectangle up on a hill at the end of a long paved driveway empty of vehicles. I park at the bottom and walk right up, heart pounding. I peek around back and see a swimming pool that no one's been looking after. I try not to think of Swimmer wandering out there and falling in. There are some empty booze bottles and cigarette butts in a can on the deck. I knock, wait a few minutes, then try the doorbell. I can't see anything through the curtains. I'm just about to leave when a window slides open on the second floor. A hard-looking woman in a pink bathrobe sticks her head out.

"You get your ass off my property," she yells down. "And tell Jackie if he drives by here again, Troy will slit Bird's throat."

I bite down hard on my tongue. "Our nephew's gone missing," I say, tasting blood. "We're talking to everyone. He's only three years old and has medications he needs to be taking. He can get real sick with the runs."

"I have no idea what you're talking about."

"You haven't seen all the posters or turned on a television?"

Her mouth tightens. "I said get your ass off my property."

"I want to talk to Troy."

She slams the window shut. I try the doorknob, but it's locked. I bang on the door and the window opens again. I see the barrel of a rifle sliding out.

"Okay, okay." I raise my hands. As I retreat down the driveway, I spy some jelly beans amongst the rocks. It rained overnight, but their colours are still vivid. I pause, look back over my shoulder, and she's still pointing that thing at me.

I peel out of there and drive straight to the police station. When I barge into Detective Surette's office, he's on the phone. I have to sit and listen to him order a deer antler chandelier from some catalogue. He tucks his credit card back in his wallet and scratches the loose skin under his chin before hanging up.

"I don't investigate missing persons." He closes his door. "You have to talk to Detective McNeil."

"That's not why I'm here."

He sits on his desk and cracks each of his knuckles. "Then what can I do for you?"

"We own land in Solace River. If there's taxes owing, I want it taken care of. And I want the old house bulldozed. We'll sleep in a goddamn lean-to if we have to."

"That's a tall order." He puts his glasses on and flips through a Rolodex.

"So's asking us to leave. We're about as welcome in Solace River as we are here."

"You'd be taking Jackie?"

"All of them. As soon as we get Swimmer."

He plucks one of the Rolodex cards. "I'll make some calls."

"There's one more thing."

"What's that?"

I think back to the other day when I fed Bird. He kept biting the spoon and when I swatted his arm, he screeched and wrenched away from me so fast his wheelchair almost keeled over.

152

"Tell me why you didn't go after the people who almost killed Bird."

Surette removes his glasses and places them on the desk. A MedicAlert bracelet on his wrist catches the sun as he folds his hands. "We're pretty sure we know who did it. But they had solid alibis, every one of them. We had nothing on them. Couldn't get a decent footprint, no weapon recovered, no witnesses."

"So he's no dummy, this Troy?"

"Not when it could send him to prison."

A few seconds pass in silence before he returns to his Rolodex. I snatch the catalogue and flip through it till I find the chandelier.

"Eight hundred dollars is a rip-off. Jackie could shoot a buck and rig you up one for a hundred."

Surette looks at me over the rim of his glasses. "He wouldn't need to shoot one. Antlers fall off."

"Sure, if you want to follow it around the forest waiting for the magical moment." I stand up. "I guess that's how it goes down here at the station. You all sit around expecting everything to tie itself up in a big fucking bow."

I slam the catalogue on the desk and walk out.

I HAVE TO DRINK THE DREGS OF A BOTTLE OF SHERRY TO work up the nerve to call West. I half expect him to tell me to take care and have a nice life, but instead he says everyone in Solace River is talking about Swimmer.

"Are they saying it serves us right?"

"Christ, no, Tabby. Give people a little credit."

I balance the telephone receiver in my neck as I open a can of chili, not sure what to say next. "Was the tavern locked when you got back?"

"I locked the register, but not the door. Weird enough, no one was in here. This town is getting lazy."

I dump the chili into a pot. I can't find a clean spoon, so I stir it with a butter knife. Then I grab the receiver in both hands and press it to my ear. I hear West toss a beer cap at the garbage can and miss. Then there's a long creak and I know which chair he sat on.

"You want me to come get you?" he asks.

I'm so stunned, I don't answer.

"You there?"

"Yeah." I reach over and turn down the burner as hot brown bubbles jump in the air. "I can't go anywhere. I'm the only one feeding Janis and Bird. Ma won't even leave the house or take a bath because she's afraid she'll miss a phone call. She'd kill me if she knew I was tying up the line right now."

On cue, Ma barges in and putters around the cupboards, muttering that there's a pay phone down the frigging road.

"Listen," West blurts. "I got my divorce papers ready to serve. Abriel thinks she's entitled to half the tavern, but the lawyer I talked to says there's no way."

I drop the phone by mistake and Ma picks it up, tells West goodbye and hangs it back on the hook. My heart pounds in my ears as I transfer the chili to a bowl and cover it with foil. I cart it over to the Musketeers, and I'm so distracted feeding Bird I don't notice he's wearing a bolo tie until I'm about to leave. When I get back to the trailer, Ma's standing outside. She's wearing a nice blouse and combed her hair a different way. Janis is sitting on the stairs behind her with a little pink sequined purse slung over her arm.

"I just got a call from the hospital," Ma says. "They don't think your father will make it to the end of the week." She won't look at me. "I was going to go up there anyway to see Poppy. She's asking for Janis."

"Are you going to say goodbye to him?"

She won't answer, just gets in the car and checks her teeth in the mirror. When we get to the hospital, she walks in ahead of Janis and me. We follow ten feet behind her as she goes up to the second floor and into Poppy's room.

"How are you doing, Poppy?" Ma asks the wall. She looks around the room and fixes her gaze on a stock painting of a basket of wine and cheese.

Poppy sits up limply and holds her arms out for Janis. Janis doesn't budge, unzips her purse and pulls out a folded homemade card. Poppy opens it and her face breaks into hard lines. She puts it on the nightstand and I lean back to read what's printed inside. It says, I STIL LUV YOO, BUT YOO BETUR SMRTAN UP.

"Daddy's almost dead," Poppy says. "I think seeing me made him sicker. He just started shutting down. First he couldn't walk, now he can't chew his food."

"Is he still talking?" Ma asks.

"He was last night."

"What did he say?"

"That he's not ready to go."

"That it?" Ma fidgets with her glasses. "Did he ask for me?"

"Just go up there," Poppy says.

Ma stands and walks out of the room. The three of us stare at the empty doorway for a minute.

"Why is there two beds in here?" Janis asks.

"I asked for another one so you can sleep over," Poppy tells her.

It's a lie. The nurse told Ma Poppy's been having withdrawal nightmares and tried to attack her roommate in her sleep. They had to move the poor woman to the other end of the hospital.

"No, thanks," Janis says.

Poppy clenches her jaw. "Go play in the lounge around the corner a minute. I need to talk to Tabby."

Janis sits down and picks up a barf tray instead, turns it over in her hands trying to figure out what it does.

"Janis Jean," Poppy warns. "What did I just say?"

Janis pretends not to hear, so I tell her I saw a book about bats in the lounge.

She looks up. "What kind of bats?"

"The gross kind."

She sighs, but then she gets up and stomps out of the room.

"That was some trick pushing Daddy in here," Poppy says. "He wouldn't let them take him back to his room. He never shut up, talked until I passed out cold. Then he made his nurse bring him back down the next morning and picked up right where he left off."

"What did he have to say?"

"He went on and on. Why he is who he is, how Grandpa Jack used to torture him. He talked about how his teacher always called him stupid, how he got fed up one day and told her he wasn't stupid, he was just hungry because Grandpa Jack was on a world-class bender and there was nothing in the house to eat. The teacher made him stand up in front of the class and eat a jar of glue for talking back to her." Poppy tucks her greasy hair behind her ears. "He said he learned to hate from birth and couldn't unlearn it, blah blah blah. It was a load of horseshit." She reaches under her pillow, pulls out a map scrawled in blue ink on a piece of foolscap. "He only gave this to me when he realized he ain't walking out of here and not a moment before. So don't go thinking it was meant for us." She covers it with her hand and motions for me to tuck it in my purse. "You know what else? He asked me to get him a priest, said it had to be a black man or a Mi'kmaq because he don't trust white men in robes."

"Did you tell the doctor?"

"Who's going to find a priest near Jubilant that ain't bleached as toilet paper, let alone one that would stand in the same room as Daddy? Fuck him. He don't deserve saving."

Maybe there's still time. I walk out and go find Janis. She's stretched out in the lounge, taking up a whole sofa.

"Look," she says, holding up the book. "These bats will rip your eyes out of your head."

A little blond girl on the opposite sofa burrows her face into her father's shoulder.

"They bite your eye out of your head," Janice says, louder, "and you have to wear a pirate patch like Bird's friend."

I confiscate the book and put it back on the shelf, but Janis snatches it back. I can't be bothered to fight her, so I let her take it.

"Come on," I say, steering her by the hood of her jacket.

When we get up to Daddy's room, Ma is seated at his bedside. She nods for us to come in. Daddy looks just like one of the bats Janis just showed me, all shrivelled and small-faced.

"He can't talk, but he can hear you," Ma says.

Janis points to herself. "JAN-IS."

Daddy grabs his elbows, moving them side to side like he's rocking a baby.

"That's right," Ma says to him. "You held her once when she was a baby." She turns to Janis. "He sang you songs."

"What songs?" Janis demands.

"Probably the one about the drunken sailor."

"How does it go?"

Daddy wheezes and grunts, trying to sing it for her.

I have only two good memories of my father and one of them is him teaching me this song. It was a summer day in Solace River and he and I were sitting on a blanket at the secret lake, right where I sat with West.

I start the song and Daddy tries to hit the bed rails in time. He's too weak and collapses against the pillow. I sing the verses that start "Put him in the longboat till he's sober" and "Shave his belly with a rusty razor," and then Janis makes one up, "Kick him in the head until he's sorry."

After we run out of stuff to sing, Janis reads Daddy the entire bat book, inventing most of it. I have to admit her version is pretty entertaining. There are spitting contests and midnight birthday parties. A sort of bat tribunal decides whether a captured creature lives or dies. Most of them die. Daddy seems to enjoy it very much for someone at death's door himself. *Poor bastard*, I think, watching the little red-rimmed eyes fly around our faces. He's going to die with his dirty soul all clogged up with glue and nobody really cares.

We all look up as Jackie appears in the doorway. He seems as startled as we are, shuffling to the corner without a word. After a while Ma asks him if there's something he wants to say. He takes off his ball cap, holds it in front of him with both hands.

"I'm about to be a father," he tells the floor. "I fucked it up three times already, but I'm trying to do better. That's something you never done, Daddy. I'm going to do right by every kid I bring into the world. I ain't even got a clue how, except to do the opposite of everything you did. You're a piece of shit," he says hoarsely. "But I forgive you."

Daddy is swallowing non-stop during this speech, the hard grooves of his cheeks sinking deeper into shadow. I glance at the phone. We could call for a priest, or a shaman. Or an exorcist.

Jackie leans in as Daddy beckons, and we watch Daddy kiss his own palm, reach up and press it to Jackie's face. Jackie's lower lip twitches and he walks out of the room so fast he knocks Daddy's chart off the hook on the back of the door. It hits the floor with a bang and Ma flinches.

As I bend down to pick it up, I realize Poppy's right. Daddy doesn't deserve it.

My first week at Raspberry, I got punched in the face for not passing the salt fast enough. When I didn't start bawling or rat anyone out, the bitches backed off. But soon they got bored again, and I noticed these three girls eyeing me, talking about how I deserved to bleed for what I said about Arlene the lunch lady. Everyone loved Arlene because she'd give second helpings of home fries. Of course, I hadn't trash-talked anyone; they were just looking for any excuse. As I walked past them to leave, I said, "I never ribbed Arlene. The poor woman's just trying to get through the day without her buns sticking together."

They looked at me blankly.

"She's got enough on her plate without me stirring the pot."

Nothing.

"If you carrot all about Arlene, go let off steam somewhere else."

When they finally got my puns, one of them chased me down the hall and demanded I come back and be funny some more. She looked like Danny DeVito, but I decided I better not start there. After a few more jokes about how I'm on a roll but I butter stop before I milk it, I told them my last name was Smith and invented a whole backstory, complete with dead parents and a loyal pit bull with whom I wandered the city streets. I was practically Little Orphan Annie, except with hickies and a cigarette behind one ear.

It didn't take me long to figure out that all the girls were from families no better than Saints. We were all trying to hide it, but it seeps out of our pores and stinks up the air around us. Sometimes, when a girl was going to be sent back to her family, she'd freak out and beg to stay. It must have been contagious, because every time I thought about Solace River I saw Daddy's swinging fist.

The counsellor assigned to me at Raspberry was in his late twenties and not bad-looking. He let me call him Pete instead of Mr. Chambers. He was stocky and pale with ice-blue eyes and nice shirts. After my tooth got fixed, he started writing me little notes about how he thought I was cute and more mature than the other girls. I'd never had a boyfriend before, and I kind of liked the attention. One day he brought me into the gym storage room and whispered that he wasn't allowed to touch me so I'd have to touch him. After that, all my "counselling sessions" were about him getting off. I found out later he was the main reason they kept me at Raspberry for so many years. He wrote in my record that I was a danger to the public, that I'd told him in detail all the violent crimes I intended to commit once I was out.

Apparently, this kind of stuff was happening all the time. Everyone from janitors up to parole officers was getting action off the girls. I found out when I started hanging out in metal shop with the senior girls who spent all their unsupervised hours making knuckle rings and slim jims. For forty bucks of Barbara Best's money, they told me everything there was to know about Raspberry. For another twenty, they cut me copies of every key for the building.

When I told Counsellor Pete I was done shining his shaft, he freaked out, thinking I was about to tell on him, and locked me in the basement. The first thing I did when he let me out was break into the kitchen and gorge myself on anything that wasn't locked up. Then I went back to the basement to get this industrial stapler I'd seen down there. I used my keys to get into his room later that night and woke him up with my mouth. As soon as he relaxed and closed his eyes, I pulled that heavy thing out from under my sweater and drove three or four metal staples straight down into his balls.

Not all the staff at Raspberry were criminals. There was one teacher I liked, Mrs. Dunphy, who taught us sewing and cooking. She wore steel-toed boots with long denim dresses, threw F-bombs around even more than we did. After I cracked her code for multiple-choice tests (the first four answers always spelled ABBA and the last four ACDC), she asked me if I came from a family of geniuses. I told her about the time Daddy put on a thrift store tie, drove to another town and impersonated a member of their school board. He purchased a hot water heater on the board's credit account, even had the store employee load it onto his truck before he promptly drove out of town, changing his licence plate on the way. Mrs. Dunphy laughed till she had to thump her chest with her fist to get some air. But then she sat me down and said I should find a way to use my powers for good.

So I did. The girls at Raspberry were always complaining that they couldn't talk to their boyfriends. We were only allowed sixty minutes' phone time per week and you could only use them to call designated family members. One night we were all sitting around the common room watching MuchMusic and the VJ announced that fans could phone in to the show, speak into an answering machine, and the message would be converted into type that ran in an ongoing stream across the bottom of the screen. I pointed out to the girls that they could receive messages this way. Soon enough, during music videos, we saw a string of fake gushing about a certain band followed by the instructions: *R.S. meet L.J. back field at 7pm 05/03.* We could barely hold in our cheers in front of the supervisors on duty. They didn't catch on for almost a year, and by then there had been eight covert conjugal visits.

IT TAKES A WHILE TO CONVINCE MA OF THE PLAN. SHE tells me that she and the kids nearly froze to the chesterfield last winter and she's saving Daddy's money for the oil tank. But she finally forks it over.

I walk into Jody's Garage and Lyle Kenzie starts toward me with a wrench in his hand, tightening his grip like he might hit me with it. I haven't had a whiff of him since the police warned him to stay away from Poppy's trailer, but I can tell he's still looking to collect.

"You ain't no cop," he says.

I hand him an envelope containing the cash and watch him count it.

"Fuck is this? She owes me a grand. If I don't get the rest, I'll go to the hospital and shoot her in the face."

"Bet you won't get caught doing that."

He yanks his pants higher, trying to think of a comeback.

"I'll give you double what she owes, cash in hand. All you have to do is talk to the people who have Poppy's kid."

"What?" He sniffs the air.

"We're leaving." I hand him the deed. "Poppy's trailer. Tell Troy he can have it."

"Who'd want that piece of crap?"

"It's the only way to show him we're serious. He can use it as a meth lab for all I care."

Lyle stares at the paper so long I wonder if he's just pretending to know how to read. Finally, he rolls it up and sticks it in his back pocket. "What the fuck do you want me to do?"

"Bring Swimmer to the trailer. We'll tell the police he came wandering back on his own and that'll be the end of it. We'll drive away in moving trucks and Troy can be king of the castle again."

Lyle smacks the wrench against his hand. "You better not be playing games."

"Don't fuck it up." I turn to leave. "By the way, your barn door's open."

"Huh?"

"The wiener's leaving the bean pot."

"What?"

"Forget it."

He turns back to the workbench muttering and I finally hear his zipper go up.

THE LAST THING DADDY SAID TO POPPY BEFORE THEY stuck the tubes down his throat was, "I was born on a Friday, going to die on a Friday." He should have put money on it.

Nobody was with him when he went. A nurse just casually mentioned it to Poppy, which pissed her off to no end. Then she turned around and did the same thing to us.

"Daddy's dead," she barked into the phone. "Can someone bring me down a bag of ketchup chips? The vending machine ate my fucking loonie."

Ma slammed down the receiver and called the main switchboard to ask what was going to happen to his body. They said if no one claims him, he'll be cremated after the weekend, so we wait it out. First thing Monday morning, Jackie and I take Ma down to the room where families are allowed to sit and watch the cremation fire through a window. Jackie puts his arm around Ma, settles in like he's at the movies.

After a few hours, the furnace man pokes his head in the little room to tell us it's taking longer than usual.

"The crisper's got to work extra hard to get through that tough black heart, hey Ma?" Jackie grins.

The furnace looks like a big pizza oven. I picture the flames devouring Daddy's hands and feet, his soft grey belly and jackal smile. After we run out of things to say, I slowly tune out all sound in the room and search my heart for the only other good memory I have of my father.

It was January and all of us kids were home sick with the flu. My and Poppy's beds had been moved into Bird and Jackie's room, where the radiators worked better. Ma was sick too and couldn't do much for us. It hadn't snowed all winter, but that morning the whole house shook with what sounded like a giant whip crack and snow started pouring out of the sky in heavy tufts. We could hear the little thuds on the windows, but none of us had the energy to pick up our heads to look. Daddy's feet came pounding up the stairs and we placed fast bets on who was going to get it. But Daddy said, "Come on! Get up!" and in two trips he peeled the four of us out of our beds, blankets and all, and parked us on the old sofa in front of the picture window.

"Wendell!" Ma called out from her bedroom. "Why are them kids out of bed?"

He banged around near the kitchen door and then there was silence. Four-year-old Jackie rolled himself into a sweaty ball, muttering, "I didn't do nothing." I copied Bird, pressing my hot forehead to the cool glass, and suddenly Daddy appeared before us in the yard. He had on two pairs of pants, a goofy-looking hat with earflaps and wool socks over his hands.

Baby Poppy giggled as Daddy started strutting back and forth. We all sat up straight as he spun around in circles, jumped up and kicked his heels then hopped like a rabbit, wriggling his nose, all the while sneaking glances back to the window to catch our reaction. He stuck out his tongue to catch some flakes then pretended he caught too much and was choking. He wrapped his hand around his throat and mouthed, "Help me." Now we were all giggling. Finally, he spread his arms, fell backward and made a snow angel. It was beautiful, except the flask of whisky in one hand made his wings uneven.

I close my eyes and freeze the memory in my mind into the shape of a plastic snow globe. I trap a tiny man inside that looks like Daddy and gently lay him on his back atop the drifts.

A green light comes on above the furnace and Jackie opens the retort door.

"He's gonezo." Jackie pulls his head back out. "Must have cased the joint and escaped before they fired it up."

"Funny," Ma says, putting her coat on. "Let's go. The police may be trying to call."

The furnace man delicately tells her he still has to pulverize Daddy's bone fragments and she rolls her eyes. Finally, we're called into a backroom where the man pours the remains into a cardboard box and places it in Ma's hands. She stares at it, then sticks it under one arm.

"That ain't right," Jackie says. "We can't let him go home in that."

"Those fancy vases are a rip-off," Ma says, already walking out. "Your father don't care. He's dead."

Back at the trailer, she sorts through a bag of his effects the hospital handed over and calculates how much she could pawn it all for. I watch her put Daddy up on the shelf next to her mother and stick her tongue out at him. Daddy hated Grandma Jean ever since she spiked his coffee with horse laxatives to stop him from taking off on Ma while she was pregnant with Poppy. He went anyway, drove off slurring curse words with shit running down one leg. The police told us later he ended up smashed up in the ditch with a deer in his passenger seat. He was taken to the hospital, but he snuck out, hitchhiked down to Maine, came back home a month later with a truck full of contraband cigarettes and a Newfoundlander named Ghoulie. The cops tried to get Ghoulie to rat Daddy out, but the man had a bay accent so thick the judge couldn't understand a word he said.

In the middle of the night, I awake and think I hear Ma crying. I wonder if she's worrying about Swimmer or sad about Daddy, or both. I knock lightly on her door.

"You all right, Ma? Can I bring you anything?"

"Like what?"

"Tissue? Cigarette? Glass of water?" She doesn't respond, so I keep going. "Valium? Tequila shot? Chocolate sundae?"

I rack my brain for things she used to like. I remember asking her once what she'd wish for if she had three magic wishes. I wanted her to wish us away from Daddy, but she wished for twenty minutes alone with Rod Stewart. I asked what her second wish would be and she said twenty more minutes with Rod Stewart, then twenty more for the third wish. I threw my hands up and asked her why the hell she didn't just take an hour with him on her first wish, and she said she'd probably need breaks in between to keep up.

I knock again. "Rod Stewart?"

"Oh, yeah, right." She loudly blows her nose. "I suppose he's just standing out there in hot pants."

I'm not sure Ma's car will make it all the way to Solace River, so I convince Jackie to pick me up in the Tercel. It isn't hard once I tell him why I'm going.

The days are warming up and the car has no air conditioning. Jackie undoes another shirt button every hour. He squirms in the heat and rolls his sleeves up.

"What's that?" I ask, pointing at the scab on his forearm.

Jackie turns his wrist so I can see the tattoo: WENDELL SAINT R.I.P.

"What the hell did you do that for?"

He shrugs and I want to reach over and slap him. I haven't told him I went to see Lyle and I'm not going to. The fact that Lyle didn't turn down my deal on the spot pretty much fingers Troy as Swimmer's kidnapper. If I tell Jackie and he goes after Troy, he'll mess the whole deal up.

"Answer me one question," I say. "Why is Troy out to get you?"

"Don't know, don't care."

"Oh, give me a break. I grew up in Raspberry. Everyone in there was innocent."

"Fine." He tightens his hands on the wheel. "I knocked up his cousin and said it was someone else. She was a goddamn liar, though. First she says she's on the pill, then when I dump her she says she's pregnant and wants an abortion. I didn't believe her, so I wouldn't give her the money to go to Halifax. She was asking for way too much. I know what those things cost. Anyways, she got one from some woman in Amherst and wound up with an infection." He takes a big wad of chewing tobacco out of his jacket and sticks it under his lip. "I went to see her in the hospital. Troy was in there and starting shoving me right in the room. He pulled a knife and the doctors kicked us out. I tried phoning to tell her I'd help out with money if she needed it, for losing work at the diner. I felt like shit, Tabby, I really did."

"Good. You deserve to. She probably can't have kids now."

Jackie goes pale, like he hadn't thought of that. "Troy went after Bird because I was expecting it and Bird wasn't. He hates Bird anyway."

"If jumping Bird was supposed to even things up, why did Troy take Swimmer?"

Jackie spits out the window. "I ratted out his brother for robbing vending machines and he did time."

"Jesus Christ. You realize everybody's fucked sideways, except for you and Troy? This is some game you're playing."

"Shut up, Tabby. You weren't here and you don't know shit." He pauses. "I'm supposed to give a squirt about his brother after what he did to Poppy? She could have been the only one of us to go to college and do makeup on stiffs. Now she's a ninety-pound junkie with half her teeth rotted out. You telling me anything I did compares to what those fucks did to Bird? I know it should have been me, all right?" He pulls over to the side of the road, drops his head to the steering wheel. His shoulders heave and he starts bawling like I haven't seen since he was a little kid and Daddy would kick him for no reason. "You should have seen Bird after," he manages. "They beat him with pipes and everything. Now they're all shooting pool and fucking women and laughing at the retard in the halfway house that can't even wipe his own ass. Bird ain't even a person anymore. What kind of brother am I if I don't do nothing?"

"But it's done. You can't change it."

"When Josie was born, Bird said, 'Jackie, I didn't know I had it in me to love like this.'" Jackie wipes his eyes hard with the backs of his hands. "He ain't never going to see those girls again."

We sit in the thick heat. A log truck blows by and rocks the car side to side. Jackie leans his head back and lets out his breath in a shaky stream.

"How did this whole thing start?" I ask.

"Nobody wanted us in Jubilant, same as nobody wanted us in Solace. People were planning on running us out before we even got there."

"Why? It was just Ma and you kids."

"Because there ain't a man or his dog that Daddy didn't rip off between here and Charlottetown. I don't even think we know the half of what he done. Ma was a mess. All she could talk about was the house, her kitchen, how she'd lived in Solace River her whole life."

"What did you do?"

"We couldn't let them make her run again."

"So, what did you do?"

"I'm not proud of everything we done, but we had to start with Troy because that little inbred hick was getting all his punk friends together to—"

"What did you do?"

"Jesus, Tabby! Nothing! We got him piss loaded and took pictures of him passed out with some hobo's hairy balls sitting on his face. We made photocopies at the library and put them up all over town. Then Bird started screwing Troy's girlfriend all the time in public where everybody would see them. Nothing. Kid stuff."

I sigh. "Sadly, the only part of that story I don't buy is that you and Bird were ever in a library."

Another truck flies past, honking at us for being so close to the pavement. Jackie starts the car and merges back onto the highway. He snaps on the radio, but I turn it back off.

"You have to get out of Jubilant. I'm working on us getting the old land in Solace River back." I let that hit him with a smack. "And by the way, I can go to college if I want to."

"What?"

"You said Poppy was the only one who could go to college."

"I meant the only one of *us*."

"What the hell does that mean?"

Jackie sticks a fresh batch of tobacco under his lip instead of explaining, so I spark up a cigarette and blow the smoke over to his side. WELCOME TO SOLACE RIVER appears ahead and I remember Daddy bragging to me once that back when the sign was made of wood, Grandpa Jack shot two nipples onto the curvy *W* with his Remington. I bet Jackie would get a kick out of that, but I'm too pissed off to share.

Ten minutes later, we pull up in front of our old house. Jackie sits glaring at it while small birds chirp in the trees. He gets out and slams his door, but it only makes them sing louder, like the Whos down in Whoville.

We enter the house and wander through looking for anything worth salvaging. In the cellar, I find an old crate of Garnet's Saint's Elixir, but the contents of the bottles have evaporated.

Jackie takes a framed picture off the wall of Grandpa Jack and Daddy taken back when Daddy was a little boy. Both of them are shirtless with the exact same scowl on their faces. The house is in the background, but the paint isn't peeling yet and the grass is freshly mowed. Grandpa has tattoos all up and down his arms. Daddy's got a pickaxe in one hand.

"I don't get why Daddy named me Jack. Never heard him speak a good word about the man till after he was gone." Jackie sets the picture on a window ledge. "Did you hear there was a big party in town when the body washed up? I guess everybody knew he fell in the river, but the cops didn't even drag it to find out. Jack was in there so long that when some farmer tried to pull him out by the ankles, the skin slid off his feet like a pair of socks."

I cringe. "What do you think made him so hard?"

"The war, I guess. Daddy said Jack was afraid of the dark. He'd go hunting early in the morning and leave before the sun fell instead of staying out in that cabin. The other men used to rile him up about it until he broke a whisky glass on someone's face. That shut them up."

On the way upstairs, Jackie trips over a cat and it claws his leg. "Motherfucker!" he yells, trying to kick it. "Can we get the fuck out of here before we get fucking rabies?"

"Just a sec."

I make him follow me to get Ma's jewellery box. He pries it open, but there's nothing inside except some cheap plastic bracelets. I slide her dress off the hanger, but it's a mess. No point in taking it, but I do anyway. I grab one of Daddy's shirts too. Jackie helps me over the holes in the floor, then we head downstairs and outside to the garage. A crow swoops down from the old power pole and caws for backup.

As we squeeze into the stuffy garage, my mind rewinds to the day I arrived. I wonder what might be different if I'd turned around and left town right then. Poppy would still be gone, which means Swimmer would still be safe at the trailer with Ma. I shiver in the sweltering air.

"Map." Jackie snaps his fingers.

I take the paper Poppy gave me out of my purse and unfold it. Daddy made a grid of the dirt floor and drew a compass rose at the top to show direction. He marked an X then shaded in the old freezer right above it with a question mark. He told Poppy that if anyone had moved it, there should still be an indentation in the dirt where it used to sit. But we can tell it hasn't been messed with. It's full of old farm machinery parts that Daddy used to weigh it down, with more piled on top. It takes us forever to slide the thing to the other end of the garage.

"Five feet," I read.

"Five feet? Christ. This better be worth it."

Jackie goes out and grabs a metal shovel from the trunk of Jewell's car. I find a rake to break up the dirt and use it to poke and claw around the bottom of the hole each time Jackie lifts his shovel. After forty-five minutes, we stop talking. Jackie tosses his shirt aside and I twist my hair up out of my face. I wish we had some water.

"Shit. I feel something." Jackie drops the shovel.

I tunnel my hand into the dirt until I feel a plastic casing. I try to pull on it, but it's stuck, so I trench all around it with my fingers. Jackie pushes me back, gets a hold of an edge and hauls it out of the dirt with the veins popping out of his neck. He drops it at our feet and we stare at a clear industrial trash bag wrapped around something the size of a stone brick.

Jackie hoists himself out of the pit then jumps down again a minute later with an old fish knife. He tears into the plastic with the blade, dumps out all the debris that's seeped inside and starts pulling out filthy stacks of bills tied with twine. He holds them in both hands, gauging their weight.

"Suffering Jesus." His eyes meet mine. "That's a fuckload of money."

WE WALK INTO THE FOUR HORSES GRINNING LIKE JACK-o'-lanterns.

"Whoa." West puts down the newspaper. "Where'd you two come from?"

He asks us what we're so happy about and I pull back a corner of the blanket in my arms to show him the money. He nods toward a couple of guys in the corner and Jackie takes the hint, grabs the bundle from me and shoves it down at his feet. We make small talk while the two men stare up at the TV trying to figure out who we are. Finally, they get bored, pay their tab and leave.

I tell West that Daddy died and he mixes the three of us a stiff drink he calls the Soulless River. I sneak a few glances at him while he's pouring, wondering if he served those divorce papers yet.

"When's the funeral?" he asks, pushing two glasses toward us.

"We're not having one."

"Your mother don't want a service?"

"My mother played a Game Boy during the cremation."

"It's weird being in here," Jackie says, looking around. "Nothing's different." He knocks his drink back without even making a face, pushes his cap back on his sweaty hairline and scans the old photographs of the tavern. He starts asking West all kinds of personal questions, like how much money the place rakes in now compared with when Clutch Kelly owned it.

"West's from Cable," I tell him. "He wouldn't know."

"How'd you wind up here?"

"I heard the Four Horses was for sale cheap," West says. "I started out in the Labatt's warehouse then worked my way up to the brewery. I learned a lot, and after a couple years I was sick of having a boss, started thinking about starting my own label. Anyhow, circumstances changed and I wound up with this dump instead."

Circumstances being, I'd like to add, that he married a selfish fucking bitch.

"Your mother name you West?" Jackie asks.

"Jackie!" I shove him on his stool.

West refreshes Jackie's drink. "West's my last name."

"Wait." I slap the bar with both hands. "Say what?"

"Never mind. I go by West."

"No, not never mind. Don't make me jump over this counter, Ronnie or Gene or whoever you are."

"Gene?" He cringes.

"He don't look like a Gene," Jackie says thoughtfully. "More like a Rick."

"Rick?" West folds his arms across his chest. "Christ. Really?"

The door opens and an old woman in a plastic yellow sun visor comes in. She hangs up her sweater and waddles over to the bar, stares at Jackie as if he's behind glass.

"You're Mary Saint's boy," she says. "I heard your father passed."

Jackie drains his drink in one swig, turns his glass upside down on the bar and starts turning it in circles.

She reaches over and puts her hand on his shoulder. "You tell your mother we're praying for her grandson."

Jackie's face flushes crimson. "Thank you," he finally mutters.

It's dark by the time we get back to Jubilant, but Jackie insists we show Bird the money. While we're sitting in the drive-through ordering burgers, he admits he hardly ever steps foot in the blue house.

"I can't stand to see Bird like he is," he says. "He can't stand to see me, neither."

When we pull in the driveway, Jackie waves to Bird in the window and Bird gives him the finger. It's the wrong finger, but Jackie gets the message.

"See," he sighs.

Bird smells the food as we're coming in the door and wheels himself to the table. The three Musketeers rip the bag of food apart. Bird gets mustard and pickles all over his face and won't let me wipe it off.

"Bird, I got something to tell you," Jackie says. "Daddy's gone. He died."

Bird keeps chewing.

"Do you understand what I'm saying? Daddy's dead."

Bird swallows the whole burger, looks up and swings his head left to right.

"Okay?"

Bird picks up the cardboard tray that held the drinks and rips it in half. He lets the pieces fall on the floor and stares at them. Then he starts rolling his wheelchair over them, back and forth, saying, "Fuck you, fuck you, fuck you."

"You know he loved us, right? Even though he was an asshole. You know how I know? He left us a whole pile of money. Look at this." Jackie pulls out one of the stacks and dangles it in front of Bird's face.

Bird stares at the money, drooling.

"We can do anything now. We can go fishing again like we used to. Me and you. Whatever you want to do."

Bird wheels over to the wall and rips off some wallpaper. "Josie."

"She's with her mother," Jackie tells him. "Remember? She's with her mother and her sister in Alberta. They moved to the country so they could have a horse to ride. They got a yard so big they can run in a straight line till Tuesday."

"Josie and Michelle."

Jackie hands me the money. "I can't do this."

I can feel the heat rising off his back.

"It's all right," I tell him. "I'll stay."

He heads straight to the door and a second later I hear the Tercel peel out. I sit with Bird until he forgets about Josie and Michelle and wants to play cards. I get the others seated at the table with him and we play a few hands.

I've got a bad feeling rolling around my insides, and after twenty minutes of trying to ignore it I tell Bird I have to go check something. I get up from the table, grab the money and beat it down the road to the trailer. All the lights are off and a note on the fridge says Ma and Janis are at the hospital visiting Poppy. I pick up the phone and dial Jackie's place. Jewell answers.

"Is Jackie there?"

"He's not here. I thought he was with you."

"Jewell, I need you to come pick me up at the trailer."

"Why? What's going on?"

"Right now!"

"I can't. Jackie has the car."

"Shit!"

"I'll borrow my neighbour's car. Stay there."

I hang up, stash the money in a loose ceiling tile above Janis's bunk. Then I lock up and wait down at the curb. After fifteen minutes, Jewell comes roaring up in a pink Mary Kay car.

I jump in and she swings the car around, accelerating so fast we dip into the oncoming lane.

"He grabbed Grandpa's guns from the garage this afternoon, said he was going to try and sell them. I can't imagine they still shoot."

"There's a Ruger in the Tercel," Jewell says. "Jackie duct-taped it under the seat."

The last Soulless River I drank sloshes in my stomach as she picks up speed. She doesn't even have to ask where we're headed, guns it to the other side of town, cuts the headlights and idles up to the foot of Troy's driveway.

"Call the police," I tell her. "Use the pay phone at Frosty's then come right back."

Before she can argue, I get out and sprint up to the house, trying to remain in darkness. Through the front window, I see broken glass all over the living room carpet. Jackie must have busted in. I climb over the windowsill, avoiding the jagged shards, then crouch low and make my way to the kitchen.

There's a small mound of marijuana sitting on a scale out in the open. Above it on the wall is that "Footprints" story printed on a plaque, the one that reassures shitheads like Troy that Jesus always has his back. I hear voices and slide a knife out of the wooden block on the countertop. I follow the sounds up the carpeted staircase to a lamplit master bedroom.

As I reach the doorway, I see the woman who turned the rifle on me seated on the floor. She's wearing the same pink bathrobe. Next to her is a tattooed man with buzzed blond hair. Troy. The wiry little prick is nothing like I pictured. I step into the room and there's Jackie standing over them, holding a pistol to Troy's head.

"Jesus Christ, Jackie!"

They all look up in alarm. Troy's grey eyes are working the angles of the room, flying through possibilities. His white shirt is unbuttoned and the thin, pale chest is rising up, down, up, down. The woman leans forward like she wants to take her chances, stand up and make a run for it, but Troy puts his hand on her leg like it's all under control.

Jackie cocks the trigger. "Go find Swimmer," he tells me.

I race around the upstairs, checking the closets and under the unmade beds. I trip going back downstairs, pull myself up using the wall and limp the rest of the way down. I check all the first-floor rooms then open the door to the basement and call Swimmer's name. It's quiet. I find the chain for the light bulb and hop down on my good foot.

There's a pile of dirty laundry on the concrete floor next to the washing machine. I see a little striped sock in the mess of towels and sheets and drop to my knees, rummaging wildly through the pile, tossing things aside until I uncover a child-sized T-shirt. I stare at it a second before I grab it and hold it up to the light. Smurfs. I stumble to my feet, half crawl back up to the main floor and scream, "Jackie! Let's go! The cops are on the way!"

No response. I put my weight on the bad foot and let the pain shoot up my leg as I run upstairs to the master bedroom.

Troy and his woman are breathing fast and shallow, like dying animals. Jackie has the gun pressed hard to Troy's temple and Troy's eyes are squeezed closed, head turned away from the barrel. There's a large tattoo on his neck of a snake eating a bird.

"JACKIE, DON'T DO IT!"

A horn honks once outside and I run to the window. Jewell sees me waving and lays on the horn. Jackie grabs my arm and pushes me out of the bedroom. My ankle throbs as we sprint downstairs and out the front door. There are sirens in the distance, getting closer. I suddenly remember I had a kitchen knife in my hand. I don't know where I dropped it. I should have wiped off the handle.

"Get in!" Jewell screams.

Jackie and I dive into the back seat, slam our doors as she starts backing down the driveway, fishtailing on the rocks. Just before the nose of the car swings out onto the road, Troy runs out of the house and hollers, "THE KID AIN'T HERE, JACKIE, 'CAUSE I FUCKING BURIED HIM!"

Jewell struggles to stay under the speed limit. "I told the cops I heard gunshots coming from Troy's address. Then I hung up."

"Stop here and let me and Tabby out," Jackie says. "Go straight to the hospital and find Poppy's room. Pretend you were running an errand in town and dropped in for a visit."

"Ma and Janis are there now," I tell him.

"Good." Jackie grabs Jewell's shoulder. "Listen to me. Tell Ma to head back to the trailer, and keep Janis with you. If the cops show up looking for me or Tabby, tell them you've been at the hospital all night and that as far as you know both of us are in Solace River."

"What happened back there?" Her voice breaks.

"I'll tell you later."

Jackie and I get out and skulk along the woods to a dark side street where he left the Tercel. He drives us back to the trailer and we sneak inside, keeping the lights off.

"Call West," Jackie says. "People saw us at the Four Horses earlier. Get him to tell the cops we had too much to drink and crashed at his place."

West barely says hello before I spit out what Jackie just said.

"Tabby, what are you getting me mixed up in?"

I give him the short version.

"You have to tell the police you saw Swimmer's shirt."

"How can I? Jackie and I will get charged for break and enter."

West lets his breath out. "This can't be good. I mean, why's the kid not wearing his clothes?"

"They must have put him in clean ones. Think about it. If Troy did something to hurt Swimmer, he's not going to leave the evidence in plain sight."

"Maybe he ain't that smart."

"He's smart enough to have gotten away with this so far, smart enough to get away with what he did to Bird."

Ma walks into the trailer and I hang up without saying good-bye. Jackie starts to tell her what's going on when two police officers pull in and knock on the door. Ma waits for Jackie and me to hide in the bathroom before she answers the door. We hear her ask the cops if they've come with news about Swimmer. They say they're looking for me and she tells them I'm with my boyfriend in Solace River, asks why on earth they're looking for me when they should be out searching for Swimmer. I forgot Ma had to lie for Daddy so many times she got pretty good at it.

When the cops leave, she draws the curtains, lights a few candles then opens the bathroom door. Jackie tells her he broke into Troy's house, but leaves out the part where he had a gun to Troy's head. I retrieve Daddy's money from the kids' room and drop it on the table. Ma takes one look at it and trails off mid-sentence.

"Daddy buried it under the garage," I tell her.

"For Christ's sake," Ma says, holding a hundred-dollar bill close to a candle flame. "There's dried blood on this one."

"He probably just cut his hand," Jackie says. He guides her into a chair and divides the money into three rough piles. "Let's count it up."

We add in silence, the exaggerated shadows of the stacks growing ever higher on the wall.

"Fifty-eight," I announce after half an hour.

Ma pushes two piles into the centre. "Fifty-six."

Jackie punches all the numbers into Janis's Hello Kitty calculator.

"How much is it?" Ma demands.

Jackie shows her six digits on the little plastic screen.

"Oh, Lord." Ma stands up, sits, stands up again and walks around to double-check the curtains are closed. She sinks back down on her chair and stares in shock at the filthy hundred-dollar bills spread out over the tablecloth.

Jackie puts his hands on her shoulders. "Let's buy you a house. You can take the kids to live there. We'll get a place big enough for Bird to have a room too, get him out of that shithole."

Ma takes his hand in hers, then reaches across the table and grabs mine. Even by candlelight, I can see that all of our fingers are soiled black.

THEY'VE UPPED POPPY'S SEDATIVES AND HAVE HER ON suicide watch. She told Ma she's going to stay alive at least long enough to murder whoever took Swimmer. They had to remove her TV because she kept seeing Swimmer's face on the news. She had a conniption when Jewell tried to wake Janis to leave, so Jewell let Janis stay sleeping in the extra bed. I go over in the morning to pick her up. When I enter the room, Janis is feeding Poppy a doughnut by hand.

"Would you tell me what the hell is going on?" Poppy asks me.

"Later."

A nurse is ordering people around in the hallway and Poppy says, "Hear that dog barking out there? If she steps foot in here, she'll be walking out without a face. She was Bird's nurse. I caught her forcing food down his throat, yanking him in and out of bed like a fucking rag doll."

"Don't say that word," Janis says, picking crumbs off Poppy's chest. "Jesus is listening."

"What word?" Poppy says. The skin underneath her eyes looks scaly. "No, he ain't." She watches me limp over to an armless chair. "What happened to you?"

"Fox-hunting accident in the countryside," I say in a bad British accent. "My steed and I took a rather nasty spill."

"Hilarious."

"I'm just trying to lighten the mood."

"Well, don't."

"Fine." I sit and put my ankle up on the metal bed stool. "Then I won't tell you we found the money. Or that we're going to move you to a nice hospital in Solace River."

"There ain't no nice hospital in Solace River."

"Then we'll get you their best private room and redecorate."

"You going to redecorate the food too?"

Janis pulls the doughnut away. "Stop your complaining or we'll leave you here."

"You sound just like Ma when you say that," Poppy tells her.

"That's who takes care of me all the time," Janis says. "Swimmer talks like Grandma when he says 'goddamnit.' I bet he's saying it a lot if the bad people won't let him in their fridge to get string cheese."

Poppy's face constricts, and I push myself back up.

"How much money was there?" Poppy asks me.

I start gathering up Janis's stuff.

"Tabby, give me twenty bucks for smokes."

"Let's go, Janis."

Poppy tries to grab hold of my jacket as I usher Janis off the bed and out of the room. Janis ignores Poppy's yelling, asks me if she can have some chocolate milk from the cafeteria. I buy her some breakfast and take her to the playground in back of the hospital. She doesn't play, though, just sits on the little wooden bridge in her sunglasses with her arms dangling over the ropes. I notice she's got two different sneakers on and it makes me feel like shit.

"So, guess what?" I say. "You're going to live in a brand new house with a big bedroom."

She perks up, but then her shoulders droop again, as if she's heard this one before. "I don't want to go live in a new house if my mother gets to live there too."

"Your mother doesn't want to do drugs, you know."

"Then why does she?"

"They change her body so that she feels sick if she doesn't take them."

Janis swings one leg. "One time I had a wedding to my big teddy bear, Lippy, that I won at the fair from bonking a frog on the head. Swimmer was the ring boy and Mama was the judge, and then we had a party after with Cheezies and danced. But that was before, when she was nice."

I see my face reflected in her sunglasses as I ask, "Did she ever hurt you?"

"Nope." Janis rests her chin on the rope. "But she set the oven on fire and I had to call the fire truck because she forgot how to use the phone."

Two little girls in matching purple cowboy boots race each other to the slides. I watch Janis eyeball the boots.

"Want to go over there and play with those kids?"

She picks at the hole in the knee of her jeans and doesn't answer.

"Come on." I grab her feet and slide her underneath the rope, set her down on the ground. "Let's go look at the Sears catalogue and see what kind of furniture they have for your new bedroom. I bet you want one of those beds shaped like a race car."

"Do they have any shaped like a pineapple?"

"Maybe."

"Are you going to live at our new house? You can sleep in my new bedroom with me and Swimmer if you want."

"Maybe I'll live at West's house with him," I say, feeling myself blush. "It's not far from your new house."

"Are you going to have a wedding to West? I will, if you don't want to."

"Hands off, you already got a husband."

"Lippy the bear? Not no more. I broke it off when he cheated around."

"Who'd he cheat with?"

"Swimmer's baby girl doll, Wendy. I poked a fork through her forehead."

"You'd marry West, huh?" I bend down to zip her coat, but she pushes my hand away.

"Grandma thinks he got a nice rear end on him, but I like his truck."

When we get back to the trailer, I tuck her in for a nap and recline on Swimmer's empty bottom bunk. I stare up at the sagging bump in the mattress where her body lies, too tired to fall asleep myself. One of the photographs she showed me the first night I stayed here is lying on the floor. I reach down and pick it up.

Daddy was right: I do look like him, eyeing the camera like I want to punch it, sunken cheeks even at that age. That was probably the summer Bird and Jackie started stringing up cats to use for target practice. The same summer Terry Profit slid his wet tongue around in my ear.

I toss the photo back onto the floor and stare at the rectangle of grey sky framed in the small window. There are dark forces attracted to us Saints like the tide to the moon. Even when I was far away pretending to be somebody else, everything I tried to grab hold of wound up getting me in trouble. I'm sure if I'd tried to dodge this whole snakepit by turning on my boot heels and leaving Solace River the same day I arrived, the darkness would have just followed me wherever I went next. I can almost feel it shape-shifting around me sometimes. If it ever finds a way in, I'll wind up just like Daddy and Poppy, with eyes like two dead fish and carnage strewn for miles.

Swimmer's pillow smells sour. There's something lumpy stuffed beneath his covers. I reach down and pull out a woman's tank top and blouse. He must have been cuddling with Poppy's clothes like a security blanket. I stuff them back where they were, feeling oddly sheepish for invading a three-year-old's privacy.

On the low dresser there's a plaster imprint of his hands like little monkey paws, and beside it a photograph of him and his sister standing in one of those cheap wading pools. Janis is flexing her bicep while Swimmer grins up at her. "He can't even swim," Janis tells everyone. Poppy told me she named him Swimmer because he was conceived through a condom. If his father doesn't know he exists, maybe he should. Janis told me Swimmer's father is named John. Probably more of Poppy's sick sense of humour.

Nobody's trying to find Swimmer except for us. That's the sad truth. It's why I want out of here and why I can't leave.

I close my eyes and try to sleep, but thoughts keep banging around my head like boots in a clothes dryer. We have to drive the darkness out, and it's not something a priest or shaman can do for us. If we're ever going to stop biting our tails, we have to outrun Daddy's ghost back to Solace River, slide into that dried-up husk of a life and start all over. It's the only way to trick the devil: hide in the one place he'd never look.

6

WEST ISN'T PICKING UP AT THE TAVERN OR AT HOME either. I've been calling for two days straight. When the phone finally rings, I rip the receiver from the cradle.

"I was starting to think you were dead in a ditch."

"If I am, the afterlife is as shitty as the real one."

It's Detective Surette.

"Sorry. I thought you were someone else."

"I'm sorry I'm not someone else too. It would solve a lot of my problems." Surette coughs. "Enough of my sparkling wit. I'm just calling to let you know that your father's house fell off the town grid."

"What does that mean?"

"It means that seeing as how it's on a dirt road with its own well water and no power hooked up since the family left, best I can tell, you're clear on taxes. I hear it's in pretty rough shape, though."

"That's why I asked for bulldozers."

"I'm working on it. You'll have to go legit if you rebuild. This is a one-time loophole."

"Fine. What's the update on Swimmer?"

"Detective McNeil's been getting a lot of false leads. I think certain people are wasting his time on purpose."

"We all know who did it."

"Nobody knows anything for sure. Not even you."

I slam down the receiver and go back to driving myself bonkers over West. I'm worried Troy found out he gave us an alibi and sent someone after him. By the time the phone rings again the next afternoon, I'm half hysterical.

"Where've you been?"

"Abriel showed up here," West says.

"What?" My chest pinches. "At the tavern?"

"At the house."

"At *your* house?"

"Well, it's not all mine. Not yet."

I wish phones had TV screens so you could see the expression on the other person's face.

"What did she want?"

"She wants to get back together. I told her I'm done with her, but she won't listen. She keeps talking to me like I've got amnesia, saying everything was my fault and she's been trying to come back all this time."

"Did you sleep with her?"

He hesitates a half second too long.

"She's making it real hard to say no, I suppose." I wind the phone cord around my finger so tight, the skin turns blue.

"Tabby, I didn't see this coming. I need to sort a few things out."

"What things?"

"I got some questions for her."

I hang up on him even harder than I did on Surette. All I can see in my head is that auburn hair splayed out on my pillow. I bet she took one look around and decided the place wasn't so bad after all with the plants and the new curtains. She probably put my apron on and started frying up eggs. Even if she's gone again, she'll always be back.

I grab my purse, bang out the door and start running down the road. I veer up the driveway of the blue house and barge in the door, shove Bird's yellowed feet into his ugly Velcro sneakers, stick his arms through his denim jacket. I wheel him down the uneven ramp to the bottom of the driveway and start along the dirt road as fast as I can go. He bumps up and down, trucker hat veering to one side of his head. When his protest noises get louder, I stop to light a cigarette. My hands shake as I push his wheelchair down the ditch into the woods. About twenty feet into the trees, I can't manoeuvre his chair any farther. I park him next to a log and sit on it.

"He said if she came back, he'd tell her to go to hell," I say. "He said he doesn't have feelings for her, that it was over as soon as she walked out the door."

Bird tries to reach for my cigarette. I hold it up to his lips for a drag and he snatches it from me. I watch him perch it daintily between his fingertips and puff on it like a little old lady. I wonder how it is he can hold a cigarette but not a spoon, and why he can rip the shit out of the wallpaper but can't put on his own pants.

I bet Ma treats him like a baby just so she can take care of him, the same way she comes in and hands me a towel the minute she hears me turn on the tap. She can't protect us from getting our brains kicked in or being raped by some motel slumlord, but she shows up with hot soup and clean towels.

I tap another smoke out of my pack and stick it in my teeth. "What the hell did I come back here for? Daddy got what he deserved. Poppy's a mess. Janis and Swimmer will be the ones on drugs soon enough. Jackie's going to wind up in jail. And Ma, well, Ma's never going to be happy, is she? And here I am a grown woman with no house, no job, no car, no husband. You want to know why it took me so long to come find everybody? I wanted to have something to show for all these years. Joke's on me." I kick my purse. "I don't even have a social insurance number, which means I don't exist, just like the house we grew up in."

My lighter's dead. I flick it ten times then whip it at a tree.

"I don't even know West's real fucking name."

The fog sinks lower into the tree branches, mingling with Bird's cigarette smoke. We sit there so long my mind wanders all sorts of strange places. I start to imagine that Swimmer's been in these woods all along, eating fiddleheads and berries and babbling with the birds. I can almost see him toddling out of the mist with pine cones in his hair.

After a while it starts getting cold, so I button up Bird's coat and wheel him back up the road.

Janis wants to come with me to Solace River. She's never been. I don't know if she's ever been anywhere. I feel uneasy leaving Ma alone, but I need to sort out where we're going to live.

"I picture it's cloudy and the water's all black and everybody looks like this." Janis twists her face into a snarl. She clambers into the front seat of Ma's car, starts rolling the windows up and down and looking under the floor mats for dimes. "Are we going to visit West at his house?"

I pretend not to hear and distract her by telling her to pick a good song on the radio. She scans through every channel twice and finally settles on Dutch Mason, sits back nodding her head like an old bluesman.

"Janis, what do you want to be when you grow up?" I'm genuinely curious.

She bolts upright. "A bagpipe blower."

"Why?"

I get the feeling she's been dying for someone to ask her this question.

"Because. You walk at parades and you have hangy things on your socks, and a purse that goes in the front, and you don't got to put on no underpants. Everybody goes 'ooh aah' and takes pictures of you. They can hear you coming for a long time, and there's a person at the back who bangs on a drum this big." She flings her arms wide. "And old men watch and cry because they wish they got to play the bagpipes and now they're too old."

"What goes in those bagpipers' purses?"

"Tissues and gum."

I point to her sequined purse in her lap. "Is that what's in yours?"

"In here?" She unzips it and shows me a one-dollar bill, a ceramic rabbit figurine and some lip gloss called Ghostberry.

"Where did you get a one-dollar bill? They don't even make those anymore. It might be worth something someday."

She unrolls it. "How much?"

"Maybe a hundred dollars if you wait a long time."

Ma's car leaks oil, so we have to stop at four different gas stations along the way. One of them has a convenience store attached and Janis unclips her belt, says she'll be right back. I stare at the door until she re-emerges with a root beer slushie, a box of Cracker Jack and some licorice twists. She's clutching a five-dollar bill and a bunch of change in one fist.

"I thought you only had a buck?"

"I did, but I told the teenager in there that a one-dollar bill will be worth a hundred dollars someday and he bought it off me for ten bucks."

I lean over and sip her slushie. "You're just like your aunt Tabby, you know that?"

"Yup." Janis nods, adjusting her sunglasses.

It must be lunch break when we arrive at the house. The bull-dozers are parked willy-nilly and there's no one around. They've already torn down the garage and the sheds and have started to pull the house apart from the back.

I paint Janis a picture. "You can have a swing set there, and a tree house back there. I bet Uncle Jackie will build you one if you ask him nicely."

"Like this?" She cups both her hands under her chin and

flutters her eyelashes. "That's what I do at church group so Mr. Northwood will let me pound the nails into Jesus."

When we get back in the car and drive into town, I realize the real estate office is only a few buildings down from the Four Horses. I spy West's truck in the parking lot and hurry Janis across the street.

We walk into the tiny beige office and she starts pawing the house models, poking her candy-coated fingers in the windows of a mock-up of a prefab called the Buckingham.

"I was thinking something more like this." I redirect her to the Brunswick. "It's got enough space, and we won't piss off the Queen."

The saleswoman is about nineteen years old, wearing a long lavender floral dress with a lace collar that might be considered a "go-getter look" on an Amish egg farm. She seems to be timing us on her watch, and at about four minutes strolls over and recites the brochure word for word.

"The Brunswick is a spacious two-level house designed for modern living. It boasts four elegant bedrooms, three bathrooms and a two-car garage."

"TWO-CAR GARAGE?" Janis screams.

The woman continues giving the specs, and after enduring an hour's worth of questions from Janis and me, ranging from "Are the appliances included?" (me) to "How many people can fit in the bathtub?" (Janis), she finally asks, "Would you like to discuss financing?"

"We'll be paying cash."

She blinks a few times. "For the down payment?"

"For the whole payment."

"We're rich," Janis explains, one hand on her hip.

I nudge her behind me. "We've received a large inheritance."

The woman gets me to fill out some forms and select some siding and floor samples. I let Janis hold all the little rectangular blocks and she shuffles them in the car, informing me which are boring and which are gorgeous. I allow myself one quick glance toward the tavern.

When we're almost off the main street, I realize Janis hasn't seen anything interesting. I find a scraggly little park and we sit and chuck sticks in the water. Then we walk to the general store for snacks and buy Swimmer a T-shirt. *Solace River: Going with the flow since 1768.* Janis insisted. It was hanging in the window next to one that said, *I Shaved My Balls for This?*

"Don't tell people we're rich, okay?" I say to her.

"Why not?"

"Because. We don't want it to get back to the sorcerer."

"Gimme a break."

Poppy told Janis we inherited the money from Grandma Jean. She should have left it at that, but instead she spun a big yarn only a crack addict would cook up. She said Grandma Jean was a princess who had been hidden away in Solace River from an evil sorcerer who wanted to steal her soul. The royal family sent the princess her inheritance when she turned eighteen, but Grandma Jean saved it all for us. This didn't jive with Janis at first. She had a million questions. If Great-grandma Jean was a princess, why did she use bad words and cut the necks off turkeys? And if she was so nice, why did she always go around spitting sunflower seeds on the carpet and making Janis pick up all the soggy shells?

She conks out in the car after ten minutes and sleeps most of the way back to Jubilant. I spend the drive trying not to think about West. Part of me regrets not going into the tavern. Maybe I should have stormed in and demanded he send Abriel packing like he claimed he would.

Just before we hit the Jubilant exit, Janis wakes up and yells, "Holy ship!"

I glance where she's pointing and almost slam on the brakes right there on the highway. It's the Rubik's cube rock. Inside new black grid lines, it's been painted solid orange on one side, blue on another. I pull the car over to the shoulder, jump out and run up to it. The remaining visible sides are slathered in green, red and white respectively. It's been solved the easy way.

"What is it?" Janis sticks her head out the car window.

"It's a sign!" I call, jogging back.

"It's not a sign. It's a painted-up rock."

"It's *a sign*."

She looks back at the rock for a minute then tilts her sunglasses down at me. "You been eating crazy crackers again?"

THE MORONS IN JODY'S GARAGE TELL ME LYLE'S NOT around. They can't believe I just walked right in. One of them asks me if I'm looking for a good time and I tell him my idea of a good time is a shower that stays hot long enough for me to shave my armpits. Another one looks me up and down and asks if I'm like my sister.

"Not really," I say. "She's a Pisces. I'm Gemini."

The first guy says Lyle won't be back until tomorrow, but in case he's full of shit, I stall by getting him to look under Ma's hood. He does a quick fix on some wires, charges up the battery and patches the hole in the oil tank. Then he gives me what he thinks is a sexy look and invites me for a test ride. I tell him I have a gyno appointment to get to and he hands me the keys pinched between two fingers, worried he'll get a yeast infection if our hands touch.

On my way back to the trailer, I take a wrong turn and wind up on a deserted road full of potholes too narrow to turn around on. It occurs to me there could be an old cabin back here where Troy's hiding Swimmer, so I keep going till the pavement turns to dirt. Then the dirt gives way to sand and I'm at a deserted beach. I turn off the ignition and unroll the windows. A cold wind wafts off the sea, swishing the eelgrass back and forth all along the dunes and weaving through the knit of my sweater. The planks from an old boardwalk are scattered like teeth punched out of a mouth, and an old lighthouse ladder is mangled into a heart shape. It's hard to tell if the storm happened ten years ago or last week.

I get out and walk along the shore trying to spot any cabins farther up the coastline. If Lyle had been at the garage I was going to tell him he had twenty-four hours to deliver Swimmer or else I'd put up every cent of the money I promised him as a reward for

Swimmer's return. The entire town of Jubilant would be scrambling to sell out Troy for that kind of cash. But now that the sea wind's blowing fresh oxygen into my brain, I can't shake what Surette said about Troy being smart enough to keep himself out of prison all this time. If Troy found out the cops were coming, what might he do to avoid getting caught? He could hand Swimmer over to one of his goons to dispose of like a sack of garbage.

I come upon a firepit littered with empty Keith's cans, sit down on a driftwood log and watch the ocean rise and fall back on itself. A seagull hops over, but when I say hello, it flinches and flies off.

Something bobbing out on the water catches my eye. It ducks behind the waves then comes back into view, disappears, re-emerges. I stand up for a better look and make out a black plastic bag knotted at one end. I watch it for several minutes until I feel queasy. I can't shake the awful thought creeping into my brain.

I roll my jeans up to my knees and kick off my boots. The first touch of my bare feet to the cold sea shocks me to the eyeballs. I make my way in till the water's at my waist and reach out my fingers far enough to grab a corner of the bag. Just as I have it in my grip, a wave picks me up and my feet can't touch bottom. I kick and pull as the current tugs at the bag. The icy water takes my breath and I start to panic, but then the next wave carries me to where I can get a footing. I tear through the plastic bag right there in the water until I'm surrounded by floating milk cartons and empty margarine tubs. I wade back to shore and drop to my knees on the sand. It's not until I'm back in the car that I start sobbing with relief.

"WHO TOLD YOU TO SLAP ALL THAT MONEY DOWN ON A big fucking mansion we'll never afford in the long run?" Jackie hollers.

"*You* decided Ma's getting a house. We can't all sit around watching *Wheel of Fortune*. We're almost out of time."

"You don't trust me with all that money hanging around, do you? You think I'm going to take off with it."

I don't answer and he storms out. I hadn't thought of that, but maybe I should have. I noticed when we were sitting side by side counting the money that he has Daddy's same tapered thumbs, the extra lines around the knuckles.

Once I hear the car peel off, I curl up on the sofa and watch drops of water break loose from the clouds. The sky surrenders and the rain heaves, smearing everything beyond the windows. I lie back and nod off until late afternoon, when I wake to the storm trying to slash through the walls. I sit up in the window and watch the wind drag the plastic swan planter across the lawn, entrails of sludgy garbage trailing out behind it.

I was dreaming about Raspberry again. This time I was walking down those hallways with the stupid murals painted to look like graffiti. I passed the grey cafeteria and started up Staircase A. We used to call this staircase Rachel Roulette because the middle landing wasn't visible to either floor and you never knew if this girl Rachel was waiting on it with her fist cocked. Staircase B was a safer bet, but it was all the way at the other end of the building. Anyhow, in the dream the whole building was empty, so I took Staircase A, turned left on the third floor and stopped at the fourth door on the right, my old room. Everything was just as

I left it: the pointless chair, the bed with the scratchy comforter, the pilled hooded sweatshirts hanging in the closet. On a little shelf by the bed, there were bottles of nail polish and a copy of the New Testament I read for kicks. I walked over and opened it, and on the inside cover where it was inscribed *This Bible belongs to*, my handwriting said: *The Bitch I stole it from*. The bed opposite mine was bare. No sheets, no pillow. In real life, that side of the room was reserved for a rotating sideshow of hateful weirdos. First there was a cutter who tried to drown her baby cousin. She was a ball of fun. When she left, the bed was stripped down to the mattress stain and remade for a pyromaniac who told me to eat shit and die any time I tried to strike up a conversation. All these psychos came and went, and I was there indefinitely. It made no sense.

On Sundays at Raspberry, family members could visit, and sometimes I would go down to get a look at people's mothers. Then I'd trudge back to my room and stand at my window staring out at the fields rippling beyond the basketball court. I used to worry that the sky and grass were just painted on the other side of the glass, that if I punched through the pane, there'd be just another room on the other side. Some nights, when I was trying to sleep, I'd imagine someone trapped in that room. If I thought about it too long, I could almost hear the breathing.

In the dream, I did it—punched through the window— and sure enough there was a dark, windowless room hidden behind it. A little girl was slumped in the corner and when she lifted her face, it was my own fourteen-year-old self staring back at me.

Talk about a mindfuck.

I get up from the sofa and wander up and down the trailer, but it's like I'm still in the dream, walking the hallways of Raspberry. I can see the fluorescent lights and practically smell the bleach on the floors. I smoke about ten cigarettes before Ma and Janis finally return from the blue house. I run over and help Janis strip off her coat.

"We have to build a ark!" she tells me, wet hair slathered to her cheeks. "Jesus said!" She disappears into the bathroom for a while and twenty minutes later I step over her lying in front of the television. I ask her what happened to the ark, and she says she didn't have the right boards.

Later that night, the phone rings and Ma tries to pass it to me. I shake my head no. It's taking all my mental power not to picture West playing house with Abriel, and hearing his voice would transport me right to his kitchen table. I'd have to watch the two of them play footsie by candlelight or some shit.

"It's Jackie," Ma snaps. "The police got a search warrant for Troy's."

I grab the receiver.

"Don't tell Ma," Jackie says, "the cops have already searched the place. They didn't find Swimmer's shirt. No guns or drugs neither. Troy must have cleaned the whole place out."

"Jackie, I don't like this. Swimmer's becoming a hot potato. What if …" My insides clench.

"Troy don't have the balls."

"How do you know? Because he didn't kill Bird? Maybe he only kept Bird alive to punish you."

"Look, just shut up for a sec. I called to tell you that I ain't mad at you no more about the house." I hear his foot tapping. "I looked it up, and property taxes are pretty low on the old dirt road, so it's just the bills we need to worry about. Did you show Ma the pictures of it in them brochures you got?"

"No."

"Don't show her. Let's surprise the shit out of her."

"Janis already told her how many rooms it has."

"She knows Janis makes shit up."

"Is this why you called?"

"No. Troy's bitch cornered Jewell after a doctor appointment, told her when the baby comes out, she better watch it every minute. Jewell came to see me at work shaking like a wet cat. I ain't thrilled about leaving, but we've been talking about how we'd like some family around for the baby, Bird and everybody. You know, when me and you was up in Solace the other day, it didn't seem as much of a shithole as I remembered. Anyway, Jewell and I are coming to stay with you guys in the new house till we can sell this one and buy our own." His foot starts up again. "So are we cool?"

"Is that your way of saying sorry?"

"Yes, Christ. I said I was."

"No, you didn't."

"Guess what, Tabby?" His voice softens. "It's going to be a little girl."

I tell him congrats, hang up and return to the table.

"What'd I miss?" I ask Ma.

"Some jackass whacking off in the cemetery."

I've become addicted to the police scanner now too. Nothing ever happens, and then everything happens at once, so we have to be on the ball. Last night, within the span of one hour, some loser threatened to choke out the family cat if his wife didn't go buy him another six-pack, a group of underage kids crashed their ATV into the lake, and a meth head stole a stack of scratch-offs from the convenience store before returning twenty minutes later trying to claim a winning ticket. The cops use code over the radio, but it's pretty easy to crack if you spent time in juvie.

"Holy shit, Ma!" Flares start firing off in my brain. "I bet Troy has a scanner."

"Yeah, so what? All the dealers do so they know where the cops are at."

I grab the phone, call down to the station and tell Surette my idea.

"You're going to cost me my job."

"The job you're *not doing?*"

"I said I'll think about it."

He must think fast, because I crank the scanner volume and within minutes the cops on duty are sent to investigate the robbery of a liquor store in Halifax: Tabatha Mary Saint. Caucasian female, mid-twenties, five foot six, 120 pounds, sighted in the Jubilant area. According to what's rolled out over the scanner in the next few days, the cops will question me, search the woods and the trailer but find no trace of the six grand I collected from the registers. They don't have serial numbers for any of the bills and the security camera at the liquor store wasn't functioning during the time of the robbery. Worse, procedure wasn't followed fast enough and there's not a single usable fingerprint. At one point, one of the cops leaves his radio on "by mistake" and we overhear him say that the whole investigation's such a fuck-up, the chief called in a favour to keep it out of the papers.

But by Saturday morning, I still haven't heard from Lyle. I'm starting to have fantasies that involve kerosene, matches and his shiny new truck. I get up early to try the garage again, but Ma stops me.

"Happy Jubilant Day." She takes a shot of Pepto-Bismol. "There's a parade downtown in an hour."

She's wearing the same clothes she was wearing last night. I don't think she's slept at all the past few nights. All she does is keep her ear to the scanner and wait for the phone to ring.

"I'll take Janis."

"No." She shakes her head. "I always do."

"Then I'll come. I can't just sit here."

I walk down the hall and duck my head in Janis's room. Her leg is hanging over the side of the bunk and I shake it gently. Three of her toes are poking out of one sock.

"Who wants to go to the parade?"

"Me." She opens one eye then the other. "Swimmer will be there. He claps when those Shiners go by in those little cars honking the horns."

She finds her sunglasses in the sheets and jumps down off the bed. I watch her dig through a laundry basket and pull out a lobster claw hat from three festivals ago. It's too small for her now. Every time she yanks it down on her forehead, it slowly creeps back up on top of her head.

"*Shriners*," I correct her.

"Nope, they're called Shiners!" she screams. "Because they shine everything! Like those little cars. If you need something shined, you call them and they drive over right away!"

I try to take the hat off her head to brush out her hair, but she squirms past me, runs down the hall, through the kitchen all the way out to the driveway to buckle Swimmer's stuffed husky dog into the back seat of the car. Then she comes back in, sets herself up at the table with a bag of tobacco and starts pumping paper tubes one at a time into Ma's sliding machine, lining up the finished cigarettes in a neat row. In the meantime Ma showers, does a few dishes, tidies up and fills a Thermos with tea. She inspects Janis's work, hands her a Baggie, and Janis tosses the smokes in, twist-ties it and places it in Ma's purse. Then they both turn and walk in opposite directions, checking to make sure all the lights and the stove are off. This must be their routine.

"Let's pick up Bird," I say as we're pulling out of the driveway.

Ma shakes her head. "Jackie won't like that."

"Why? He wants Bird to stay inside peeling the walls off every day?"

"He don't want anyone to know how bad off Bird is."

"That's the whole point. Everyone needs to know. Let them talk about how Bird can barely hold his head up and Troy will realize he won the war a long time ago."

She clicks her tongue but stays silent as I pull in to the blue house. Bird is sitting out on the porch. I bring him down, lift him out of his chair, and Ma folds it up and puts it in the trunk. As

I'm wrangling him into the back seat, I suggest we squeeze in the other two Musketeers, but Ma says we better not.

"They're too unpredictable, those two. I took them with me to get groceries once and they attacked each other in the pasta aisle. There were noodles goddamn everywhere."

Once we're on the road, I glance in the rear-view mirror and say, "Hey, Janis, you should tell everyone at the parade we're moving to Solace River."

"Why?"

"So when they see a big house riding on a truck, they won't think it got lost from the parade. They'll say, 'Hey look! There goes Janis Saint's brand new house!'"

"Yup." Janis nods. "They'll say, 'There goes the fastest house in the world!' Right, Uncle Bird?"

He turns his head side to side, drooling.

It takes a while to find a place to park and then we have to walk along the street trying to find an empty spot to watch the parade. Every time Bird sees a little girl with pigtails on either side of her head, he grunts and starts pointing. Ma has to say, "No, Birdie. That's not Josie," every time.

I ask someone where we can buy festival hats and he tells me to go to the festival kiosk. We walk all over hell's half acre before I realize the "kiosk" is just two sawhorses with a sign taped between them. It's manned by the town stoner, a teenage boy who looks like he's fast asleep except for the big greasy grin. Once he remembers why he's sitting there, he sells me a headband with light-up antennae, but then it takes him five hundred years to figure out my change.

I clamp the headband crooked on Bird's head, trying to make him look as pathetic as possible. I spy some kids with plastic lobster bibs and buy one of those too. Ma has no energy to fight me. She just looks down at the lights bobbing around on Bird's head and sighs.

Finally, a troupe of ten majorettes comes marching around the corner. The chubby, freckle-faced kid keeps dropping her baton. She throws it in the air, misses right in front of us, and sighs, "Fuuuck." She picks it up, shakes it angrily at the sky and yells, "Seriously?" then yanks out her wedgie one-handed and runs panting to catch up with the others.

"She said the F-word," Janis informs everyone around us.

Two teenage girls are carrying the parade banner: TOWN OF JUBILANT: PRIDE AND PROGRESS. One of them has a lit cigarette in her hand. Ma points to her.

"That's Frosty's daughter."

"His name's not Frosty," I tell her. "That's just the name of his store."

She lowers her voice. "Progress, my ass. That Frosty's still renting out porn movies on VHS. He tapes them off the Quebec channel, and he don't know French, so he makes up the titles. They all got 'Miss Frenchie' in them."

The Jubilant Lobster Fishermen's Association's float has a bunch of people in sou'westers standing single file under a sign painted UNEMPLOYMENT LINE. Some lobster traps tied to the back of the truck drag empty along the pavement. The crowd falls silent as it passes.

When the pipe band comes into view, I tap Janis on the shoulder.

"I know," she snaps, shrugging me off. She steps off the curb and gives each piper a thumbs-up.

"You really think you can blow that much air into those bags?" I ask.

"Yup," she says. "I blew up six hundred balloons for Swimmer's birthday party."

"Six hundred?"

"Probably seven hundred."

The Jubilant Day Queen has a big hickey on her neck, which didn't make her think twice about an updo. She waves to the crowd in white gloves like she's been doing this her whole life. As if Ma and I didn't just see her half an hour ago bumming change outside the liquor store, screeching to someone in a car, "Where's Jimmy at? He said he was getting hash for the Gravitron!"

"What's the Gravitron?" Ma asked me once we'd passed.

"It's a carnival ride that looks like a UFO and spins around at warp speed blasting Mötley Crüe songs until everybody's pinned to the walls. Then sometimes one of the workers will do tricks, skulking sideways across the seats or flipping upside down. You'd be surprised at how often those tricks get carnies laid."

"I'm sure I would," Ma barked. "What's the hash for? That sounds like enough on its own."

WHEN THE PARADE CLEARS, THE CROWD JAMS THE street. Janis takes out one of her drawings of Swimmer, unfolds it and stops different kids to ask if they've seen him. She says, "He's

wearing a yellow shirt in this picture, but now he might be wearing a blue one, or an orange one, or a green one. But not brown.
He won't wear brown shirts, because brown makes him need to
poop." She runs up to a little boy who looks like Swimmer from
behind and grabs him by the hair.

"Control her," the boy's mother says to Ma. Then she narrows
her eyes. "I know who you are."

"Do you know who I am?" I ask. She starts to make a snarky
comment, but I lean in and whisper, "You open that tacky lipstick
mouth again, I'll find out who your husband is and fuck his ever-
loving brains out."

It was the only thing I could think of. She yanks her son away
and as soon as they're at a safe distance, she spins around and
gives me the double middle finger.

Looking around, all I see are idiots stuffing their faces with
hot dogs and cigarettes, pushing their baby strollers, hollering at
their older kids who are whining because they blew all their junk
food money on face tattoos. Camouflage gear seems to be the
prevailing fashion trend and I can't imagine the draw. A three-
hundred-pound woman in a camo skirt will not blend into her
surroundings. Even if she was standing in a thicket, she'd be hard
to miss with the rhinestone belt and the seeming inability to stop
screeching, "Mama's getting on the hooch!"

I take a look at us, and we're no better. Ma didn't even comb
her hair. Janis looks like she's dressed as a hobo for Halloween,
with two different shoes on again and a bright orange stain on
her shirt front. I find some Wet-naps in my purse and clean her
up a bit, tuck in her shirt.

We make our way down the road to the fire hall parking lot where the carnival games are set up, and Ma starts making that furball noise in her throat. I ask her if she wants to go home, but she shakes her head no. She silently weeps as we walk around watching people whack moles and toss rings. I buy some wilted cotton candy that no one eats and try to smile every time Janis looks up. Ma tells me there used to be a big tug-of-war match after the parade, but the Jubilant Day Committee banned it after last year's accident.

"What happened?"

"Buddy had the rope twisted around his wrist," Janis jumps in. "The other guys pulled the rope over and saw a bloody hand hanging off it. I said to the newspaper, 'That's the craziest thing I ever seen in my life.' After the ambulance drove away, they had to bring a fire truck out and hose all the different-colour barf off the street."

"She didn't see it," Ma says. "We were in the bathroom changing Swimmer's diaper. But she did tell the reporter that. We have the newspaper article at home with her name in it."

"Wait." Janis sticks her arm out in front of us. "I see something for Uncle Bird."

She turns and wheels Bird up to the craft tables and we overhear her ask how much the tissue paper angels cost. She talks the old lady down to two dollars then zips her sequined purse back up. She grabs a delicate angel from the lady's outstretched hands and drops it into Bird's lap. I turn my head as Bird starts ripping the thing to shreds.

Angela from the Lighthouse is leaning against the fire hall. She's got those leopard shoes on again. She looks right at me, but

I don't seem to register. She must have been drunk as a porcupine that night.

Janis pulls up her shirt and shows me she wore her bathing suit under her clothes so she can go in the dunk tank. We take her over to the rickety old thing and when it's her turn, she climbs up on the swing and sways back and forth in her sunglasses, trash-talking grown men. No one knocks her down and after half an hour Ma starts to get impatient in the heat. Her nerves are so fried I can almost smell the sizzle.

"Oh, yeah, right," Janis groans when Ma buys a ball from the man. She barely gets that out of her mouth when Ma fires it underhand and smacks the orange target dead-on. The seat collapses and Janis vanishes. She stays down extra long on purpose. Eventually, her head pops up and she crawls out of the booth dripping wet, fake gasping for air. I ask her how it was and she puts her hand on her chest, huffing away. Ma tells her it's time to leave and she drops the act, gets a panicked look on her face.

Janis grabs Bird's chair handles and pushes him with all her strength up to the auction booth. The auction's over, but the auctioneer is still there packing up.

"I bet she's asking him if she can sing into his microphone," Ma says.

We watch as the man lifts Janis up onto his platform, switches on the microphone and places it in her hands.

"Hey, everybody!" she yells into it, then "WHAT?" when the man tries to tell her not to press it directly to her mouth. "I'm Janis and this is Uncle Bird. Say hello, Bird." She crouches and shoves the microphone at Bird, but he's half asleep. She stands back up. "Does anyone here know where's my little brother, Swimmer? I have a picture right here." She holds up her drawing. "See. He has brown hair and he's only this big." She pushes the palm of her hand down six inches from the ground. "And he likes Dolly Pardon and dogs and candy."

I look around and notice people are actually listening. The guy working the dunk booth has stopped selling balls while she's talking. Some elderly women are shushing people and pointing up at the platform.

"If you have him up at your house, please give him back." Her lip trembles and big tears start rolling down her cheeks. "Because he's my brother. We have to go to live at Saw-liss River, but we can't go without Swimmer because he won't know how to find us and I have his husky dog from Grandma Jean." She puts the microphone down and it makes a big thump into the speaker. Then she wipes her eyes with the backs of her hands, picks the mic back up in both hands and presses it right up to her mouth. "And if anyone wants me to, I can sing a song."

Ma goes over to collect her.

EVERYBODY'S QUIET ON THE DRIVE HOME. I GET OUT AT the blue house with Bird, draw him a bath and feed him supper. The Musketeers are having a music night. The fat one's strumming an old guitar with three strings and making up lyrics, most of them about how he's a sharp-tooth man that ain't gonna go down to the river. Eye Patch Stanley grunts along, tapping the table off time with a wooden spoon, as Bird rocks back and forth, dancing in his chair. After his bath, he makes me put his antennae back on him. I sit for one more song before I say good night. Halfway across the field, I turn to see the colourful lights on Bird's head swaying in the window.

I kick my boots off in the trailer and the phone rings a single time. I run over to pick it up, but there's a dial tone. Two minutes later, same thing. Ma says it's been happening for the past hour. I wonder if it could be Lyle trying to send a message. I put my boots back on without explaining, get in her car and speed down to Jody's Garage.

Lyle's there. He sticks his neck out as I arrive, looks up and down the street, then tells me to park around back. He lets me in a side door, locking it behind us.

"Well?" My heart is thrashing around my chest like a bird trapped in the house. I look for somewhere to sit, but everything's covered in car grease.

"They want money for the kid." Lyle's eyes are bloodshot and there's booze on his breath. "Six grand."

My knees almost give out with relief. I jam my hands in my jacket pockets to hide how badly they're shaking. "Six grand. That's a lot of money." I try hard to look surprised.

"That's what it will cost to buy back the *Wanda Lust*." Lyle slides a mickey of fireball whisky out of his jacket and unscrews the cap. "Course, getting the real Wanda back might not be so easy."

"Am I supposed to know what the hell you're talking about?"

"Jimmy's lobster boat. When he got out of the clink, he sold it to pay down his debts. Wanda left him because he had no boat to put down traps. No traps, no money. She's up in Black's Point fucking some DFO asshole while he's drinking himself stupid. He takes his empties down to get the deposit back just so he can buy more booze." He gestures to a stack of empty two-fours in the corner. "Everybody's saving bottles for poor fucking Jimmy."

I have no idea who Jimmy is or why Lyle's telling me all this, but I take the whisky when he offers it just so he'll keep talking. The first sip burns my throat.

"*Wanda Lust*, get it? Jimmy's old boat was called *Crack of Dawn*," Lyle says. "'Cause he was doing this girl, Dawn."

"So Jimmy is Troy's brother, the one who got caught ripping off vending machines?"

Lyle realizes he just fucked up, telling me all these names. I see the hamster wheel in his brain struggle to make a full rotation. He wipes the sweat from his forehead.

"Whatever," I say. "You'll get the six grand plus your cut as soon as we get Swimmer. We can trade off tomorrow morning."

"You-all get your shit packed up first. They want proof you're getting gone. You got three days." He snatches the flask back.

"Fine." My hands start to shake again, so I pretend to fish around in my purse for my keys ."Did you see him?"

"Who?"

"Swimmer."

"I don't know nothing about nothing."

MA'S LYING ON THE SOFA WHEN I GET BACK, THE PUPPY sweater she knitted for Swimmer draped over her chest.

"We're getting Swimmer back."

"What?" She sits upright. "When?"

"It worked this time. Troy wants the six grand he thinks I stole. As soon as we get the moving trucks packed up, Swimmer's all ours."

I show her where I keep the money hidden in the kids' bedroom in case she has to hand it over to Lyle.

"What if it's a trick?" she asks.

"It's not."

She dials Jackie and talks so fast he can't possibly make out a word. I pry the phone from her and she collapses into a chair, laughing and crying at the same time. I tell Jackie everything Lyle said. I expect Jackie to balk when I tell him to get packing, but he says Jewell's already wrapping up her knick-knacks in newspaper. He has us on speakerphone and she yells in the background, "Are you kidding me? I can't wait to turn the corner in the grocery store and not run into one of his exes with one of his kids."

The only thing Jackie wants to know is how we're going to get the six grand back after we hand it over.

"We're not," I say.

"WHAT? We're just going to give that fucktard Daddy's money?"

"It's not Daddy's money and you know it."

I hang up with a tidy click and he doesn't call back. As soon as my adrenalin subsides, I'm so tired I can hardly keep my eyes open. I crash the instant my head hits the pillow. All night long my dreams stick together and pull apart. I wake before Ma and Janis and start making a list of things we need to do to get out of Jubilant for good. First off, I have to make sure the old house in Solace River comes down before the concrete guy shows up to pour the new foundation. I leave a note and sneak out to Ma's car.

The highway is deserted this early and my mind is free to bounce around. I start wondering what West is up to, but thinking about him gives me a pain in my chest, so I crank up the radio and try to get interested in a CBC documentary about the collapse of the cod fishery.

I reach Solace River around noon. Victory Road is full of puddles. I roll down the window and the air is warm and fresh from a recent rain. When I round the bend, my heart gallops. All I see is a dark field of mud where the house used to sit.

I park at the top of the driveway and the foreman waddles over. "You must be Tabby," he yells over the banging.

I shake his hand through the window and he tells me it'll take about three more days to get the whole mess gone. I ask him if his guys could cut that time in half if I gave them each a hundred bucks cash right now.

He raises one thick eyebrow. "For a hundred bucks each, these fellers will probably have her done before the liquor store closes tonight."

I count it out and he says, "Hold on. I saved something for you." He goes off toward one of the trucks, returns with an old yellowed copy of the *Solace River Review* under one arm. "The boys found it in the walls, thought maybe it was there for a reason." He passes it through the window.

I thank him and hang around a few minutes to see my money start to work its magic. When I pull back out onto the road, I pause for one last look at the pile of debris. I can't help but think of the suffering those walls held in over the years. Now all that misery is free to blow out over the river and settle deep down in the sediment.

I glance down at the newspaper on the passenger seat and pick it up. Halfway down the first page there's a story about Grandpa Jack winning the house in a card game. The paper's so parched it's ready to disintegrate, but I can still read the faded type. It says Private Jack Saint and his infant son were renting a room in town when the woman who owned this house passed on. The place was in poor condition, but the land it sat on was viable. The woman's son put word out that he was willing to trade the house and property for some healthy livestock or a year's worth of manual labour. Grandpa Jack apparently tracked the man down in a barber's chair and proposed a game of poker. The terms were set that if the man won, Jack would pay him 10 percent of his military pension every month for the rest of his life. But if Jack won, he would simply take the drafty old firetrap off the man's hands. The enterprising Private Saint must have been born under lucky stars, the article says.

Of course, it fails to mention that Grandpa Jack threatened a priest who'd already offered the man some fine horses, and that his violent temper preceded him when his boots came stomping into the barber shop. It also left out the part where Jack plied the farmer with Pusser's rum and had the ace of spades beating like a telltale heart under his left thigh until it miraculously found its way into a winning full house. Grandma Jean told me the real story. I'm sure her version is much closer to the truth, even if she added the more poetic details.

Part of me thinks I should burn the newspaper with my cigarette lighter right now, let the history go down with the house. My other half, the Saint half, thinks we should frame it on the wall in the new house.

When I hit the main road, I come to a dead stop. Left or right? My mind and body duke it out till my foot presses the accelerator and I steer toward town. I cruise slowly down Main Street then speed up and zip past the tavern. I do that three more times, back and forth, but I can't see a thing through the frosted windows. Finally, I just park the car and walk in on shaky legs.

West is alone, counting up the bottles in the beer fridge. He doesn't see me until he turns to crank up the stereo. I take a stool as he slowly removes the pencil from his teeth and sticks it behind one ear. He pulls down a bottle of Jim Beam and I think he's pouring me a shot, but it's not for me. I watch the muscles in his jaw twitch as he flicks it down his throat.

"They're going to give us Swimmer back." My voice sounds warped, like a vinyl record left out in the rain.

He goes right back to counting like I'm not even there. I stare at the backs of his thighs straining against his jeans as if he wants to run, and it's the damnedest thing, I just start bawling. Everything that's happened in the last weeks comes crashing down on me.

West comes around the bar, drops his clipboard on the counter and takes the stool next to me. He places his fingers under my chin and turns my face toward him. "What's the matter?"

I shrug. He wipes some snot off my nose with his sleeve, pushes my hair off my forehead and grabs onto my eyes with his. He sits there staring into me through a whole cycle of the dishwasher and three John Cougar Mellencamp songs.

"Why do you look at me like that?" I whisper.

"Like what?"

"Like I'm somebody."

"You are somebody." He presses his lips to my forehead. "You're Tabby Saint."

He closes up the tavern and I tail his truck to the house. Abriel's white Rabbit convertible is in the driveway, so I have to park on the street. I finish my third cigarette in a row, flick it in the gutter and join West in his driveway. He's nervous, jingling the spare change in his pocket.

"Ready?" He puts his arm around my shoulders and steers me inside before I can answer.

There's music playing and laughter at the end of the hall. When we walk into the living room, Abriel is standing at the stereo with a drink in her hand. She looks the exact same as in the picture. She's wearing a halter sundress and I can tell she's still got the body. Her mouth drops as she looks from me to West then back again. Danny is seated on the sofa smoking a joint with a man who looks enough like Abriel to be the brother West mentioned.

"Well, isn't this cozy?" Abriel says to West, ice cubes popping loudly in her glass. I can tell she's well on her way to getting drunk. She sets her drink down, grabs West by the arm and points a long fingernail at my chest. "You stay right there," she orders me.

I follow right behind them into the kitchen as the volume

lowers on the stereo. I glance around the room and everything looks mostly the same except for Abriel's car keys hanging on the hook and a lipstick kiss on a Post-it Note stuck to the fridge.

"What's going on, baby?" Abriel whispers to West. "Why is she here?"

"I want her here." West leans his arm against the cupboard as if he needs it for support. "Abriel, you can't stay. I told you. I want a divorce."

"My name is on this house."

"Fine, take it."

"Excuse me?"

"Take it. Or I'll buy you out and you can get your own house."

She's shocked silent.

"Sounds fair," I say.

"Who the hell asked you?" She spins around. "What kind of person are you, anyway, going around sleeping with other people's husbands?"

The gold flecks in her eyes match the tones of her dress and I wish I wasn't wearing Ma's old *Where's the Beef?* sweatshirt.

I walk over to the fridge and rip off her lipstick kiss. She screams like I pulled her hair.

"Tommy!" she yells. "Get in here!"

He appears around the corner with Danny right behind him. "What's going on here, West?"

"None of your business, Tommy," West says. "As fucking usual."

I open the fridge door to reach in for a beer. Abriel tries to grab it from my hand and West wrenches it back, takes another for himself.

"Tabby and I are going to drink these outside. The rest of you go home."

"I *am* home!" Abriel screams.

"Well, Tabby's sleeping here tonight, so you'll have to take the sofa."

She starts calling him every name in the book and a few more. He takes me by the hand and pulls me out the door, leads me around to a little back porch I didn't even know existed. He twists the caps off the beers with the inside of his elbow and hands me one, sits down and pats the spot next to him. The window's open and we can hear Abriel say she's not going anywhere, that I'm the one who'll be leaving.

West doesn't drink his beer, just holds it between his knees. He's staring up at the moon, but I can tell he's not really looking at it. He told her she'll have to take the sofa if I stay, which means she's been sleeping in his bed. I want to ask where he's been sleeping, but I don't. I just sit there not looking at the moon either. After a while the two men drive off and West finally drops his shoulders. He takes a sip of his beer, and I take a sip of mine.

ABRIEL STICKS AROUND ALL THE NEXT DAY, PEACOCKING up and down the hall. She runs outside in a bathing suit in the pouring rain, comes in all breathless and dripping, asking West to open a mustard jar with her tits in his face.

While I'm boiling rice at the stove, she paints her toenails at the kitchen table, tells me she's been in love with West ever since she was in junior high school and he popped a wheelie on his bicycle outside her house. When she goes back down the hall singing "Stand By Your Man," I glance out the window to make sure West isn't coming before slipping off my panties and straining the rice through them. When the three of us sit down to supper and West asks me why I haven't got any rice on my plate, I just tell him I'm cutting back on starch.

In the morning, she and I walk into the kitchen at the same time. We hesitate then both go for the coffee maker. She snatches the pot from me and turns on the tap. I can tell she's starting to smell defeat. She's already wearing a little less makeup. The cat wanders in and looks to each of us before trotting over to me and rubbing himself along my shins.

"Oh, fuck you," she snaps at him. "Asshole."

I pick him up and stroke his back while the coffee percolates. Drip, drip, drip. Purr. Purr. Purr.

"Well?" She glares at me, slamming two mugs down on the countertop. "Do you take sugar or are you goddamn sweet enough?"

Finally, she and West sit down and have a big talk about money. The bedroom door is shut, so I have to stand on the other side of it to listen. She sobs, "What am I supposed to do now, baby? What about me?"

I want to burst in and yell, "Who cares about you, you lying, cheating, leaving, skanking, can't sing, can't cook, MANIPULATING FUCKNUT?"

When the door opens, I pretend I just happen to be in the hallway getting the vacuum cleaner from the closet.

SARAH MIAN

West walks Abriel to her car, so I start vacuuming in the living room where I can keep an eye on them through the front window. She drives away in that white car looking a little too satisfied for the deal to have been fair. West comes back in and I unplug the vacuum cleaner in time to hear a giant fart.

"I heard that," I call out. "So you hold it in while she's here and let it all out for me?"

He comes in and flops down on the sofa. "Sorry. I couldn't relax until she was gone."

"Why not?"

He rakes his hair back with one hand, looks up at me and sighs. "I felt we were dangerously close to a threesome."

"What?"

"It seemed like it was headed in that direction."

"WHAT?"

His mouth contorts into a smile.

"Hilarious." I cross my arms. "Did you get the answers you wanted or what?"

"That low-life she took off with said he'd take her around the world, but he left her alone all the time to go gambling. They went to Niagara Falls once, that's it."

"So?"

It pisses me off that he forgave her so easily. Here he is at the tavern every night trying to make the numbers work and she probably made off with half of everything he owns just for pouting her lip.

"I've never been to Niagara Falls," I say.

"Me neither," he yawns.

I sigh as loud as I can, but he's already drifting off.

WHEN I PHONE MA IN THE MORNING, THERE'S BEEN NO word from Lyle. It's day three. I tell her I have to run a quick errand and then I'll be on the highway. I head over to Victory Road to wait for the trucks to arrive with the first of the prefab parts, but when there's no sign of them by 9 a.m., I give up and dart into town. Ma gave me my birth certificate when I first got back and told me I'll need it to get my social insurance number if I want to get a job. It turns out you just mail an application in and they send you a plastic card with your number on it. It arrived at West's house yesterday and he told me I can use it to open a bank account and deposit the money rather than leave it sitting in the trailer.

The bank manager isn't even curious why I've never opened a bank account before. On the phone she told me that, other than my SIN, all I needed was a reference letter from a client in good standing. Now she says, "Oh, how do you know West?" then walks away to photocopy something without waiting for an answer.

After the bank, I duck into the tavern to show West my shiny new bank card. He holds it up to the light, pretending to check if it's a fake.

"Nice. Now you can get your licence and stop driving my truck around illegally."

"I can't go completely straight. What would people think?"

I tell him I'm on my way to get Swimmer and he stops smiling.

"Are you sure you don't want to involve the police?"

"If I do, Troy will get arrested, Jackie will be ahead in the Game of Fuckheads, and it will start all over."

"I'll come with you."

"No." I shake my head. "Lyle might spook if he sees someone he doesn't recognize."

West knits his eyebrows. "Be careful."

He breathes on my bank card and polishes it on his ass pocket before handing it back. I tell him what Janis said about Ma checking out his rear end.

"Oh yeah? I do clenching exercises while I'm standing behind the bar. It's nice to know someone's paying attention."

"Wait. So, you're serving drinks to Hells Angels, listening to them talk about motorcycles and putting bullets in people's foreheads or whatever, and the whole time you're standing there squeezing your cheeks?" I shake my head. "You have got to be a Gene."

"Gene can't multi-task like that."

"When are you going to tell me your name?"

"About two weeks after you stop bugging me about it."

7

THE RAIN FOLLOWS ME ALL THE WAY BACK TO JUBILANT. Ma's got clothes on the line soaking wet. She and Janis are putting things into boxes and marking the contents on the outside with a black Sharpie. At least three of them are designated *CRAP*.

"Why are we keeping crap?"

Ma glances at the boxes. "I got no clue what Poppy wants and don't want."

I reach into one and pull out a pair of ripped fuchsia nylons, a pamphlet explaining how to identify magic mushrooms in the woods, and a troll doll with no arms. There's also a kitten calendar from five years ago, a pack of rum-sticky playing cards, one silver earring and two cans of dried-out playdough. I pick up the marker and make it *FREE CRAP*. When the rain dries up, Janis and I put the boxes out at the end of the driveway and they're gone within ten minutes.

The only things we hold on to from those boxes are some Styrofoam heads left over from when Poppy was learning how to do hairdos on corpses. "For Uncle Bird," Janis says, lining them up on the windowsill. "To chop up." Every time I turn the corner and see the eyeless faces, I think of Troy and his gang. I've been obsessing about where they have Swimmer stashed. For some reason, the way Troy had his hand on his woman's knee the night Jackie almost shot their heads off makes me think they're treating him decent. Sometimes I picture Swimmer in a rec room laughing and chasing around a battery-operated frog. I don't know why.

Yesterday I saw one of Janis's posters yellowing on a telephone pole. Poppy's been getting letters from other mothers of missing children, but we don't mention it to her.

"What would she write back?" I ask Ma. "'Dear So-and-So. Sorry about your tragedy, and thank you for your prayers, but I know where my kid's at. See, I went out to score a few weeks ago and he was taken by this low-life Troy whose teenage cousin was knocked up by my brother and almost died from having a rusty coat hanger rammed up her hoo-ha. Now, you'd think that putting my other brother in a wheelchair and getting me hooked on crack would be payback enough, but you know how it is with guys like Troy.'"

"Jesus." Ma sits down and rubs her temples. "When you put it like that."

I pick up a U-Haul truck so Troy's spies will see it parked and ready. Jackie and I decided that if it comes down to it, we'll stay at a motel in Solace River until the new house is finished.

Janis immediately sets about making the U-Haul her new pad. She hauls her toys in there and dances on the steel floor wearing tap shoes she made herself by crazy-gluing beer caps to the bottoms of her fuzzy slippers. When she asks me if I want to come over to her place and gossip, I'm curious enough to take her up on it.

"What's the news?" I ask, climbing in. "Lippy the bear still being a dog?"

"I chucked Lippy in one of them junk boxes. All the stuffing came out of his head after I ripped his ears off."

"Why'd you rip his ears off?"

"Because he said he was working late when he was really out partying."

"Is that the gossip?"

"No."

"You said you had gossip."

"No, I asked if you wanted to gossip."

"And I said yes, so what's the gossip?"

She thinks. "Want to know what Auntie Jewell told Uncle Jackie?"

"I already know. They're having a baby girl."

Janis puts her hands on her hips. "Everybody knows that."

"Well, what then?"

"Auntie Jewell told Uncle Jackie if he didn't get rid of the naked pictures of his ex-girlfriends, she was going to cut his wiener off and feed it to her neighbour's iguanas. I seen them once. Axl and Slash."

I laugh.

"Be quiet!" Janis scolds. "It's a secret."

"If it's a secret, how do you know?"

"Because I was on the toilet and Auntie Jewell thought I was Uncle Jackie in there. She said it right by the door, and I yelled,

'It's me, Janis!' And she said, 'Oh, sorry, Janis. That's a secret, okay, honey?' And I said, 'Can I finish having my pee now?'"

"You didn't say anything else?"

"Nope."

"Because you knew it was too good to keep a secret."

"Yup."

"Let's go tell Ma."

Janis pushes me out of the way. "I get to say it first!"

By late afternoon, the U-Haul is packed up with anything worth taking. Some of Jackie's furniture is in there too. He brought it over and loaded it on, said the rest of his and Jewell's stuff is sitting in his driveway. After he's gone, I take a sneaky drive by to make sure. He's not lying. He must have packed up as soon as I relayed the message from Lyle because he's got a utility trailer loaded and hitched onto the Tercel. The tarps tied down over it are pooled with the rain that's been turning on and off for days. I stare at the wet blue plastic flapping in the breeze, turn around and drive right back to the trailer.

Janis and I stare out the window for hours on end, as if Swimmer might magically descend on a rainbow cloud. We play Scrabble, eat Kraft Dinner off paper plates and grow more uneasy. Janis starts picking fights with Ma and me for no reason. She hides Ma's Game Boy and won't tell her where it is. I ask her what her problem is and she smashes a biscuit with her fist. Then she "accidentally" drops both Ma's and my toothbrushes in the toilet.

"Do you need a time out, missy?" Ma asks her.

"Time out from WHAT?" she screams, kicking over the stand-up ashtray. "Who's Missy?!"

"Be careful with that! It belonged to Grandma Jean!" Ma rights the heavy base and reattaches the brass doe and fawn that had been peacefully basking at a pond of butts.

"Janis," I say. "Come here."

"Why?" Her face is streaked in tears and orange cheese powder.

"Just come here. I'll give you five bucks."

She stomps over with her arms crossed. I try to lift her sunglasses, but she kicks me. I somehow manage to get her into my lap and start rubbing her back in big circles until she stops struggling.

"Swimmer's on his way," I tell her. "He has to walk slow because of his big pumpkin head. Maybe if we sing his favourite song, he'll hurry up. What do you think it is? 'I Believe in Santa Claus'?"

She won't uncross her arms. "I DON'T believe in Santa Claus."

I don't blame her.

"How about drunken sailors? You believe in those, right?"

She thinks for a minute. "Yup."

We sing Daddy's song until she finally falls asleep. I put her in pyjamas and tuck her in bed. She snores like a smoker, all raspy.

"Thank you," Ma says when I come back out. "I was about to call Troy and tell him he can have her too."

"Don't joke about that."

She makes tea and we sit in the near dark with only the lamp on. It makes it easier to see outside whenever we hear a car coming.

Where the fuck is Lyle? My head is pounding. I get up and pace around the bare walls. I'm worried. Maybe Mrs. Dunphy from Raspberry was right. I'm too smart for anyone's good. My plan was so solid, no one thought about a backup.

I stop in front of two white rectangular outlines left on the wall where the velvet paintings were hanging. "Why the hell does Janis think there are palm trees in Toronto?"

Ma glances over. "Poppy talks about moving there and taking the kids. She says she'll make ten times more money in the big-city clubs. She made it sound like a fairyland so Janis would get excited. I worry myself sick over it. I got no way to stop her from going and I won't know if the kids are okay, or if she's dead or alive."

"There is *one* way to stop her."

"What's that?"

"You become Janis and Swimmer's legal guardian."

"Take Poppy's kids away from her?" Ma jams her teabag in and out of the hot water. "She won't let me do that."

"Just on paper. She's going to lose them if you don't."

We both stare at the two empty white spaces.

"Why ain't that Lyle here by now?" Mama tosses her teabag on the table. "We did everything they told us to."

"Maybe they're waiting for us to leave."

"How the hell are they going to bring Swimmer back to us if we're not here, Tabby? Use your head."

"I am using my head. Stop yelling at me." I sit. "I don't know why you keep making tea. You never drink it."

"I have to do something."

I suddenly notice how gaunt she is. Her cheekbones have sunk in and the jowls are weighing down all the loose skin. I think back, and I haven't seen her eat anything in days. I get up and go to the cupboards, but all that's left on the shelves is a half-empty box of Shreddies, a few teabags, a bag of loose tobacco and half a pack of cigarettes.

"Go ahead," Ma says. "Jewell's picking me up a carton tomorrow."

"I'm looking for food. Maybe you forgot what that is." I snatch the pack anyway.

Ma clasps her hands together and presses the thumbs between her eyes. "Tabby, I did try to find you. After we came to Jubilant, I got a phone hooked up and called all over. Barbara Best had moved and unlisted her phone number. She didn't even write me to tell me you weren't with her no more. I think she was afraid your father was going to come after her, and he would have, too. After I told him what I done, he put a shotgun to my head. I had to tell him Barbara's last name was something different so he couldn't find you."

I light a cigarette for myself and set another on the table in front of her.

"That day she came to get you," Ma says, "I tried to stop her. I screamed and hollered, chased that car all the way into town, but you were gone. So I kept telling myself it was the right thing." She shakes her head. "Now I wish I could take it back."

We're quiet for a long time. I finish my smoke, crush it out and say, "Why don't you go to bed? I'll stay up and keep watch."

"I ain't moving till I know where Swimmer's at."

I switch off the police scanner and she flicks it right back on. I pace a bit more, check the phone to make sure it's still working. Then I dial Jackie.

"Hello?"

"Have you heard anything?"

"No."

I lower my voice. "Promise me you haven't contacted Troy."

"I haven't done shit fuck all. I'm just sitting here in my gitch banging my stupid head against the wall." His words slur together. "But I swear to fuck, if Swimmer's not back in his bed by midnight, I'm going to jail tomorrow for what I'm going to do to that psychopath." His voice catches. "Tabby, if that happens, I need you to look out for Jewell. Move her to the new house and make sure she gets a good doctor."

"Put her on the phone."

"Shut up and lisssen. I'm sorry you got messed up in this. You were right. It's all on me."

I hear the phone bang onto the table and some muted noises. Jewell picks up the receiver and whispers, "Don't worry, Tabby. I slipped something in his drink. He's not going anywhere."

"Thank you." I sigh with relief. "I'll call if something happens."

I hang up and hear a thump down the hall. I freeze, listening. The noise turns into a scurry and Gord the Ferret pokes his head into the room. I exhale and sit back down at the table. Ma's just staring at the unlit cigarette in front of her.

"I miss my granddaughters," she tells me. "Bird's girls. I don't talk about them because it upsets your brothers, but I dream about them all the time. Same as I used to dream about you."

"You dreamt about me?"

"All the time. Now I dream about your father. Last night he came floating into my room and I asked him to find Swimmer and bring him back here. You'd think that bastard could do one little thing for me, but no. Not even in a goddamn dream world. He just hovered over my bed like a bad fart."

She gets up, marches over and pulls Daddy down off the shelf, slams his box on the table, flips open the lid and starts pouring his ashes down the sink.

"Ma, don't!" I leap up. "You'll clog the drain."

I grab her arm, pry the box from her hands then watch in horror as she dips her pinky finger in the little grey pile and brings it to her tongue.

"Jesus, Ma! Would you sit down? You're scaring the shit out of me."

I scoop as much of Daddy as I can back into his box. As I'm hiding him in the refrigerator, I hear a faint knocking sound on the side wall of the trailer.

"That's probably your father now," Ma says. "He wants to slap me for that one."

"Shush for a second."

"Pissed you off, did I, Wendell?" Ma hollers.

"Shh!"

I hear the knock again and decide it's the ferret, but then it trots through the kitchen right in front of us. I run to the door and fling it open, switch on the outside light. It takes a minute for my eyes to adjust enough to make out the silhouette of a familiar beer gut.

"Lyle?"

He steps to one side and a tiny shadow slowly detaches itself from his. I see the disproportionate head and lopsided stance.

"Swimmer?"

A plump little arm waves to me.

"I found him in the woods," Lyle mutters.

Ma runs past me faster than I've ever seen her move. Her sweatsuit is just a blurry streak. In the same second, she has Swimmer wrapped in her arms, screaming at Lyle, "Get off this property, you shit stick!"

As soon as she has Swimmer safely inside, I run in and grab the two sweat socks full of cash from the ceiling hiding spot.

"Troy's," I say, tossing the white sock to Lyle from the doorway. "Yours." I toss him the grey one. "Now fuck off."

He misses both. I straddle the doorway to keep an eye on both him and Ma. Lyle dumps out the socks, rips off the elastic bands and counts both stacks. Then he gives me the finger and takes off running. In the darkness, I hear an engine start up, and a second later his Ford roars past.

Ma starts toward the phone with Swimmer still in her arms.

"No way!" I yell at her. "You call the police, this never ends."

We take Swimmer into the living room and Ma strips him down. He has a skinned knee, but that's it. She rocks him back and forth while he talks non-stop, trying to show us what he has in his hands. He's got fistfuls of little Happy Meal toys, and a bunch more in a plastic bag tied to the belt loop of his pants.

"They must have fed him McDonald's every meal." Ma clicks her tongue.

We hear a crash. Janis has woken up and overheard. She comes charging down the hall yelling, "NO FAIR!"

Swimmer runs to meet her and they smack into each other at the corner, falling backward in opposite directions.

"Hi, Swimmer." Janis hitches up her pyjama pants. "We're moving to Saw-liss River."

"Sawus ribah?"

I call Jewell, tell her what happened, and she pulls up in the Tercel within a half-hour. I see her struggling to get Jackie out of the passenger seat, so I go out to help. We practically have to hold him up. He's loose as a goose. I ask Jewell what she gave him and she says just some NyQuil. When I have to remind him to put one foot in front of the other going up the stairs, she confesses, "And a couple Xanax."

In the living room, we all surround Swimmer like he's a meteorite crashed down from another planet. He doesn't seem to notice he's been gone. We try to ask him what it looked like where he was, and he just keeps saying "Swimma McDono" and something about a dinosaur blanket. Janis is sorting all his new toys into piles. She keeps counting them to be sure exactly how many times he got to eat McNuggets.

"Ma called Lyle a shit stick," I say.

Jackie slurs, "Jewell called me a dick hat once."

"More than once," Jewell says, patting his knee. She reaches out and strokes Swimmer's hair. Swimmer closes his eyes and rests his head on her baby belly.

"Should we put this little guy to bed?" she whispers.

"No!" Ma shakes her head. "I need to look at him for a few more hours, make sure he's really here."

I call and leave a message for Detective Surette, tell him Swimmer wandered home safe and sound. Surette phones us back and sighs loudly into the phone. "I need you to fill out some paperwork and I'll have to see the boy myself."

In the morning, we take Swimmer to the hospital. He checks

out fine, so we carry him up to Poppy's room. Jackie arrived first and told her everything. As Ma and I walk in with the kids, she looks up and screams, "What's wrong with his face?"

I tell her Janis kicked off the day by drawing a pair of eyeglasses on Swimmer with a permanent marker. Ma made me promise to leave out the part where I walked into the bedroom just as Janis was about to pour nail polish remover over his forehead to try to get them off.

Poppy pulls Swimmer onto the bed and squeezes him to her rib cage. She keeps him pinned there for five minutes, crying so hard it makes him wail too.

Jackie swats her with his hat, nods at me. "Tabby worked the whole deal out with Lyle."

"We should do three cheers for Aunt Tabby!" Janis jumps up. "That's what we do at church group. Like when Julie G. showed us that God's love is all around us. I didn't see nothing but the chalkboard, but I like doing the three cheers."

"I think we're taking you out of church group," Jackie says. "It sounds weird."

"Then you better learn to bake Smartie cake," Ma tells him. "Because that's the whole reason she goes."

DETECTIVE SURETTE IS TORN BETWEEN DOING HIS JOB and making it easy for us to leave town. I know which way he leans. He makes us wait while he talks to Swimmer alone in his office. Swimmer stares at him seriously from behind his new spectacles, but Surette doesn't get much more out of him than we did. Something about the lady and marshmallows, and a motorcycle man. Obviously no one's buying that Swimmer toddled around in the woods for two weeks, but Surette knows the score. He knocks on the window to get my attention.

"That's enough for now," he sighs. "Detective McNeil's on his way." He gives Swimmer a Big Foot candy from his desk drawer, takes a handful for himself. Swimmer holds out his palm for an equal share and Surette reluctantly taps a few more out of the bag. He points to the door and Swimmer slides off the chair with his mouth full.

I've never met McNeil. Ma says he's a tit, and she's right. He's way too blond for it to be natural, asks a bunch of standard questions and tells us we're free to go. As Ma's buckling Swimmer into her back seat, Surette comes out of the station and beckons me.

"Sometimes I wish I still smoked." He pats his shirt pocket.

I hold out my pack to him and he looks at it for a few seconds before slowly sliding a cigarette out. He sticks it under his nose, inhaling deeply, then changes his mind and hands it back.

"Everything all right?" he asks.

"If you're asking if we're leaving, don't worry. In a few hours, Jubilant can go back to being the quiet little fishing village it never was."

I march back to the car and start the engine. Through the windshield, I see him still standing there with his hands in his pockets watching two pigeons peck at each other in the parking lot.

"Janis," I say. "Moon that cop, would you?"

She unclips her seat belt and stands up on the back seat. I honk the horn and Surette looks up just in time to see her bare butt coast past his face.

WE DO A QUICK WALK-THROUGH OF THE TRAILER BEFORE we go.

"It looks naked," Janis says to me, running her hands along the walls. "Like a hot dog that got no ketchup on it."

"Do you want to say goodbye to your room?"

"Nope." She kicks the front door shut on our way out, scrambles up into the passenger seat of the U-Haul and pumps her fist.

Ma is parked in front of us in her own car with Swimmer and Bird. We pull the vehicles out of the driveway, wait one behind the other on the shoulder of the road till Jackie and Jewell's Tercel comes struggling around the corner hauling that rickety trailer. It looks like they've got a blue whale under the tarps. They putter up and Jackie motions for me to roll down my window.

"Where's Poppy?" he asks.

"We'll come back for her in a few days."

"No fucking way. The hospital in Solace River said she can transfer any time."

"Say *frigging!*" Janis yells at him.

Jackie leans across Jewell's belly and says loudly, "There's no *frigging* way we're leaving your mother behind, so let's go get her skinny ass."

"Say *butt!*"

"*Butt* I say *ass!*"

Ma and I follow Jackie to the hospital and park in front. Janis runs in to tell Poppy we're springing her and Ma follows to collect Poppy's things.

Poppy herself's outside within ten minutes. She jumps into the U-Haul holding her hospital robe closed.

"Think you could have got a bigger truck?" she jokes. It's the first time I've seen her smile.

"SO LONG, SUCKERS!" Janis hollers at the rolled-up window.

"You trying to make me go deaf, Janis?!" Poppy snaps. "I got enough problems."

"Sorry," Janis says, blushing.

"What?" Poppy teases. "WHAT? I can't hear nothing!"

Once we're on the highway, Poppy tells me a reporter showed up at the hospital but the nurses wouldn't let him in.

"The cops must have issued a press release about Swimmer being brought back," I say. "Don't mention it to Ma. She's worried sick that if the press finds out all the details and how you're in the hospital and everything, it might tip off social services."

"I know." Poppy gnaws her lip between her teeth. I can tell she's been doing that a lot because the skin's all rubbed raw. "She wants me to let her be Janis and Swimmer's legal guardian."

Janis taps her. "Grandma's going to be my new mother?"

"No, baby," Poppy says. "I'm your mother no matter what."

Janis puts the hood up on her jacket and crosses her arms.

The Legend of Glooscap Motel is a long, green one-level building atop a gravel hill on the far side of the river. I stall at the

Ernie Ells Bridge and wait for the other two vehicles. We convoy over the river, honking our horns like crazy.

"Solace River, here we come!" I exclaim.

Poppy sighs. "Like it or not."

WE USED TO HAVE A COLLECTION OF LEGEND OF GLOOSCAP towels and sheets in our old house, so Daddy probably stopped in here once or twice for a drink. We decide we better not check in under the name Saint.

"How about Snuffleupagus?" Janis says, jumping down from the truck.

Jackie gets the keys and I help sort out the sleeping arrangements. Ma and Janis will share one double bed, Bird and Swimmer will take the other. Jackie and Jewell get their own room a few doors down.

After everyone's settled, Jackie takes Poppy to the hospital and I get in Ma's car and drive over to West's. I pause in the driveway, trying to block out the memory of Abriel's white Rabbit parked in this same spot. When I look up, West is completely naked in the doorway flexing his butt cheeks. I go in and he massages my shoulders while I rehash everything that happened back in Jubilant. I don't plan on getting back in the sex saddle until we sort through what happened with his wife, but I'm so tired I fall asleep before it's an issue.

When I finally wake up, it's past 1p.m. I drive back over to the Glooscap to check on things. The motel hasn't been renovated since the fifties. The rooms have green carpet and orange drapes, and the television sets still have rabbit ears. Janis thinks she's at Club Med.

"I got to have a bubble bath without Swimmer in it," she brags through a mouthful of Cracker Jack. "They have little soaps and shampoos and if you want more, you just pick up the phone and ask. And guess what? They chuck your glass in the garbage every time you use it and bring you a brand new one."

"What makes you think that?"

"Auntie Jewell took me and Swimmer to play the video game and when we got back, these were all sitting right there all wrapped up, and the ones with the chewed-up animal crackers were gone."

She hands me one as proof. Glooscap's slogan is written fancily on the paper band: *We are the only motel in town!*

I take a look around and spy Daddy and Grandma Jean sitting on top of the TV set. Ma said she wants to bury them both back behind the new house and buy little headstones. The boxes are almost identical, so I guess it's a good thing about those Cheerios getting in with Grandma.

"They got Jell-O at the restaurant," Janis says, jumping on the bed. "Buddy said it might be orange today. Want to go check?"

Ma's in there with Swimmer and Bird. She seems to be in the best mood of her life, chatting like I've never seen to the staff in the restaurant, adding a gold-rimmed cigarette to the waitress's tip. Swimmer's apparently become a celebrity. There's an article about him in the Solace River newspaper. I read it three times, but it doesn't mention Poppy at all. It says the circumstances of his disappearance and return are still unknown to police.

"Jackie won't let me see the new house till it's done," Ma says. "He went over there and offered to help out to try to speed things up." She pats Bird's shoulder. "Took this one with him and parked him with a hard hat on. I guess they got into a fight about how to level floors," she laughs. "Just like the old days."

"You been in town yet?" I ask.

"What for?" She sticks a spoon into the mashed potatoes on her plate and brings it to Swimmer's mouth. She's been feeding him like he's a baby ever since he came back, just like she did with Bird after his accident.

"Aren't you wondering what's changed?"

"Nothing's changed."

"Some things have. There's a gas station now."

"Whoop dee frigging doo." She drops the spoon on a plate.

I look down at Swimmer. The eyeglasses are finally fading, but there's still a black ring around one eye. He reminds me of the dog from the Little Rascals.

"Look what I learned him," Janis says. She puts her palms out and he slaps ten, coating her hands in his mashed potatoes.

"Hey, Swimmer," I say. "Do you want to come with me and meet West?"

He nods. "Mee Wes."

Ma stiffens.

"It's fine, Ma," I say. "We'll be just down the road."

I lift Swimmer out of his booster chair and take him back to the room to change his clothes. I change too and put on the dress Poppy gave me. When we come back out to get in the car,

Janis is leaned back in the passenger seat with her arm dangling out the window.

"Grandma said I could come."

"Grandma's not the boss."

She gets out, slams the door and goes stomping back into the motel. I wait a few minutes and she reappears with her purse, climbs in and hands me a five-dollar bill.

"Gas money."

"Oh, I get it. You're just using me for a ride to your boyfriend's house."

I start the car as she slathers Ghostberry lip gloss all over her mouth. Then she clicks the cap back on and pumps her fist.

The air finally smells like summer and it's hot enough to have all the windows down. When we pull into his driveway, West comes out of the house bare-chested carrying a giant box over his head. Janis and Swimmer scramble out of the car to see what's in it. They watch wide-eyed as he pulls out a plastic sprinkler set and sets it up for them on the lawn.

"Fank yoo." Swimmer grins up at him.

"You're welcome, buddy."

Swimmer holds his arms open and when West bends down to give him a hug, Janis tears across the grass and flings her arms around West's neck. I almost can't believe my eyes. I've never seen her willingly touch anyone. She announces that she has to do a safety inspection, walks around tapping all the star-shaped nozzles and then tells West to let her rip.

He turns a tap on the side of the house before joining me on the front steps. We sip near-beers, watching the kids run back and forth through the spray. Janis keeps trying to make Swimmer pretend he's drowning so she can save him, but he won't hold still.

I turn the label on my bottle. "What's with the fakes?"

"Abriel thought I should cut back." West takes a sip of foam.

"Hell-bent on your self-improvement, that woman. Meanwhile, she had a rye and ginger in her hand the whole time she was here." I pause. "I'll bet that wasn't the only thing she had in her hand."

He frowns. "I guess I wanted to see if there was a chance." He rolls his bottle back and forth between his palms. "Like, maybe if we still had the sex part."

"Maybe if you still had the sex part what?"

"I woke up one morning and looked at her face and she don't even look like the same person to me. She crawled all on top of me, and after she said she wanted me to take her dancing. And you know what I thought? Me and Tabby should go dancing. I told her that, too." He takes another sip.

I start to ask him why the hell he made me picture that, but I'm distracted by some guy traipsing around in wrestling pants across the street. He drags a lawn chair all over his yard trying to find the perfect spot for a sunburn. Finally, he sets up smack dab in the middle, pours a drink from a forty of white rum and sets the bottle on the grass beside him. He sees us and gives a little air guitar riff.

West laughs. "My neighbour, Dennis. He's been on a bender since his cat died. God love him. He used to have a mullet, but then he grew it all out long, said he wanted to party in the front too." West catches my expression and starts massaging his neck.

"Here, give me that piss." He snatches the near-beer from my hand and takes it inside.

When I glance back across the street, the neighbour draws a heart in the air and blows it at me. I think about joining his party in the front so I can get a real drink.

I watch the kids playing then look up at the blue sky and over at West's fresh-washed truck gleaming in the driveway. I can't help but think this scene would be perfect if I weren't so fucking pissed off.

West comes back out and hands me a Ten-Penny. He's holding a bottle back at his thigh, hoping I won't notice he got himself another fake. I open my mouth to protest, but Swimmer screams out and we both snap our heads to look. Janis is lying on her belly gnashing at his heels like a shark. So much for playing hero.

West sits down and puts his arm around me. "Christ," he says, "you sure know how to wear a dress."

He leans in for a kiss. I follow his laugh lines to those copper eyes and can't help but kiss him back. Then he leaps up to start the barbecue.

After we eat cheeseburgers, the kids and I say goodbye and head over to the hospital to visit Poppy. There are wildflowers sprouting up all along the road and we pull over and make a bouquet of lupines and some bright violet ones I don't know the name of. I tell Janis they're called Grandma Jean's Crown Jewels. This gets her going again.

"Why'd the wizard want to skin Grandma Jean alive?"

"He didn't want to skin her alive, he wanted to steal her soul."

"What's a soul?"

"You tell me. You must have learned that in church group."

"Oh yeah. I know what that is."

"What is it, then?"

She scratches her elbow. "Jesus said not to talk about it too much."

"Sure he did."

THE ROOMS AT SOLACE GENERAL HAVE GOTTEN A FACE-lift since Ma was in there with that infection all those years ago. Poppy's got a big clean window and two comfy upholstered chairs.

"Prize!" Swimmer says, running to the bed.

"SA-PRIZE," Janis corrects him.

"You look good," I say to Poppy.

She does, too. She's gained at least five pounds in the past week and looks like she got some sleep last night. When she takes the flowers out of Janis's outstretched hands and sticks them in her water jug, her hands don't even shake. I help Janis and Swimmer scramble up on either side of her and they start pawing the tarot cards spread out on her lap.

"What's your future?" Janis asks.

"I have to stay in here for a long time," Poppy tells her. "Longer than I want to. But I seen a counsellor yesterday, and they have a program to help people like me. The sessions are right here in the hospital twice a week. Isn't that great?"

"Dat's gweat!" Swimmer says.

Janis doesn't answer.

"How'd you learn to read cards?" I ask.

"On the soap I watch, this rich woman always goes to a tarot reader to find out if her husband's cheating on her. I thought it would be a handy skill to have. I mean, shitloads of women want to know if some asshole's lying to her face, right? So I asked around and this girl I used to dance with says her grandmother's been reading cards forever, learned it from her own grandmother. I call up the old witch and she says to come on by with a box of wine and a couple cartons of Player's. She taught me everything she knew."

"Let's do Aunt Tabby's fortune," Janis insists.

Poppy gathers up the cards and hands them to me. "Shuffle."

I stare at the deck sitting in my palm and questions start to churn. *Will Ma ever be happy? Is Jackie capable of being with one woman? Will Poppy stay clean? Is Bird going to see his daughters again? Will Janis learn to play the bagpipes?* I swallow. *Do West and I stand a snowball's chance in hell?* I hand the cards back. "I'm afraid to ask."

Janis rifles through the deck and pulls out a card with a picture of a man and a woman facing each other under a giant sun. She points to the woman. "This is you, Aunt Tabby." She taps the man's head. "And that's West."

"How do you know it's West?"

She rolls her eyes. "Because that's the same face he makes when he looks at you. It's like you're his favourite TV show."

Jackie is threatening to bust some heads. He went to the bank to deposit the money in my account and says the assistant manager made up a bunch of new rules when he told him his name.

"Fucking Freddy thinks he's king shit walking around in green leather shoes," he says to me. "I asked him where he found those, the douchebag bin at Twat 'n' Co?"

I take the money and go down myself. He's right. The teller suddenly has a list of questions. She calls Fucking Freddy over, and I have to explain that I've been saving my babysitting and dog-walking money since I was knee-high to a gas pump. He makes me nervous and I end up depositing only half the cash. I glance down at his feet, but now he's got penny loafers on.

"That your retirement fund?" I ask, pointing to the coins in the slots.

He crosses his arms and tells me Jackie's lucky they didn't press charges. He points to a life-sized cardboard cut-out of a smiling old lady and says Jackie knocked it over as he was leaving the bank.

"Is there a law against assaulting a piece of cardboard?"

"There certainly is. It's called destruction of property."

I walk over to it. The sign attached says *We Treat Our Customers Like Family.*

"Aw, come on. Nana's fine." I pat her shoulder and her head droops. "A little shaken up is all."

He narrows his eyes at me and I almost give Nana another smack. The other clerks start whispering to each other as I walk out. Now *I* feel like busting some heads. I march down the side-walk and stop at Beula's Beauty Parlour.

"Beula!" I yell, punching the door open.

"She don't own this place no more," a voice says.

A woman in a paisley dress emerges from the back. I recognize her face. I saw her through the window that first day I visted Solace River. She sets down her diet soda and motions to one of the swivel chairs. They're the same minty green colour they always were, slightly more faded and dye-stained. I sit and dig my fingernail stubs into the vinyl armrests.

"You been in here before?" she asks.

"Twice. The first time, my mother was laughed out the door for having the nerve to ask for a job." I feel my face grow hot. "The second time, I was about eleven years old and won a contest for guessing how many pop caps were strung around the school Christmas tree. The prize was getting my hair done at Beula Dean's. I saved it up until there was a Valentine's Day party at school, came in with all these pictures I'd drawn of the hairstyle of my dreams. Beula told me my win had expired." My ears are burning. "She wasn't even busy. She was leaning on the counter doing a scratch ticket."

The woman walks over to a cooler and pours me a Dixie cup of water. Her earrings jingle like tiny gold bells as she hands it to me. "Beula got alopecia now."

"What's that?"

"It makes your hair fall out. Baldy won't even leave the house because that expensive wig she ordered from New York City turned blue when she washed it." She winks. "How's that for poetic justice?"

"I'd rather she died in a fiery car crash or drowned in the bathtub."

"I might be for hire if business stays slow."

I look around. The framed posters on the walls of fashion models with blue eyeshadow and pink pearl necklaces are even more outdated than they were when I was a kid. The place is spotless, though.

"When did you take over?"

"October. I tried to buy it years ago when I heard she was looking to sell, put in a nice offer. It got back to me that she didn't want to sell to a black woman. Then, wouldn't you know, as soon as that first lock of hair fell into her tomato soup, guess who's calling me up." She sits down in the chair next to me and laces her fingers between her knees. "This time my offer wasn't so nice."

I raise my paper cup to her, stick my other hand out. "I'm Tabby Saint."

"Olivia Sparks." She shakes my hand and scoops up her soda. "You live around here?"

"I used to."

She squints, waits for me to say more. Then she gestures to a machine at the back that looks like a torture chamber.

"You want your nipples pierced? I bought that piece of junk and it just sits there. You look like you could use … something."

"How about a drink?" I drain the Dixie cup and crush it. "A real drink."

She glances at the clock, drumming her fingernails on the soda can.

"Come on," I say. "They're free down at the tavern."

"How so?"

"I'm with West."

"For real?" She slaps the countertop. "It's about time somebody hit that."

THE NEW HOUSE HAS BEEN VANDALIZED. SOMEONE spray-painted *Dirty Money Bastards* along one wall. Jewell calls West's house to tell me.

"They spelled it *t-u-r-d-s*, the morons. Jackie's managed to scrub most of it off, but now he's on the warpath."

"Where is he?"

"I don't know. He went stomping out of here in his fighting shirt."

"Is that an expression?"

"No, it's a slippery old football jersey with no buttons to grab on to."

"What's he going to do, pick a fist fight our first week back here, let everyone know the Saints still haven't developed opposable thumbs?"

"He's all talk most of the time."

"Let's hope this is one of those times."

I hang up the phone, haul my boots on and stomp down to the tavern. It's packed inside and I can smell the beer sweating out of everyone's pores. I forgot it was Saturday night. West is busy, but I get his attention over the bar. He nods over at Jackie brooding in a corner.

I go over and tap Jackie's shoulder. "Saturday night all right for fighting?" I yell over the music.

He gestures at three hard-looking men standing in front of the dartboard. "I came down to meet the welcome wagon."

"Picking out the new Troy, are you?"

"No. I came to put a stop to this right here. And don't say that name to me. You say that name enough times, I'm on the highway back to Jubilant."

"Drop it. You're even."

He stands up. "We'll never be even."

He walks up to the bar and I see West hesitate a half second before grabbing five Oland's from the fridge, plunking them on the bar and snapping the caps off in a line. He shoots me a wary look as Jackie heads over to the dartboard.

I scout the exits and squeeze my eyes closed, but all I can hear is Aerosmith playing on the speakers. When I open one eye, I see Jackie's beers have found their way into the men's mitts. I can't hear their conversation, but I can tell no one's gearing up for a fight. I know what that looks like. It starts with chest puffing, followed by warnings and insults. Then the warnings turn to threats, then crazy eyes, then whoever's about to throw the first punch takes off his jacket. I always wondered why there's such a lead-up. If I really wanted to whoop someone, I'd just come at them like a flying squirrel, but I've seen guys seven feet tall with spikes on their collars follow this same stupid ritual, giving the other guy every opportunity to take back what he said about the frigging Leafs.

Jackie beckons me over. "This is my sister, Tabby." He hands me the extra beer.

The men smell like leather and fried fish. One of them is wearing a wool sweater in this heat. He looks me over as he takes a gulp of beer.

"I seen you yesterday," he says. "In the bank."

"I went to settle some accounts," I tell him. "Our father just passed away after he was in a taxicab accident and we got a big chunk of insurance money. We're using it to put up a new house on our old land."

What the fuck? Jackie mouths.

"Anyway," I continue, "the money's all gone now and we've got a niece and nephew who eat like wrestlers. Plus Jackie's got one on the way, so we're looking for work. You know if anyone's hiring?"

The tall one with the shiny bald head pulls out his wallet. "I got a one-year-old." He slides out a photo of a chubby toddler with blond pigtails. "Ain't she something?"

"You hitting on my girlfriend?" West thumps him on the back. I didn't even notice him approach.

"This your woman?" Shiny Head turns to me and rolls his eyes. "Fuck. West don't do nothing these days except talk about you. I used to come in here to talk about me. Now it's the girl-friend this and the girlfriend that."

I raise my eyebrow at West. "What's the this-and-that part?"

"Never mind," West says. "Who needs a drink?"

"Give me a Dory 72 and Coke," Shiny Head says.

West gives him a look. "You ain't no Dory lush."

"How do you know?"

"Because your clothes are clean and you still got all your teeth."

"Ah, but the night is young."

I notice Wool Sweater getting agitated. When West walks away, he says to Jackie, "That new house you put up is pissing off a lot of people."

"Why's that, now?" Jackie asks.

"I think you know why."

"If it's about my father, I know he wasn't nothing but a dumb drunk who stole whatever wasn't nailed down, but that bitch is dead. Ding dong the merry-o. Let's all move on."

"We don't want any trouble," I cut in. "We came back to Solace River to have a nice place for the kids to grow up."

Wool Sweater glances around the room. "Let me put it this way. There's people looking to get back their losses."

"You're starting to piss me off." Jackie raises his voice. "I've had to deal with every shit pile Daddy ever left and I didn't even know the man past growing up. Yes, I know he cheated people. I *am* one of those people. Tell your 'party' if that ain't good enough, they can dig him up and kick the fuck out of his bones. I'm done with this shit."

"Just watch your back is all I'm saying."

I grab Jackie's arm, and once we're out the door and halfway up the road, I realize he's not resisting. I let go, sit down on the curb and let out a small, tight scream.

Jackie glances back down the road, spitting tobacco over his shoulder. "Those guys don't scare me."

"No?" I push my hair back hard from my face. "What about the guys behind those guys?"

"They probably don't exist. Forget it. Poppy read them creepy cards of hers. She said it's going to be smooth sailing from here."

"Well, then." I stand back up. "If Junkie Jane's creepy cards said so, what am I so worried for?"

"Come on, now. It ain't fair to call her a junkie when she's trying to get clean."

"Why are you always defending her?"

"What?"

"I'm your sister too."

"I know that."

"You don't even think I'm a Saint."

"What are you talking about?"

"You said so yourself."

"When?"

A porch light snaps on and a little old man comes out of his house with his hands on his hips, street lights glaring off his glasses. Without waiting for him to ask us if we know what the hell time it is, Jackie and I split off. He heads straight up toward the motel and I cross the street toward West's. What I really want to do is run back and karate-chop the fucker in the neck.

I feel like I'm ten again. Bird and I never fought as kids, but Jackie and I were like Sylvester and Tweety Bird. I remember one time I overheard Jackie telling Bird that I took off with Daddy's good hammer. He'd lost it in the woods while he was building a love shack for his little girlfriends and was hoping I'd get the beating for it. People sometimes say they see red, but I saw actual flames. I picked up a brick over my head and came running at him with it. Bird saw what was happening and pushed Jackie out of the way, held me down and made me use my words. He told Jackie to go find the hammer, and the little jerk must have found it, too, because a few days later my school books went missing and reappeared nailed way up in the trees where only Jackie was crazy enough to climb. I had detention three times for forgetting my books until Bird chucked rocks up to make them fall down. I stayed up all night thinking about what I could do to get revenge. I got out of bed early and spread margarine inside Jackie's ball cap and shoes. That didn't seem like enough, so I drew a big dick on the back of his windbreaker with whiteout. Later that day at school, he walked up behind me in the hallway with a pair of scissors and cut off half my ponytail.

When I get back to West's, I ransack the hall closet looking for that framed photograph of him and his bitch wife. I eventually find it stashed in a box under his bed, take it out back and smash it on the fence post. I let the broken glass slide off and stash the metal frame in his neighbour's garbage. Then I rip the photo to shreds and flush it down the toilet. One of the pieces has Abriel's eyeball on it and I watch it go around and around, giving me the stink eye one last time before she's sucked down to the sewer.

I sit in the living room, chewing on the skin around my fingernails and trying to relax. Before West gets home, I slip back outside and pick up all the tiny glass shards I can find in the moonlight so he doesn't cut his foot while he's watering the lawn.

NOW THAT IT'S TWENTY-THREE DEGREES OUTSIDE, THE real estate lady is wearing a black turtleneck dress and riding boots. She has a gaudy, gold-painted clip in her hair that slips down toward her ear as she counts our money. She counts it at least eight times and then she can't get Ma and me out of there fast enough.

"I hope she buys some new clothes with her cut," I say in the car. "Something that shows us she's a woman but still a professional. I'd put her in a white sleeveless blouse with an olive green skirt." I keep chatting away, making up different paper-doll outfits for our salesgirl so Ma won't notice I'm driving in the opposite direction of the motel. When I pull in to the legal aid office building, she bolts upright and grabs the dash.

"What are you doing? Turn around!"

"This is where you have to go to apply for legal guardianship of Janis and Swimmer."

"I can't go in there. They know everything your father's ever done. As soon as we walk out, they'll be saying the Saints are all the same, that we can't take care of our own kids."

"Things are different, Ma. Daddy's gone, the house is gone. You'll see. People are going to melt when they meet Janis out pushing her uncle Bird around, asking the store clerks if they have any bubble wrap he can pop."

Ma takes a small bottle of lotion out of her purse and coats her finger with it. She slides her wedding ring up and down until it comes off and gently sets it in the glove compartment.

When we walk into the office, a woman in a shiny tube top is screaming at the person behind the desk. A man comes out from the back and tells her the police are on their way. "We're getting a restraining order this time," he says. "You and your family can't come in here making threats." After she throws an artificial bonsai tree at him, he looks over and gives us an apologetic smile. "Sorry for the disruption. We'll be right with you."

"See?" I whisper to Ma. "The Saints who?"

LATER THAT NIGHT, WE MEET UP IN THE MOTEL RESTAU-rant to dicuss what to do with the rest of the money. Jewell offers to transfer her bank account from Jubilant to Solace River and deposit what's left in her name. In total, there's about three grand. Along with Bird's disability cheques, it should keep everybody going until Jackie finds work.

Jackie and I don't say much to each other, but I stopped being mad at him after I remembered what happened after he cut off my ponytail. He kept it and used to wave it in front of my face, and I constantly searched his and Bird's room for it. I never found it, but in one of his drawers I discovered a cash box and a homemade fundraising letter for a fake Little League team. Jackie had been going door to door asking for donations and had already collected forty-eight dollars. To make it look legit, he had his pledgers sign their names and write down the amount of their donation. I saw that Mrs. Glen had pledged fifteen dollars. When I showed Ma, she had a conniption.

I look at him smugly across the table, remembering Ma dragging him by the ear up to all the neighbours' houses. She made him give back every cent. Apparently, he'd been saving up for a gun that shoots out a grappling hook.

"So, it's all worked out," Jewell says. "Once a month, Jackie's skanky exes are going to come here to pick up their child support and bring the kids so he can spend some time with them. I'll conveniently be anywhere else."

Ma asks Jackie if he's okay for child support payments for now and he tells us he already found work. There's a new call centre going up just outside of town and he got on with the construction company that won the contract.

"I heard once it's up they're going to need shitloads of people in there answering phones," he tells me. "You should check it out."

A few days later, I see a notice tacked up at the grocery store: CALL CENTRE JOBS! INFO SESSION 9 A.M. SATURDAY AT THE LIBRARY.

On Friday night, I'm so nervous I get the runs. When I walk into the library the next morning, I see about thirty people sitting around waiting. I recognize a few faces from the old days at the Doyle Street Country Club. They're holding cookies on napkins, drinking coffee out of Styrofoam cups. I seat myself on a squeaky chair and everyone turns to stare.

"Hi, my name's Tabby and I'm an alcoholic."

Most laugh at my joke, but a few shoot back, "Hello, Tabby," in unison. The awkward silence seeps back in.

Finally, a woman in a bright blue pantsuit introduces herself and gets the ball rolling. She explains a bit about the job, which is fielding calls from customers experiencing glitches with their computers. It doesn't sound so hard. All the solutions to the problems are in a manual that employees keep at their stations.

At the end of the session, I hand in an application. The woman thanks me for my interest, tells me I'll be contacted if I'm selected for an interview. I compliment her pantsuit and she writes something at the top of my paper, which I'm hoping is, *I like her.*

Before I head back to West's, I walk into the Frenchy's thrift store and try on some pantsuits. They're all too dowdy, but I find a dress with a matching jacket that's pretty sharp. I try it on and stare at my reflection. I feel like I'm wearing a Halloween costume.

"Now that's a power suit," the saleslady says. "You can go all the way to the top in that outfit."

I wouldn't have far to go. In the info session, they told us their incentive program is that employees with the highest customer satisfaction rating each month get to put their names in a draw for a gift certificate to Swiss Chalet.

West comes home from work as I'm ironing the outfit for the third time, and I tell him everything I learned about the job.

"You know anything about computers?" He looks skeptical.

"The woman said I don't need to. I just need to know about people."

He watches me flatten the collar of the jacket and run the iron over it.

"Folks get pretty pissed off when shit stops working. Are you sure you can keep your cool?"

"Try me." I unplug the iron. "Pretend you're a client."

He looks at me blank-faced.

"Clients are what we call the callers. Probably so they'll think we're in an LA high-rise instead of downwind of the Solace River landfill."

"All right." He puts his fist up to his ear. "Ring."

"Clien-Tel. You're speaking with Tabby."

"It's about damn time," West barks into his fist. "I've been on hold for twenty Jesus minutes!"

"Are those the same as regular minutes?"

"You getting smart?"

"If I was, I'd leave this dead-end job and go work for Microsoft. Can I assist you with a computer issue today, sir?"

"The fucking thing is fucked."

"Can you describe for me exactly what it's doing?"

"The screen's jammed and I'm about to bash it through the wall."

"Well, don't do that, hon, or you're going to have two problems—three when your wife comes home. Now, I can help you un-jam that fucker, but first I'm going to need the serial number, so do me a favour. Put the beer down and go look at the sticker on the back of the grey rectangle majigy."

"I don't drink beer. It's Scotch."

"Really? Now I'm impressed. Here I took you for a simple beer man. What's your name?"

"Larry."

"You're kidding me? I got a brother named Larry."

"No you don't," West says.

"I do for the rest of this call. See, now Larry isn't going to fight with me. We're practically blood."

West grins. "Yeah, all right. I can see you being real good at this. Just don't cuss in the interview and you'll be vacationing in a Swiss chalet in no time."

"No, it's a gift certificate to the Swiss Chalet *restaurant*."

"What? Solace River don't even got one of them."

"I know. We'd have to drive all the way to New Minas."

"That ain't even worth the gas money."

"Then we'll sell it."

"Hold on, now. I heard their chicken's pretty tasty."

"Well, don't count your chickens yet. I have to get the interview first."

Jewell types me up a resumé and pays the motel clerk to fax it to the Clien-Tel head office. She doctors all my previous experience to make it look legit and adds a waitressing job at a restaurant that doesn't exist. She gives her motel room phone number as the reference number for my fake former manager, Wendy. Every time the phone rings, she chirps, "Sunnyside Café, Wendy speaking," just in case it's someone from Clien-Tel. Whenever Jackie calls to check in from the construction site, he asks Wendy what colour panties she's wearing.

The woman finally does phone and Jewell tells her I was the best waitress they ever had, that I never broke a glass or stole nothing, and that I could shoot the breeze with everyone from welfare drunks to lawyers. It must have done the trick, because later that night I get an automated phone call asking me to press one if my name is Tabatha Saint. I do and a robot voice gives me an interview time slot.

I feel less nervous this time, until I put on the dress and the little matching jacket. I'm a wreck walking in and after the interview's over I go straight to the tavern for a drink. The door is held open with a boulder. West hears my heels on the floor and his head darts out from the back. His smile sinks when he sees the look on my face.

"Beer?"

"No, thanks."

"How about a hug?"

"How about a fucking margarita?"

"I knew it!" He leaps over the bar and lifts me up into the air. When he sets me down again, he says, "Margarita? Where do you think you are, woman? I don't even got straws."

THE JOB DOESN'T START FOR ANOTHER MONTH, BUT I find ways to keep busy. Jewell's making a quilt for the baby and I offer to help. She's using pieces of Janis's and Swimmer's old baby clothes. I pull out Ma's yellow dress and Daddy's shirt, and we cut out patches from them too. Quilting gives us tons of time to talk, and I discover I can ask Jewell anything.

"How come Ma was so close with Bird's kids, but she never sees Jackie's?"

"Well," Jewell sighs, "when Jackie and I started going together, his exes banded together and threatened to cut off access to the kids. He calls the exes the three Cs because of their names, but I'm not so polite. Anyway, they were just trying to get his attention, but it spooked your mother so bad she stopped trying to see the boys. Losing Josie and Michelle was really hard on her."

I finally have to ask Jewell what she sees in Jackie.

"It's not what I see," she says. "It's his smell. I can't get enough of it. He walks into a room and I scratch the eight every time."

That's pool slang. It took me a while to catch on. Jackie told me Jewell used to run the table at the Lighthouse for ten bucks a game, said she even has a fancy cue engraved with her initials. I asked him if he ever played her and he said, "Fuck, no. She'd hand me my nut sack."

One day I was telling her how West finally ripped out the soggy walls of the shower and installed an enclosure, and she said, "If I was you, I'd stick my rock with that man."

"I envy you, Jewell," I confess. "You coupon, you win at bingo, you somehow managed to turn my womanizing fuck-up of a brother into a decent person. You make heart-shaped sandwiches, for Christ's sake. I don't even get why West wants me around."

She knots her thread, bites off the loose end and spits it out. "Tabby, look how much you've done for this family. West has two eyes in his head. He can see you don't just skip out on people when things turn to shit. Not like that skank ex-wife of his. What's her name—Magical?"

"Abriel."

"Umbilical?" She scowls. "Whatever. Who cares."

I finish the patch I'm on and start packing up to leave when she asks me not to. "I feel like maybe the baby's coming." She presses in on her belly with her fingers. "Can you stay with me a bit longer? Something feels off."

"Where's Jackie?"

"They all went to the lake for a swim."

"What do you mean, 'something feels off'? Off what? What's off?"

Jewell watches the clock while I pace in front of the window. Half an hour goes by and she says, "I think I'm okay. You should probably get home for dinner. West's going to wonder where you're at."

"I'm not leaving you here."

"Then I'll come with you. I'm dying to get a look at this man." She grabs her purse and I help her up into the truck.

On the drive, I keep an eye on her belly, but she suddenly seems fine, staring at the sunset and humming along with the radio. When we get to West's, I see Ma's and Jackie's cars sitting in his driveway.

"What are they doing here?"

Jewell shrugs. I go around and help her out of the passenger side and she doesn't say a word.

"SURPRISE!" Janis yells before my foot's even in the door. Behind her I see Ma, Jackie and Swimmer seated at West's kitchen table. I recognize the extra chairs from the tavern. Bird's parked in his wheelchair at the far end and West is standing at the counter holding a cake lit with candles. Jewell snaps off the lights and they all start singing "Happy Birthday." Except for Bird. He's singing the theme song from *Hockey Night in Canada.*

I make a wish and blow out every candle. West winks at me then goes to the stove and starts yanking lobsters out of a giant pot while Jewell lays down newspaper so we can just toss the shells on the floor as we eat.

"Remember when Daddy stole all them lobsters out of someone's traps up in Yarmouth?" Jackie asks, butter grease on his chin. "He found a buoy close to shore, dove down and pulled a few up with his bare hands. Then he kept on going under, swimming them to the bank two and three at a time and chucking them into his back seat. He come home with his hands all sliced up, had about twenty of those friggers crawling inside the car. We ate lobster for a month. You remember?"

"I wasn't there," I remind him.

"Oh." Jackie looks down at his plate. "Right."

Ma clears her throat. "Your father made a saltwater tank in the living room. Poppy gave all the lobsters names and put bath toys in with them."

"Wait a minute," Janis interrupts. "Lobsters don't come from water."

"Sure they do." Jackie nudges her. "Where did you think they came from?"

She turns pale. "The woods."

"You ever seen a lobster in the woods?"

"They go down in tunnels under the trees."

Jackie breaks off a crustacean leg, slurps the meat out of it next to her ear. Janis says she's going to be sick, pushes her chair out and takes off down the hall. She wanders back as West starts cutting the cake.

"Want to know where ice cream comes from?" Jackie asks her. He starts describing cow udders and she covers her ears.

Out of the corner of my eye, I watch Bird trying to feed cake to Swimmer. He keeps missing his mouth, mashing it into Swimmer's chin, until Swimmer gets fed up, grabs a hunk and dumps it on Bird's head. Janis runs over and scolds them to save a piece for Poppy. I look around and there are lobster carcasses and cake smears all over the kitchen.

"Sorry," I mouth to West.

"For what?" he mouths back.

After dinner, we have a few drinks and I get to hear about more of Daddy's stunts that I missed. My favourite is the one where he stole a cop car and dropped it back off at the station in the middle of the night filled with empty beer cans.

After everyone leaves, West won't let me help clear the dishes. After he's washed up and put them all away, he joins me at the table. I lean forward and brush the hair out of his eyes.

"How did you pull this party off?"

"You can thank your brother."

"My brother? Which one?"

"Bird." West tries not to smile. "He put the whole thing together."

"I'd sooner believe Bird stood up and danced the Macarena than I'd believe this was Jackie's idea."

"Jackie called me up to say he was picking up a bunch of lobsters. Then he called three more times, told me Jewell was baking a cake and asking me what kind of ice cream I think you'd like and all that."

"Wow," I say. "I'm shocked he even remembers what month I was born in."

"I have something for you." West jumps up and goes down the hall. I hear a crash and he comes back carrying a big, odd-shaped box. It's so large he had to use three different kinds of wrapping paper on it.

"What—"

"Shut up and open it."

I find an edge and tear into the paper, tossing green and yellow pieces over both shoulders. The cardboard box beneath is taped shut, but West is already standing over me with his pocket knife. He slices the seals then stands back as if something's about to come flying out at us. I open it and reveal a vinyl case. I undo the clasps, lift the lid and feel my heart rise up and stick in my throat. The sheen of the thing is almost blinding. I reach down and gingerly lift it into my lap, running my fingers along the curves of the wood and the gleaming silver keys.

"You bought me a red guitar."

I finger the tag hanging off the neck. West blushes as I flip it around and read the two words he's written in big, loopy letters:

Love, David.

8

Ma is making a big show out of the blindfold.

"For Christ's sake, Jackie, I'm going to break my neck." She flails her arms as he steers her across the parking lot toward her car, pushes down on her head like a cop to guide her into the back seat. She's still talking as he slams the door and drowns her out.

Janis and I jump in and wave to Jewell behind us in the Tercel with Bird and Swimmer. Jackie didn't want Jewell to see the house till it was completely finished, but I gave in and snuck her out there last week. We walked through all the rooms gaping at our reflections in the shiny wood floors and appliances.

"Your mother's going to *shit her pants*," Jewell announced.

"She better, or Jackie's going to be heartbroken."

Now I glance at Jewell's belly in the rear-view mirror. It's gotten so big she can practically steer with it. "Got any baby names picked out yet?" I ask Jackie as he climbs in the driver's seat and pulls out of the Glooscap.

"Don't get me started," he says. "She's got this book full of dumb-ass names. Cellophane, Poseidon, stupid shit like that. Duplex, Dynamo."

"Cellophane?"

"How about Flipsy?" Janis suggests.

"Just don't name her something that rhymes with something else," Ma harps.

She thinks she has to talk louder because she's wearing a blindfold. I glance in the back seat and see her gripping the door handle like we're about to crash.

"Then why in the hell did you name me Tabby?" I ask her.

"I named you and your sister Tabatha and Lollipop because I knew you'd get called Tabby and Poppy. I like double letters. I really wanted to name you Hannah, because it's spelled the same backwards and forwards, but your father yelled, "Hannah banana! Hannah banana!' until I couldn't stand it no more."

"And scabby, crabby, shabby Tabby never crossed his skull?"

"You're lucky you were born at all," Ma says. "I made him pull out."

"Nice, Ma." Jackie checks the rear-view mirror to make sure Jewell's not directly behind us before he spits tobacco out the window. "We're glad you're here, Tabby." He reaches over and messes up my hair.

I adjust Daddy and Grandma Jean on my lap. Janis and Swimmer drew all over the boxes. Amongst a lot of scribbling, I decipher what looks like a cat puking on a dog and a man with a green moustache.

Once we're on Victory Road, Jackie can hardly sit still in the driver's seat. He punches my arm excitedly as the house rises out of the trees then parks at the bottom of the driveway so Ma will get the full effect. We both take a good look. The siding is almost the same colour as the paint of our old house, though we chose it for the name more than anything: Halo Yellow.

The Tercel pulls up and I help Bird into his chair as Jackie arranges everyone in a line facing the house.

"Can we please enjoy this moment fart free?" Jewell requests of whoever laid one.

"All right, Ma." Jackie rips off the blindfold. "Feast your eyes."

Her gaze travels from the porch up to the peak of the roof then down again. She takes in each of the gleaming windows staring back at her and puts one hand on each of Jackie's and my shoulders for support.

"Oh my," she finally gasps.

"Come on!" Janis yells, grabbing her arm and hauling her up the driveway. Jewell waddles behind them as fast as she can, not wanting to miss a moment of Ma soiling herself. Jackie takes Bird's chair handles and pushes him slowly up to the house, pausing to show him the wheelchair ramp he built himself. Bird nods his head side to side, running his hands along the wooden rails on the way up.

I hang back with Swimmer and watch them all vanish through the front door. The sun has set fire to the tops of the evergreens behind the house, making them shimmer as if there's gold tinsel strung in their branches. It's Christmas in July.

I pick up Swimmer in my arms. "What do you think?"

He nods his approval, contentedly sucking on his fingers.

The only sound for miles is the occasional round of laughter seeping from the house until Ma's voice comes bellowing out of one of the second-floor windows: "MY OWN BATHROOM? YOU'RE SHITTING ME!" I can't help but be reminded of the words Barbara Best lodged in my head all those years ago.

"Music is everywhere," I whisper.

Swimmer's fingers fall out of his mouth as he tilts his head back and smiles at me. I smile too. Then I set him down on the ground, take his wet little hand in mine and walk him home.

ACKNOWLEDGEMENTS

In big marquee lights:

Thank you to the members of my writing group, Ryan Turner, Stephanie Domet, Carsten Knox and Jaime Forsythe, for your steadfast company in this crazy racket.

Thank you to the earliest readers of my writing, Marie Fennell and Erin Smiley; to the Writers' Federation of Nova Scotia; to the Banff Centre; and to the grant jury at Arts Nova Scotia for believing in the work that I do.

Thank you to Greg Hollingshead for beating the crap out of me (crap sentences, I should specify); to my amazing agent, Carolyn Forde, with whom I would rob a bank after witnessing such skilled precision (backup plan?); and to HarperCollins for fulfilling an exquisite promise to treat creator and creation as an inseparable entity.

Thank you to the wise and wonderful Padma Viswanathan. Your allegiance to this novel moved mountains. You have given me a rare gift, and I promise to someday do the same for another writer.

Thank you to my friends. Some of you are actual family members; the rest, just as close. You surround me with support even when the going gets tough, and it makes all the difference. Every one of you is crucial.

Thank you, Shawn Truman Bent. You've renewed my faith in love. You make me laugh so hard it disturbs the peace, and while I split my time in imaginary worlds, you do all the cooking, cleaning and wood chopping in the real one. It will be an honour to marry you.

A couple of years ago, an article in *The New Yorker* condemned author acknowledgements as a waste of space. I say the world needs more gratitude, not less. Ditching the acknowledgements would be like showing your film and not rolling the credits afterwards, or putting out an album without naming the audio engineer or any of the background singers. And so, a final shout out:

To Nova Scotia, you beautiful blue bastard. I am proud to come from a place where everyone says thank you, thank you, thank you.